I0601229

ISBN:

978-1-0670738-4-8 (Epub)

978-1-0670738-5-5 (Print)

BAD BLOOD

HELLHOUND HEAT SERIES

SHERILEE GRAY

CONTENT NOTE

BAD BLOOD contains scenes that include extra large penetration, knotting, blood, gore, violence, explicit sex.

PROLOGUE

Roxy

December 10, 1425

GRIPPING at the stone wall with bloody fingers, I slid and stumbled down the dimly lit hall, clutching the gaping wound across my side, and desperately tried to keep my insides from spilling out. Shrieks of rage and bloodcurdling roars echoed from the room behind me.

Oh gods.

Pressing the back of my bloody hand to my mouth, I retched violently. How could this be happening? My world had simply stopped turning.

I squeezed my eyes closed as images from that room, from what I just walked in on, flashed like a horror show through my mind. I clung to the wall, forcing myself to stay upright. I'd lost too much blood; my legs were on the verge of giving out. Somehow, I managed to claw myself toward the staircase, calling Lucifer's name.

My veins burned hot as I collapsed on the floor, unable

to stay upright any longer, but as my blood drained from the gaping wound at my side and onto the stone floor, only ice remained.

"Roxy?" Lucifer's voice sounded distant. His arms surrounded me as he scooped me up, carrying me into another room, and kicked the door shut behind us.

He laid me on the bed, and I blinked up at him, at the shadows dancing across his face from the candlelight and crackling fire in the hearth. I opened my mouth, but the words wouldn't come. I couldn't speak them out loud. His gaze slid to my side, to the mess there, then back up. He didn't ask me who had caused my injuries or what happened, he didn't need to.

"Y-you sent me to that room," I rasped. "You knew."

"Yes," he said without hesitation. "You needed to know the truth."

His words pierced through my chest, and if I wasn't busy holding my intestines inside my body, my hands would have been gripping my chest, because it hurt. It hurt more than being cut open with a blade made from blessed silver, burning and still eating at my flesh now.

A howl full of pain and rage echoed in the distance, and Lucifer's yellow gaze met and held mine. For a moment, just a flicker of time, I thought I saw regret in their depths, but then it was gone.

The unmistakable sound of rustling wings had Lucifer spinning around, fury rolling off him. The angel stood just inside the room, holding a knife still dripping with my blood. The door slammed shut behind her. "Give her to me," she demanded through clenched teeth.

"You can't have her," Lucifer said, his voice cold, deadly.

An earth-shattering roar exploded nearby, threatening

to bring down this building. Seraphina was preventing Lothar from leaving her room, or trying to.

A smile curled Sera's lips. "I'll give you what you so badly want, Lucifer, even though you sent your hound to seduce, then steal it from me, and I will spare their lives, but I have conditions."

"Spare their lives?" Lucifer vibrated with rage. "You think I'll just stand by and allow you to harm them and do nothing? You overestimate your powers."

She smirked. "Maybe, but if you succeed in killing me, you will make yourself a target. I may be a traitor, but unlike you, I am still one of them." Her gaze sliced to me and she tilted her head to the side. "But very well, you can keep her. Death would be too easy anyway. Give me the hound's head, and I'll give you your trinket."

"No," I gasped, shaking so hard I had to clench my teeth. "Don't hurt him. Don't—"

"Even after what he did? You still love him, don't you?" Evil glee filled her eyes. "Fine. Here is my final offer. I will give you the gem, Lucifer, and you and your throne will be safe, at least for now. But only if you give me the biggest quadrant in Hell, make a place for me here, and—"

"What more do you think you deserve, Sera?" he said, ice dripping from his voice.

"I deserve compensation for the way you treated me. You tried to manipulate me, steal from me." She slid her thumb over her bloody lip. "You sent one of your precious little play things to attack me."

"You already know you've lost. Providing you with refuge would be a kindness, one you do not deserve," Lucifer said.

She shook her head. "Maybe, but it's the only way I'll hand over this..." A small, intricately carved wooden box appeared in her hand. "You can't leave Hell to chase me all over the realms, Lucifer, and as long as I have this, you'll be looking over your shoulder. All it would take is a whisper in the right ear, an enemy, a disgruntled demon willing to do my bidding—"

Lucifer snarled.

"Give me my quadrant, and—" She smiled, her gaze darting to me and lighting with glee. "—make the hound forget he ever loved her. Make him forget who Roxana is to him. Let her suffer unrequited love for eternity, and the prize is yours."

The roaring and snarls reached new levels. Lothar had busted out of Sera's room and was at our door now, and the sound of his huge body colliding with it, over and over again, made me jolt and tense. The only reason he hadn't gotten through was because Lucifer was preventing it.

"You dare to threaten what is mine?" Lucifer said.

"Hurting what you love, hurts you." Her gaze hardened. "And oh, how I'd love to cause you pain."

Seraphina wasn't strong enough to kill Luci, but she still held in her possession something that could.

The threat to Lucifer, to his throne, would never be gone if he let her leave with that box. Sera was desperate for power, and the rare gem inside that she'd stolen when she'd fled Heaven had the ability to destroy him. The archangels would be coming for her, her delusions of grandeur wouldn't be tolerated, but as long as she possessed that jewel, as long as she was able to evade them, she was a risk to all of us. If she managed to overthrow Lucifer, the world as we knew it would end. I tugged at the leg of Lucifer's pants with a bloody hand.

He leaned in. "What is it, my precious one?"

My throat was raw, but I forced out the words. "D-do

4

what you must. You can't let her take it with her. The risk is too high."

He leaned closer. "Are you sure?" he asked as he carefully moved my hand from my side, getting a closer look at the damage Sera had caused.

"Take his memories away," I choked out, pressing a shaking hand to my chest, because the agony of being forced to love Lothar from afar had to be less painful than the agony of my shattered heart now. I could not live in this torture one more moment. It was unbearable. "Take them." My chest felt as if it were caving in, as if the organ in there ceased to beat and had crumbled to dust. The bleeding and burning slice down my side was nothing compared to my breaking heart.

"That wound in your side may never heal," he said gravely. "And if it does, it could still take years." He ran the backs of his fingers down the side of my face. "I could try to turn back time, to before this happened," he said softly. "It won't be easy, not when an angel was present..."

I squeezed my eyes closed, and the images were still there, still flashing rapid fire through my mind. Against all odds, fate had chosen a mate for me, something that shouldn't have been possible. Handmaids didn't have mates, Lucifer had made it so. I'd had so many hopes and dreams, but they'd all been scorched to ashes now. I shook my head and gasped. "I would rather be f-forced to bind my body, to hold my insides in every day for eternity, than go back. Going back won't change the truth." I gripped his hand. "Y-you need this, you need what's in that box. L-let me do this for you."

Lucifer's gaze searched mine. "You're sure? Once too much time has passed, you know I can't undo what has been done."

I nodded as another howl echoed just beyond the door. I grabbed Lucifer's hand. "Give Sera what she wants. Make him f-forget what happened here tonight, make him forget what we are to each other."

"Roxy, my sweet child, you can't want that," Lucifer said, brushing back my blood-soaked hair.

"Just do it. Please—"

"His beast...a hound's instincts are strong, Roxy."

"C-can you suppress it?"

"I can, but this can never be reversed. If Lothar was to ever learn the truth of this day, of your connection, the consequences would be dire," he said. "This can never be undone—"

"I don't care. Please, just do it."

Lucifer stood and turned to Seraphina. "It will be done."

She held up the small box. "I want to see it done for myself."

Lucifer's gaze slid to the door, and a moment later, a massive hound burst through, charging into the room, his huge paws leaving bloody footprints, his eyes blazing red.

His gaze found me, and he shifted immediately, blood-soaked fur giving way to bare flesh. Lothar stared down at me, nostrils flared, chest heaving, and there was unbearable pain in his eyes. He bared his teeth, struggling, trying to talk, but his beast still had his throat. When he opened his mouth, instead of words, he roared and snarled.

"Do it," I said to Lucifer.

Lothar roared again, but this time, I heard part of my name as he struggled to take control. His face flashed between beast and man, his body contorting, his skin rolling with the urge to shift back, but he fought it. He stumbled to the side, then his gaze flashed gold.

Lothar stormed toward me, but Lucifer got in his way, facing off against the blood-covered hellhound.

"You can't stop me," Lothar said, finally forming words, even if they were garbled.

"I'm afraid I can," Lucifer said and lifted a hand.

All it took was one simple movement, nothing more than a wave, and Lothar stopped. He blinked at Lucifer, shaking his head as if he were trying to clear it. Lucifer laid his hand on Lothar's shoulder, and his wounds closed before my eyes.

"You can head back to your quarters now, brother," Lucifer said to him, opening a gateway back to Hell. "When you wake, you'll forget you were ever here."

The hound nodded, then without even looking at me, *without seeing me,* he walked through the opening and back into Hell.

"It is done," Lucifer said, and his hand shot out. The box Seraphina held flew to him. He snatched it out of the air and quickly checked inside, making sure the gem was there.

A flash of bright light filled the room, and when it subsided, Sera was gone.

"Where is she?"

Lucifer's gaze came back to me. "I'm sure she'll soon be back to take her place in Hell. Sera will hold me to my bargain."

I didn't want her here. I didn't want to see her smug, evil face ever again.

His yellow gaze held mine. "I can repair your broken heart, I can take all you are feeling away. Sera will never know. There is no reason for you to suffer this way."

I shook my head. Despite what Lothar had done, I couldn't let Lucifer take my pain away. The thought of erasing the love I felt for him was unthinkable—it was all I had left of us now.

I coughed, tasting blood as agony wracked through me.

"I hope, my precious one, that you will not live to regret this decision," Lucifer said as he scooped me up off the bed and stepped through the gateway to Hell, closing it behind us.

It was my job to protect Lucifer and his interests. It was what I was created for, what all the handmaids were created for. He came first, always.

Regret would be pointless.

What was done, could never be undone.

CHAPTER
ONE

Roxy

Present day

POE STRAINED AGAINST HIS CHAINS, mouth opening to scream as I carved into his flesh, but he only managed a hoarse croak. I'd been working on the demon for several hours, after torturing Tarrant until he passed out.

Still, neither was talking.

Lucifer was convinced they didn't know where Beelzebub was. I refused to believe it. They had to know something. I needed them to talk. They were B's little helpers, and if anyone knew where that traitor had run off to after his failed attempt to usurp Lucifer's throne, it was them.

The only sound in the room now was my leather jacket creaking as I leaned in and pressed the tip of my blade into the delicate flesh below Poe's right eye. "You want the pain to stop, don't you, Poe?"

His gaze bored into mine, full of fear and fury. "Yes," he croaked past his wrecked throat.

"Then you need to talk." Desperation filled me. Time was almost up. If I could get him to give me something, freaking anything, I wouldn't have to go on this hunt for the missing lord, I could just go pick the prick up from wherever he was hiding, bring him back to Hell, and be done. I swallowed thickly. I wouldn't have to spend the gods only knew how long with Lothar tracking down the giant red traitor.

He licked his bloody lips. "I-I don't know a-anything."

"Losing an eye isn't fun. You know this better than anyone. They take a really long time to regenerate." He flinched. "I'm about to make mincemeat out of both of yours, Poe, and there's only one way to stop it." I gripped his jaw. "Tell me where Beelzebub's hiding."

His mouth opened and closed several times. "No… please. I-I don't…kn-kno…"

"What are you doing, Roxy?"

I froze, and my gaze sliced to the door.

Lucifer stood there, his yellow gaze shadowed by his gloriously thick black lashes. He was dressed in black jeans and boots, leaving his chest and all that heavily tattooed skin on display. He slid his thumbs into his pockets, and the silver rings he wore glinted in the flames from the wall sconces. He didn't speak, just tilted his head to the side, studying me.

I huffed. "Before I'm sent off on some wild goose chase, I decided to give torture one last crack."

His lips curled up on one side. "You thought you could extract information that I couldn't?"

I dropped my blade from below Poe's face and straightened. The demon slumped in relief.

Sliding my knife into its sheath, I curled my blood-stained hands into fists. "Anything's possible."

Lucifer chuckled. "I suppose, but there is no escaping what must be done, Roxana."

He rarely used my full name, but when he did, it meant he wouldn't be swayed. He opened the door, stepped out, and held it open for me to follow. I had no choice but to obey, but I scowled and stomped out, making sure he knew I was doing it under duress.

We headed back along the cavern toward his quarters, and as we walked, the emotions swirling inside me like an out-of-control hurricane shamed me. Lucifer was my king. My creator. My everything. Love was a paltry word for what I felt for him, which was why the burning hot rage I felt toward him right now filled me with guilt.

He opened the door to his quarters and strode across the main room, opening the double doors on the other side that led to his private gardens, doors that only those closest to him could see, and again, motioned for me to follow.

Mini, his cat, slinked out with us, curling around Lucifer's legs when he stopped beside his favorite olive tree.

I wiped my expression clean. I was behaving like a petulant child. I was a warrior first and foremost, and I would behave like one. Which meant I bit back everything that sat on the tip of my tongue. It was hard, so hard, especially when it felt like there was a jagged ball in the center of my chest playing pinball with my ribs and tearing shit up.

His gaze slid to my hip, where the bottom of the scar peeked out between my jeans and shirt. It was the only scar on my body. It should be impossible, but the weapon that caused the wound had been special, one that was capable of killing me. It had taken years for the deep slice to heal, and the jagged and ugly scar was a constant reminder of... so many things.

"I still have nightmares about what you went through," Lucifer said and cupped the side of my face. "My precious child, my sweet Roxy. I remember the pain in your eyes and the horror. I know what that night cost you. Do you truly think I would harm you purposely? That I would send you on this hunt with Lothar if I didn't think it was the only way?"

It hurt being angry with Luci. I hated it. Tears sprang to my eyes. "I'm sorry," I choked out. "I did doubt you," I admitted. "I'm just...I'm scared."

A gentle smile curled his lips. "You are my fiercest warrior, my most brutal torturer and skilled seductress. You have faced down enemies that would make lesser beings piss in their pants. You, my precious one, are Roxana the Blade, a formidable handmaid to Lucifer, the king of Hell, and one of my most beloved creations. There is nothing you can face that you will not defeat."

I let his deep voice resonate over me, through me, then covered his hand with mine, looking up at his handsome face. Every sharp line and angle was as familiar to me as my own reflection. "I'll do whatever it takes to carry out your orders, Luci. I won't let you down."

"You never have, Rox. I know you're angry with me right now, but I hope when this is all over, you will be able to forgive me," he said and pulled me in for a hug.

I wrapped my arms around him, the guilt gnawing wider inside me, because he was right, of course. He sensed exactly how I was feeling. Lucifer knew everything. All the things he'd just said were very nice, but the anger, the hurt, was still there because he did know how hard this would be for me, and yet he was making me go anyway.

Everything Lucifer did was for a reason, though, and questioning him, doubting him, was disrespectful and disloyal. These volatile emotions made me feel so awful, so ashamed. "You know I love you," I said as a hot tear streaked down my face.

He swiped it away gently. "Of course, I do. And I love you, too, so very much," he said, his thumb sliding down to my jaw. "You will get through this, Roxy. I promise."

I nodded, but for the first time in my very long life, I doubted him. I doubted my king.

And when he wrapped me in his arms, holding me tighter, and a pained sound rumbled from his chest, I knew he felt that too.

Lothar

"Lucifer always has an ulterior motive, which means he has to know more than he's letting on," Warrick said from his spot on the other side of my quarters.

War was right. Lucifer liked to play with people and situations, but this was different. "I agree, but when it comes to his throne, he's not gonna want to mess around. It would be in his best interest to share everything he knows. If he has any info on Beelzebub, I fucking hope he decides to fill me and Rox in on it."

War nodded and his brow lifted. "I'm surprised he chose Roxy to go with you, honestly. He likes to keep her close."

I was just as surprised. I shoved a couple pairs of jeans in my bag with the rest of my clothes and zipped it up. "Yeah, especially since we have no idea how long this could take."

If truth be told, I wasn't looking forward to it. The handmaid had been giving off some serious vibes lately, ones that rubbed my beast the wrong way. Well, more than usual. I slid my favorite knife into my boot sheath, swung my bag over my shoulder, and we headed through the dens and upstairs to the clubhouse aboveground.

"You need anything, just call," War said. "And keep me updated, yeah?"

"Will do," I said as my alpha gripped my hand and pounded my back with the other.

I'd said my goodbyes to the rest of the pack last night over a few drinks. The parking lot was empty when I walked out, most still sleeping it off. I headed to the chiller behind the workshop and grabbed the deer Jagger had caught, butchered, and bagged for Kurgan. Kurgan was still refusing to see Jag, blaming him for keeping him from his female, so Jag was giving him time, and we were taking turns dropping off his meat.

When I walked back around front, Asher was there, waiting by her bike.

"You come to see me off?" I said as I strode up to her. "Gonna miss me, huh?"

She slugged me in the chest. "I'll live." She smirked. "And okay, I'll admit, I might miss you a little bit, but only because you buy the best hooch and don't act like a pussy when I drink you under the table."

I chuckled. "You keep saying sweet shit like that to me, you'll make me blush."

She rolled her eyes. "Idiot."

Ash was a high-ranking alpha female from the Silver Moon wolf pack. I'd known her for quite a few years. But we'd gotten tight after we'd almost hooked up one night at a party here at the clubhouse—almost—because she'd changed her mind by the time we reached my quarters. She said if we fucked, she'd never talk to me again, and she liked me too much to freeze me out. After that, we started building her bike, and now we went for rides, drank good whisky, and hung out whenever she wasn't busy with her pack.

I hadn't expected to feel this way for anyone apart from my brothers. There was this deep sense of loyalty when I was with her, and though she didn't need it, a protectiveness. I could admit, for a while, I'd hoped she'd turn out to be my mate, but then she'd confessed she'd been mated before. He'd died a long time ago, which meant anything between us, beyond the physical, was impossible. She was beautiful, tough, bold, funny, but after her confession, I knew that what I felt, with my limited emotions, was the same thing I felt for my brothers, and no more.

I let my power flow through me, preparing to open a gateway to Hell.

Time moved faster belowground, and I wasn't sure when I'd be back.

"Take care of yourself while I'm gone, yeah?" I said to her.

She smirked. "Of course. No one fucks with me. And I expect you to do the same."

Oh, I was coming back. I was going to find that fuck, Beelzebub, and I was going to drag his ass back to Lucifer—even if that meant bringing him back in several fucking pieces.

CHAPTER
TWO

Roxy

"HERE, DRINK THIS." Ursula handed me a vial from her bag. "You look like something just barfed you up."

I took the small bottle filled with the best hangover cure ever invented and, without a word, drank it down greedily.

Ursula was my sister. I loved her, and I was so glad she was coming with me, at least for the first couple of days, but right then I needed her to shut the hell up because I was fighting really hard not to empty my stomach all over the cavern floor.

Her elbow dug into my side. "Hey."

I ignored her and kept walking.

She elbowed me again. "The last thing you want is to appear weak when we meet up with Lothar. Pull it the fuck together."

"I'm not worried about Lothar. I'm hungover, that's all."

"Bullshit."

"Uma was making my drinks stronger than everyone else's. Blame your twin for my messy state."

Ursula scowled. Uma was two minutes younger than Urs and had spent their entire lives trying to best her. The two hated each other with a passion. "That traitorous hag needs me to fuck her up again. She's getting too cocky lately." She glanced at me, her bright green eyes seeing too much. "But that's not why you're all quiet and moody. This"—she waved her hand at my face—"droopy expression is about Lothar and this fucked-up mission Lucifer's sending you two on."

My fingers curled around the strap of my pack, and I forced a smile, shaking my head. "It's not a problem, honestly. I see Lothar all the time. How is this any different?"

"You're going to be with him twenty-four seven for a start. And you're not fooling me with the bubbly, smiley, Roxy sweetness. Don't try to bullshit a bullshitter. I know you, Rox."

I shrugged, even as my belly clenched uncomfortably. "I'll be fine." Beelzebub had been making moves to overthrow Luci, and no one tried that shit and got away with it. Beelzebub had run, leaving his cohorts high and dry. But I was determined to haul his big red ass back in record time. I was just struggling to understand why it had to be me and Lothar who did it.

Urs snorted. "Right, that's why your eyes are still all puffy after your drunken crying jag last night."

I spun to her. "My what?" I shook my head vehemently. "I did not."

"You were hugging that fucking ratty old leather jacket of his and listening to eighties hair bands."

Crap. I woke up hugging the jacket, and she was right, my eyes were puffy this morning. I inwardly cringed. I only let myself hold it...I winced, sniff it, once a year. I'd tried several times to throw the beat-up old jacket away, but I couldn't bring myself to do it. The only reason it hadn't disintegrated completely from age was because I'd gone to great lengths to care and protect the centuries-old leather. "I'm fine, Urs," I said again, giving her another wide smile.

"It's December 10th."

My smile fell. "I know what date it is."

"And so does Lucifer." She shook her head. "This whole thing couldn't come at a worse time for you."

You could say that, since it was the anniversary of my world shattering into a million pieces. "I've got it under control. Promise." And maybe if I told myself that over and over, it would eventually be true.

Ursula growled under her breath. "Why the hell is Lucifer making you do this?"

I wish I knew, but nothing I said had changed his mind. He'd insisted he wanted me, one of his best warriors, and Lothar, his best tracker, on the job. I got the feeling there was more to it, but as always, Lucifer only divulged what he deemed necessary. He always had his reasons, and I was usually fine with that—when I wasn't on the receiving end of his mysterious ways. "Luci would never intentionally hurt me," I said, parroting what he'd said to me earlier. "I know whatever his reasons, they're good ones."

Urs muttered under her breath.

We were still in Lucifer's quadrant, which meant we had to travel on foot to put space between us and his quarters. No one could open a gateway close to Luci, it was a safeguard that had been in place for centuries, and as we

20

rounded the final corner and the meeting point came into view, my heart danced a freaking jig.

Taking a deep, fortifying breath, I dumped my pack on the ground and leaned against the stone wall to wait.

"He better not be late," Urs said, tightening her vibrant red ponytail, then leaning against the wall beside me.

"He won't be." Lothar was always punctual.

Light flared across from us right on cue, and a gateway flashed open. I straightened, waiting for Lothar to step through. He was standing on the other side, in the clubhouse parking lot. He turned and said something to someone before they came into view.

Asher.

The wolf shifter he was fucking. Well, I assumed they were fucking. They spent a lot of time together, what else could they be doing? She grinned at him, and he pulled her in for one of his wonderful tight hugs.

My throat tightened and breath hissed through my teeth as feelings that I'd repeatedly stabbed to death gasped and fought, struggling for air.

"Keep the knives sheathed," Ursula muttered.

My fingers were curled around the hilt of my knife, the grip punishing. I hadn't even realized I'd reached for it. I didn't know what was going on, but my control was slipping more every time I saw him. Urs was right, I needed to get my shit together, and I needed to do it fast. Quickly releasing the hilt, I shook out my hands.

Asher stepped back, and Lothar turned to the gateway and walked through.

"Hey," he said when he saw us. "Am I late?"

"Yes," Urs said at the same time I said, "We just got here."

The gate closed behind him as he frowned. "What's up, Urs? You just here to see us off, or are you coming as well?"

"I'm tagging along for a couple days, then I have somewhere I have to be. Why? Disappointed?"

His frown deepened. "Why would I be?" He hooked a thumb under the strap of his own pack.

Why would he be, indeed.

"I need to drop this meat off to Kurgan first, then we can head out." He lifted a huge black trash bag. "So we got a game plan?" he asked me. "Any luck with Poe or Tarrant?"

"They're not talking, no matter how many times I peeled off their skin." I took a shirt from my pack and tossed it to him. "Beelzebub's stench is all over that."

Lothar grabbed it and scented it. His eyes glowed, turning distant.

"Anything?"

"Nothing concrete. The trail's faint, broken."

I nodded. "I thought as much. Our best option until you can pick up something concrete is to head to Asmodeus's quadrant," I said, ecstatic when my voice came out strong, if a little hoarse from all my drunken crying. "Since he's super tight with Beelzebub."

Lothar's brows lowered. "Can't see that fucker sharing anything with us."

Ursula grinned, and it was wicked. "Asmodeus loves our Roxy. If anyone can get him to talk, it's her."

"I'd planned to carry Rox," Lothar said, "so we could move quicker, but if you're coming, we better get going, his quadrant's four or five days' travel if we're walking."

My stomach flipped. How the hell was I going to get through this?

"Nah, we planned for that," Ursula said. "Gus is coming. Maddox said he could spare him for a couple days. I'll text and tell him to meet us at Kurgan's quarters."

Lothar nodded, and we headed through the caves. My gaze skimmed down his muscled back, down to his tight ass and strong legs. The male had a swagger that was pure arrogance, and he didn't even try—it was built in. He was created with that confidence and it never wavered. I forced myself to look away and smiled when we rounded the corner and saw Zurriah.

She was standing at Kurgan's door, about to go in, then changed direction when she saw us, striding over and giving me and Urs a hug.

"That for Kurgan?" she asked, looking down at the bags Lothar carried.

"Yeah, from Jag."

Zuri had made a huge difference in her brother's life, now that she was finally able to be with him. She visited him every day, had taught him to read and write, and was working with him on his self-control. Lucifer had expanded his quarters, and he had a few more comforts now that he didn't immediately tear everything to shreds. She was also doing what Willow had done with the hounds above-ground, watching movies with him and teaching him about emotion and social interactions. He still had outbursts and was still more in tune with his beast than any hound I knew, but he was making progress.

She unlocked the door.

"I'll take it in," Lothar said.

Now that the other hounds knew about Kurgan, they were trying to get to know him, to make him feel part of the pack—not easy when he was forced to be locked up down here. When the door opened, I caught a glimpse of the main room. One of the first names he'd asked Zuri to teach him to spell was Lenny. Now his female's name was written all over the walls in different colors, along with beautiful sketches of her and of things and places I'd never seen before.

Kurgan was on the other side of the room, his skin slick with sweat, doing pull-ups. He did that a lot, and I wasn't sure if it was to cope with the helplessness and rage he had to be feeling or if one day he planned to tear it all down. Either option was equally possible.

Lothar disappeared inside with Zuri, and by the time he came back out, Gus had arrived.

Loth lifted his fist for Gus, and the much younger hound pounded it.

"Brother, good to have you with us for a couple days," Loth said.

"Mad said if I didn't get the fuck out of his face, he'd toss me in the burning river," the younger hound said in his matter-of-fact way.

Lothar's lips twitched. "Yeah? He say why?"

"I ask too many questions," Gus said.

Ursula smirked. "Questions are welcome here, pup. Anything you want to know, you just ask Loth. That's what big brothers are for. Isn't that right, Loth?"

Gus was still basically a pup, only around a year old. Hounds made by Lucifer, like Gus, were created full grown, body and mind. We considered him a pup, but mentally, he was more like a naive, emotionally stunted, overly horny twenty-year-old human, only way more aggressive and, on occasion, bloodthirsty.

Lothar shook his head at her. "Sure."

Gus brightened. "I have one now."

"Of course you do," Loth said.

He nodded. "When you mount a drystan demon, which hole do you stick your co—"

"Not the right time, pup," Loth said while Ursula cackled. "Later, when we stop to rest. Right now we need to shift and get moving."

Gus nodded, stripped, and shifted. Urs gathered his clothes and shoved them in her pack. Lothar stripped as well, shifted, then lowered to his belly and turned my way, his golden eyes hitting me. I had to stop myself from taking an abrupt step back.

Nope, no way was I riding on Lothar. Urs was about to get on Gus's back, but I shoved her toward Loth before she could get on and quickly threw my leg over Gus's back.

"Smooth," Urs said under her breath, then strode over to Lothar and scooped up his clothes and bag.

She was right, that was way too obvious. I needed to be more careful. Urs bounded up onto Loth's back, and as soon as she touched him—my blood turned molten in my veins.

Oh no, I didn't like that.

Not at all.

Gritting my teeth, I gripped Gus's fur tight. "Let's go."

He yapped, and we took off at top speed.

As long as we stayed in front, and I didn't have to see them, I'd be okay.

At least I freaking hoped so.

We'd ridden for hours before Lothar finally stopped for the night.

Ursula jumped off his back, and when Loth shifted, she tossed him his jeans. "I'll get us dinner," she said and strode into the trees.

Skull Forest was one of many. Yes, the name was utterly unoriginal, but it was literal, making it easily identifiable since the ground was covered in the skulls of ancient demons. Hell was vast, had multiple levels, and passed through a variety of different landscapes—and despite what people thought, it wasn't hot all the time. This was only one of several forests we'd pass through before we reached Asmodeus's quadrant.

I dumped my pack on the ground and stretched, then sniffed my shirt and grabbed a hunk of my hair and did the same. I stunk of brimstone. Sighing, I shook out my hair, and ash drifted to the ground around me. I was covered in a fine layer of hellfire soot from the pits we'd passed during the ride here. I freaking hated feeling grimy.

Lucifer had shelters all over Hell, but nothing close for tonight, so we'd have to rough it. Sliding off my jacket, I paced around, getting my blood flowing again after sitting astride Gus for so long.

"I like looking at you," Gus said from his spot against one of the trees.

"Do you now, pup?" I said and bit back my laugh.

He nodded. "Your breasts are very nice. They look soft, and your ass is—"

"Okay, Romeo, that's enough. You need to learn when to keep shit to yourself," Lothar said, his voice a gravelly rumble.

That roughness sent little zips of electricity through my belly and shooting down between my legs—and nope, no fucking way could I allow that. My anger spiked.

"I don't need you to speak for me," I fired at him. "I've been dealing with males who want to fuck me all on my own for thousands of years." *What the hell are you doing? You sound insane.*

26

His head jerked back. "Not trying to piss you off, Rox. I was just—"

"Well, don't." There was no stopping me, apparently. The growing, and yes, irrational, anger was unstoppable. "Whatever you thought you were doing, just don't."

He straightened from gathering firewood and his head tilted to the side, his golden gaze moving over me as if he were trying to figure me out. His perusal was too much, and my gaze dipped to his wide, muscled chest. It was dusted with dark hair. Hair I knew was soft to the touch, and nestled among it was a darker patch of skin, a scar that he'd carried for so long it was as if he'd been created with it. Did he think that? Did he ever wonder where it came from?

"Roxy?"

My gaze sliced up to his face, clashing with his. "What?"

His chin jerked back again, his frown deepening.

Shit, I really needed to pull it together. This was why I avoided everyone this time of year. This snappy, surly bitch routine was not me. I was the bubbly, happy, fun one. I was the handmaid who all the hounds adored because of the liberal hugs I dished out. Lothar was looking at me now like I was possessed by some evil, deranged mutant. Well, I felt possessed, honestly.

"Sorry, I'm just a bit cranky," I said and strode over to him, tilting my head back. "I shouldn't have taken it out on you." Then I wrapped my arms around his waist, giving him a hug like I always did, even though I didn't want to right then. I hadn't wanted to hug him for months, honestly. Touching him had seemed far too dangerous recently.

He immediately wrapped his big arms around me, hauling me against him, giving me the kind of hug only a hellhound could dish out.

"All good, babe. You had me worried there for a minute."

I laughed, even as my heart squeezed in a way that was painful. There was a reason that bards and poets wrote of heartache—it was real. The organ beating in the chest was the center of it all, love, pain, and yes, heartbreak.

I'd worked hard to lock everything down when it came to Lothar, because I'd had no other gods-damned choice. For a really long time I'd successfully bottled my emotions up tight. I'd locked them behind a steel door and thrown away the key. Why was this loss of control happening now?

I released him and quickly stepped back. "There's a swimming hole not far from here; I'm gonna go wash up."

He nodded. "I'll get a fire going." He gathered the firewood he'd collected and dumped it into a pile, then opened his hand and hellfire licked up from his palm instantly. He aimed it at the pile, and blasted it, setting it on fire.

I grabbed my soap.

"I'll go with you," Gus said, quickly standing.

"Sit your ass down," Lothar barked at him.

Gus did as he was told but didn't look happy about it.

"Sorry, pup, not this time," I said as I headed off.

It took everything in me not to sprint away, gods, not to keep on running. Lately, that steel door I'd been relying on so heavily felt as if the hinges were rusted and loosened, that the door was flaking away, and all that volatile and brutal emotion I'd locked up tight was slipping free. It wasn't all of a sudden though, was it? I realized now, that it had been slowly decaying without me realizing it, and I was terrified it was too late to seal it back up.

I rubbed my hands over my arms as goose bumps lifted across my skin. What I was feeling right now, the lack of control I had over it—and what it would mean if I wasn't able to lock it back up—was too much to even contemplate.

But still, despite all of that, a small, twisted, pathetic part of me that I hadn't been able to smother wanted to fucking bask in it. The masochistic little bitch wanted to let every emotional wave crash into her, let it pull her under and drown her because, sweet Lucifer, I'd missed it. The way Lothar made me feel was intoxicating and terrifying all at once.

I wasn't sure what to do, because for the longest time, I hadn't allowed myself to feel anything around him. I still didn't want to, because nothing could come of it, but I didn't know how to shore up my defenses—or what had weakened them in the first place.

The clearing opened up ahead and I spotted the swimming hole. My sisters and I had bathed here more times than I could count. The water came from an underground spring and was clean, fresh, and warm. Shoving all the unsettling thoughts from my mind, I stripped off and sank into the water, sighing when the warmth immediately soaked into my skin.

Dipping my head under to wet my hair, I popped back up, grabbed the soap I'd put in easy reach, and lathered up my hair. I usually used a coconut-and-lime-scented shampoo, but I was traveling light. I dipped under the water to rinse it out—

Someone fisted my hair and wrenched my head back, hard. A sharp blade flashed toward me.

I flipped in the water, and whoever had hold of my hair was thrown off-balance, plunging into the pool with me. They still had hold of my hair, and I grabbed their other wrist to stop their blade from slashing my throat under the water. Shoving my feet against the rocky side of the swimming hole, I ran up it and flipped again. Their fingers slipped from my hair, as we changed positions, and I finally got a look at my assailant.

Verahn demon.

Still gripping his wrist, I slammed it against the rock edging the pool, once, twice. The knife clattered out of his hand, and in one quick move, I snatched it up, locked my arm around his throat, and stabbed him in the chest three times. The demon shrieked as I slashed through the tendons behind each of his shoulders, then did the same behind his knees, before I yanked his head back so I could see his face. "What do you want, why are you here?"

Demons hanging out here in the forest was no big surprise, this was Hell, they were everywhere. Sensing them close, or in the hound's case, scenting them, wouldn't set off any alarm bells, because normally they wouldn't be stupid enough to attack me.

More demons rushed forward, surrounding me. Verahn were built for fighting, which was why a lot of them made up security for most of the lords and some other immortals as well.

I tossed the flailing demon from the pool and bounded out. "How very impolite of you," I said and smiled brightly. "Attacking a girl while she's trying to take a bath. Why don't you tell me who you are and what you want and we can talk?"

"Your head for a start, then..." His gaze trailed down my naked body. "We'll see what else pops up."

"You're not going to give me your name? No problem, I'll call you...hog face. Hey, hog face, did you just imply that you were going to rape my decapitated body? That's pretty fucked up. You know that, right?"

He opened his mouth and shut it, confusion covering

his extremely swinish features before he snarled. "Shut the fuck up. We're going to kill you, bitch."

I giggled. "No, you're not."

He waved around the cleaver he was holding but looked unsure all of a sudden. Then one of the very lonely brain cells in his thick skull betrayed him and convinced him that he had this. "You don't have your backup with you now, handmaid. There are three of us and only one of you. You're fucked."

"You know what, hog face, you're kinda adorable when you say stupid shit." I lifted my hands. "I'll give it to you, you have balls, no doubt big, pink, disgusting ones, but still, kudos to you. Question?"

He snarled.

"I've been wondering something since you showed up."

He scowled, his gaze darting to his friends, then back to me. "What?"

I tilted my head to the side, then dropped my gaze to his groin. "Do you have one of those little weird, curly pig dicks as well?"

He roared and charged.

THREE

Lothar

I RAN TOWARD THE SCREAMS, pounding through the undergrowth as I sprinted to get to Roxy. She was a warrior, immortal, but that didn't mean she couldn't be killed if someone got the jump on her and managed to take her head.

There was a loud splash just as I burst through the trees and into the clearing.

I stopped so abruptly, my boots skidded in the damp soil a couple feet.

Roxy stood at the edge of the pool, naked and covered in demon blood. One verahn was flailing on the water's surface and gasping for air. Another with severed tendons flopped around on the ground at her feet, and there were two more piles of ash, demons she'd already taken out.

Ursula sat on a rock a few feet away, picking at her nails with the tip of a clean blade.

"What the fuck happened here?" I rasped.

Urs grinned over at me. "I only caught the highlights."

"You did this on your own?" I said to Roxy. I knew she was one of Lucifer's best warriors, that all the handmaids were deadly as fuck. Logically, I knew that, but I hadn't seen the small female fight in a long fucking time.

Ursula rolled her eyes. "We're not damsels, Lothar. I know you hounds get off on that shit, but you're barking up the wrong tree if you think, at any time on this hunt, you'll be forced to *save* one of us."

"I know that," I said, planting my hands on my hips, while I worked at slowing my heart rate.

Roxy ignored us, jumped in the pool, and shoved the demon's head underwater, holding him there for several minutes before dragging him, spluttering, up to the surface. "Who sent you?"

He made a bunch of garbled sounds. Scowling, she wrenched his mouth open, then cursed. "No tongue. It's been cut out. A while ago by the looks."

She tossed him out of the pool and leaped out after him. Water sluiced off her curvy, naked little body as she leaned over him, gripped his hair, and, ignoring his screams, hacked off his head.

Fuck, I couldn't look away, and even more disturbing, the front of my jeans started to get seriously tight. The demon turned into ash as Rox spun on the other demon flailing on the ground. "Okay, hog face, time to talk."

Hog face?

"This the one with the pig dick?" Ursula asked.

It took everything in me not to intervene, but these were not the kinds of females you got in the way of. It would be seen as a serious insult. They didn't need me for protection. I was here to track, but fuck it was hard to stand back and not kill something. Hounds were deeply protective of females, and it went against everything in me to do nothing.

"Yep, and if he wants to keep the curly little thing dangling between his trotters, he'll start talking," Rox said as she strode toward him, the knife in her hand flashing as she expertly spun it. "He was the only one doing any talking earlier, maybe he's the only one with a tongue? Is that it, hog face?"

Roxy straddled his flailing body and grabbed his jaw.

Fuck me, she was gorgeous and sweet, but seriously bloodthirsty, and something about that, yeah, it did it for me—*was* doing it for me. She dragged her hand down the demon's bloody chest and grabbed his dick. The demon's eyes flared.

"Who sent you?"

He bit his lips together, refusing to talk.

In a flash she slapped his balls hard, then squeezed. "Who, motherfucker?"

He shrieked.

Fucking hell. I shifted from foot to foot, my throat feeling tight all of a sudden, my gut knotting. *What the fuck?* Why the hell was I getting hard over Roxy? Yeah, she was gorgeous, and her body was...shit, perfection, but I'd never wanted to fuck her. Not only would that make shit complicated, it just seemed wrong.

For a start, her scent was—there was no other way to put it—repellent to me. There was something seriously off with it. I didn't know why, but every time I got a whiff, I wanted to get the hell away from her. It wasn't bad, just really fucking not *right*, at least to me. Which made no sense, because Roxy was the sweetest, funniest, cutest, and, fuck, sexiest little assassin I'd ever laid eyes on.

The demon shook his head, then his eyes rolled back so only the whites were showing.

Roxy's face screwed up. "Ew, are you getting off on having your balls slapped, hog face?"

Ursula, who had closed in and was looking down at him, shrugged. "Some males like it rough, Rox, you know that. Use your blade. We want to make this fucker scream, not moan."

The demon convulsed under her, light flashed behind his eyes, and then—he vanished.

Disappearing from under Rox, leaving nothing but thin air.

"What the fuck just happened?" I growled and closed the space between us before turning in a slow circle. "Where the hell did he go?"

I scented the air, pulling his stench into my lungs, then closed my eyes, using my powers to search for him. My mind spun, location after location zoomed in, then flared back out, chaotic, confusing, but never able to pinpoint one place, as if the demon was being bounced from one location to the next in a split second, so many, too many.

Snarling, I shook my head. "Whoever took him, they're scrambling shit so I can't see where he's stopped."

"Fuck," Ursula muttered.

Roxy yanked a shirt over her head. "Someone sent them to take me out." She looked up as she tugged on her jeans. "They waited until I was alone, and they went for my head."

"Not many would be that fucking stupid," Ursula said. "Going after one of Lucifer's personal guards is dumb enough, thinking they could take you out, even on your own, was fucking suicidal."

"The reward must be good," I said, unable to look away

as Roxy pulled her dark hair over her shoulder, wrung out the water, then quickly braided it.

She wasn't wearing a bra, and the thin fabric showed her tight little nipples as clear as day and—what the fuck was I doing? Was I losing my ever-loving mind right now? I wasn't here to check out Roxy. I was here to do a job. "It had to be Beelzebub. He has to be behind this. Who else? He'll have his spies everywhere, watching, waiting for Lucifer to make a move, which means he knows we're coming for him."

"You can't tell me that guy was important. He was a crappy fighter with below-average intelligence. The only reasons to snatch him away would be to make sure he didn't squeal, and no doubt for intel on our little party." Roxy finished lacing up her boots and straightened. "Which means, we're going to have to outsmart and outmaneuver the big red weasel."

Jesus, the shit that came out of her mouth. My lips actually twitched.

She blinked up at me with her big blue eyes. "What are you smirking about?"

I shrugged. "Just you." My smile widened. "The shit you said to that demon?" I chuckled, the sound surprising me.

Then Ursula was cracking up as well.

Roxy scowled at Urs. "Whatever." Then her gaze sliced back to me. "And when did you find your funny bone, all of a sudden? That's all I need on this trip."

I shrugged. It had happened slowly, I guess. But then I seemed to understand emotions better than some of my brothers. And sometimes, I thought I felt more than I should as well.

It started when Relic was born. Siring a pup had altered me in ways I hadn't expected. Also, having mated brothers and their females and pups at the clubhouse had changed things. The ability to feel humor had slowly developed for many of us, though. It was a surprise, but it also made life a lot more enjoyable.

"We better get back to camp. Gus is alone and he's still just a pup," Rox said, then spun and jogged away.

I followed her and Urs, covering them from the rear. Rox had a soft spot for the pups; she always had. When Relic was born, she'd kept him with her constantly. When I'd go and check on him, he'd either be napping in her bed or she had him strapped to her chest, carrying him everywhere. I fully believed she was the reason he was such a good male, and why my son's emotions had been more developed than the rest of us.

Not that I'd ever called him son, not to his face, anyway. Yes, I'd sired him, though not because I was mated but because Lucifer wanted to experiment. I'd donated my seed, that's all. We'd never had a father-son relationship, that's not how it worked with us. He was a brother, like all the other hounds in the pack. But since he'd mated Fern, I'd felt a shift in him toward me. We'd always been tight, and I'd naturally been drawn to him. A part of me had always felt some closer connection, but things between us had changed again.

With his mating, not only could Relic understand emotion, he felt it. More than once since, I'd wished I knew what he was feeling toward me, because I didn't miss that he looked at me differently now. He sought me out, asked me to hang with him more often, and on occasion with him and Fern. I'd watched Dirk and Elena, and War and Willow with their pups, and honestly, I felt cheated I'd never experienced what they were.

I kind of wished I felt what they did, that I could return what I could only imagine Relic was feeling.

I reached the clearing to find Roxy fussing over Gus. She was holding his head to her chest, rubbing his back and making him promise her to be safe and stay close to us. The pup was nuzzling her tits, looking more than a little pleased with himself.

"Gus," I barked.

Roxy jumped, her eyes flashing. "What's your problem now?"

"The pup doesn't need to be soothed, he's fine."

"He needs hugs like the rest of you, isn't that right, Gussy?"

The little shit nodded, making her chest jiggle. Yes, we craved hugs and affection, needed it, but Gus was taking it too fucking far.

"Having his face buried in your tits is not the kind of hug the pup needs, Rox." My voice sounded deeper, gruffer, but seeing Gus all over her was starting to piss me off for some utterly fucked-up reason. Probably because although Roxy was many centuries old, and tough as fuck, she still had this naivety about her, this innocence that made no sense and always made me feel more protective of her than any of the other handmaids—which again, made no sense.

She blew out a long breath and shook her head, before her gaze sliced back to me. "Gods, you are *such* a dick."

My brows shot up. "You think I'm a dick?" Rox had been acting weird with me for a while now, I kept asking her if something was wrong and she kept denying it, but she'd never said shit like that to me before.

She shoved Gus away and shot to her feet. "If it acts like a dick and looks like a dick, then it's probably a dick," she said and planted her hands on her hips.

I studied her. "What's really going on here, Rox? You've been giving me attitude for months, and I haven't missed that you try to avoid hugging me when you come to the clubhouse, and only do it when you absolutely have to." I crossed my arms. Yes, her scent fucked with me, and I kept our hugs short because of that, but I didn't like that she didn't seem to want to hug me anymore, when she used to always come to me first. "We're going to be traveling together for a while, babe. You got a problem with me, we should probably sort that shit out now."

"I hugged you earlier, if you'll recall," she said.

"Yeah, and you snapped my head off then as well." Her gaze sliced to Ursula, and the other handmaid subtly shook her head. "What the fuck was that?"

Roxy's gaze shot back to me. "Nothing. Like I said earlier, I'm not pissed at you, I'm just pissed off in general for *reasons* that don't concern you."

"Nah, I call bullshit. It's not just now. It's been for months, at least when I'm around. I'm the only one out of my brothers you're giving the cold shoulder to, Rox."

Her face flushed a dark pink, and her eyes glittered brighter. She wasn't embarrassed, she was flat-out pissed. "You want to know why?" she fired at me.

"Rox," Ursula growled.

"Yeah," I said.

"You really want to know why?" she repeated.

"Yes," I bit out.

Ursula stepped forward. "Rox—"

Roxy's hand shot up, silencing her sister. "No, he needs to hear this." She pointed at me. "People underestimate me all the time, Lothar. They think I'm too soft, that I'm some goofy, ditzy idiot, that they can manipulate me—"

"No, they don—"

"Yes, they do, but at least your brothers don't try to take advantage of it."

My head jerked back. "You think I take advantage of you?"

She huffed out a humorless laugh. "I sought you out, Lothar, all the time, you know I did, to hang out, to have a drink, to just sit and gab, but you always, *always* brush me off...until you want something, then you put on the charm, that's when I get the grins and the winks and the hugs. I'm sick of you treating me like a fucking moron. That a good enough reason for you?"

Had I done that? I planted my hands on my hips, my gut in fucking knots. Yeah, shit. I had. I avoided her because her scent fucked with me, but I knew she had a soft spot for me. My brothers said shit about it often enough. She was right, wasn't she? I brushed her off, and I put on the charm when I wanted something from her, info or some other bullshit. "I'm sorry, Rox, if I hurt your feelings. I didn't mean to..."

She snorted. "You haven't hurt my *feelings*. I'm just sick of playing the fool, and I'm not going to do it anymore." She sat down and yanked Gus back, pressing his head to her chest and running her fingers through his dark blond hair.

"Rox—"

"I'm done talking about this," she said. "I'll take first shift. Everyone needs to get some sleep while they can."

I studied her for a moment. I didn't like Roxy angry with me. I wanted her smiles and her hugs again, not this, not her resentment. We had possibly weeks of being together ahead of us. I had to fix this. Somehow, I had to make things right between us.

Roxy

THERE WAS A SWEET, heavy scent in the air as we approached Asmodeus's quadrant. It surrounded us before we even reached his vast orchard.

"I've never been here before," Gus said. "I like the smell."

"It's the pomegranates," I said. "Asmodeus makes moonshine out of them and supplies it to most of Hell."

"No, he barters the liquor to get what he wants. He doesn't do it out of the goodness of his rotten and blackened heart," Lothar said to Gus as his long legs ate up the road beside me. His gaze slid to me. "Is he expecting us?"

Not a fan of Asmodeus, then? Not many were. "No, we decided a surprise visit would be best." I attempted to sound like my normal self, but it wasn't easy. I'd barely stopped myself from saying something I shouldn't the night before. I had no idea why these feelings had resurfaced after so long, after centuries of successfully forcing it all down, but the volatile emotions were back with a vengeance, and I was so fucking angry with myself, but even more so with Lothar—no, I was furious with him for something he had no idea he'd done, and I was struggling to contain it.

Honestly, I wanted to punch him in the face. Worse. These feelings churning inside me were getting harder to control. My gaze dipped to his chest, and my stomach churned. I quickly looked away.

Ursula nudged me, her brow quirked.

I shook my head. No, I wasn't going to smash my fist into his face, though I wasn't sure how much longer I could hold myself back, which was seriously freaking me out. I wanted to scream at him, rail on him for what he'd done. It had happened so long ago now, but it felt fresh again, and I fucking hated it.

"Will you answer my question now?" Gus asked Lothar.

Lothar's shoulders stiffened. "What question?"

"About the drystan demon, when you mount one, which hole do you—"

"The one you are directed to," Lothar said quickly. "They all have different preferences. Wait for them to tell you before you go sticking your dick where it's not wanted."

Gus nodded, looking pleased. "Makes sense."

"Got some personal experience with that, have you, Loth?" Ursula asked, smirking.

I bit my lip so hard to stop myself from saying something that I tasted blood.

Lothar shrugged a massive shoulder. "Who hasn't?"

A shriek of rage tried to crawl out of my throat and I choked it down.

"True," Urs said and shrugged.

"Lothar?" Gus said.

"Yeah, Gus."

"Can I ask you another question?"

Lothar dragged in a deep breath. "Sure."

"Do all hounds have mates?"

"Don't know, pup. I assume the fates have one selected for all of us."

When his voice deepened like that, my belly went all swirly and my heart squeezed like it was two seconds from complete failure. *Just stab yourself in the head and put yourself out of your misery.* I felt Ursula's gaze boring into me and I studiously ignored her.

"What does it feel like to find your mate?" Gus asked.

Lothar shook his head. "No idea, brother. From what I've heard, you just know. You want to be with them all the time, your protective instincts are heightened, and you're closer to the beast than ever before."

"And the urge to fuck is all consuming, yes?" Gus said.

"That's what I hear." Lothar shook his head. "You got a one-track mind, pup."

"What does that mean?"

"It means, all you think about is fucking."

Gus nodded. "Don't you?"

Lothar cursed under his breath. "Next question."

"Is Asher your mate?"

I stumbled, and Ursula grabbing my arm was the only reason I didn't go face-first into the gravel.

Lothar's head turned sharply to Gus. "No. Why are you asking me that?"

"Fender told Mad that you're together all the time."

"Asher's a friend."

My fingers curled around my blade before I knew I was

doing it. A friend he stuck his dick in and spent all his time with.

"When you mount your mate, what does knotting her feel like?"

Lothar cursed again. "No fucking idea."

My stomach started churning again. "Let's change the subject," I said before I could stop myself.

"It's gotta feel good, right?" Gus said.

"Yeah, pup, it's gotta feel good," Lothar said, more growl in his voice now.

Yep, all it would take was one sharp, deep stab right at the base of my skull, jiggle it about a bit, and blessed release from all the insanity in my head. It wouldn't kill me, but it would be nice and quiet in there while my scrambled brain healed itself.

"I want to find my mate," Gus said.

Lothar glanced at the younger hound. "One day, I'm sure you will."

Gus's chest puffed up. "If I had a mate, I'd protect her."

Lothar nodded. "You would."

"And I'd mount her every opportunity I got."

"Fucking hell," Lothar muttered.

"Pup, we need to get you laid," Ursula said, smirking. "How do you function being that horny all the time?"

Gus shook his head, expression serious. "It's not easy."

Urs burst out laughing, and even in my sour mood, I couldn't hold my giggle back—then Lothar's rumbling laugh reached me, and my gaze sliced to him. My stomach flipped again, then heat spiraled lower.

Gods damn it. I was in serious trouble.

And so was Lothar.

·)))· ◐ ·((·

The trees were gnarled and ancient, their branches laden with vibrant reddish-purple fruit. These orchards were so vast that we were still a full day's travel to Asmodeus's keep when night fell.

Lothar decided we should stop and camp for the night, which was probably a good idea. I needed my wits about me when I was with the attention-loving lord. When I visited, he expected the bubbly, high-energy brat he liked me to be. Hopefully, we hadn't been spotted. I didn't want him being tipped off about our visit. Az sucked at thinking on his feet, and when I questioned him about Beelzebub, I didn't want him to have time to come up with some lie to cover for his treasonous bestie.

The fire crackled as I spread out my bedroll.

"Gonna do a perimeter check," Loth said and strode off.

Good, I needed a break from the infuriating hound. His continual presence was making me seriously twitchy. Kicking off my boots, I slid into bed, checked Gus was asleep, then turned to Ursula. "Promise you won't sleep while I do." I'd woken the night before, standing a few feet from Lothar. He'd been asleep, thank the gods, and I'd high-tailed it back to my bed.

"I got you, Rox," she said from her spot, leaning against the gnarled trunk of a pomegranate tree. She sliced open one of the fruits. "You start walking and talking in your sleep, I'll toss a rock at your head."

"Thanks, Urs," I said and put my hands behind my head, looking into the darkness above us, so dense, limitless.

"You doing okay?" she asked.

"Not really," I said, not bothering to lie. "I feel...angry, and I don't know how to lock it away again."

"You got any idea what's changed? Why you're feeling this way again all of a sudden?"

I shook my head. "Could just be spending so much time with him, I guess." Though I knew that was a lie, and it had nothing to do with the date and the twisted anniversary I had to suffer through every year. If I was honest with myself, I'd been slowly feeling a change over the last few months, maybe even longer.

"Do you wish things could be different?" she asked, almost gently, hesitantly. Ursula was never hesitant and she sure as hell wasn't gentle. "That you'd done things differently?"

"No...I don't know." I rubbed my hands over my face. "It's too late now. What's done is done, right? There's no going back, there's no changing the past."

"You could have," she said. "Why didn't you?"

Yeah, Lucifer had offered to make things right back then, or at least try. Attempting to send me back in time, giving me a do-over, wouldn't have been easy, not with an angel present. Their powers interfered with Lucifer's. I'd chosen not to try, but there were no guarantees it would have even worked if I'd said yes.

It was too late to go back and try to fix this mess now. At the time, the pain had been too much, had cut too deep. I hadn't been thinking clearly. I hadn't been thinking at all, and I'd agreed to the unthinkable. The result had nearly been the end of me. I'd refused Lucifer's help at first, but in the end, I let him use his powers to dull the sharpest edge, but not take my pain away completely, never that. If I hadn't relented, I wasn't sure I'd still be here.

The whole thing was just too awful to think about. If

Lothar ever learned the truth, not only would there be devastating consequences, but he wouldn't want anything to do with me, anyway.

That was the real reason his instincts told him to avoid me. That's why he always turned me down when I asked him to hang out at the clubhouse, why he ended our hugs as fast as he could. Even though he had no memory of what went down, somewhere deep in his subconscious, he was still trying to get the fuck away from me.

My hand slid down to the center of my chest, attempting to ease the ache there, and I squeezed my eyes closed.

"You get any sleep last night?" Urs asked, again far too gently.

I shook my head. Exhaustion was like a heavy cloak I'd been carrying all day. After I'd sleepwalked, I'd forced myself to stay awake.

"Use this. Two drops," Urs said, tossing me one of her vials.

I took it, doing as she said. Urs wasn't a witch, of course, but she had a well-stocked bag of tricks, along with the tools of her trade. Within minutes of taking her sleep tincture, blessed darkness was creeping in from the edges of my mind.

I eagerly let it take me away.

Excitement filled me as I jogged through cavern after cavern, until I finally reached Lothar's door. Without knocking, I slipped into his quarters and stripped out of my leathers. Crossing the room as quietly as I could, I lowered to the edge of his bed, but before I could get in properly, his long thick fingers locked around my throat from behind and he tugged me against him, so my back was pressed tight to his front. His arms wrapped around me, and he buried his face against my throat.

"About fucking time, kitten," he growled against my ear.

My eyes snapped open, and I blinked up at the darkness above me. I hadn't dreamed about him in a long time, and oh gods, didn't want to now.

That's when I became aware of the hard, solid body under me, radiating heat like a furnace. That's when I also realized it wasn't darkness above me, it was below me. I was staring at a black T-shirt, and I wasn't lying on my pallet, I was lying *on top* of Lothar. I froze. *Oh fuck.*

Oh *fuck.*

As slowly and carefully as I could, I lifted my head. *Please let him be asleep.*

My gaze slid over his chin, up to his nose, then higher, locking on heavy-lidded, golden eyes that were staring back at me.

I was definitely going to stab myself in the brain. There was no other option. "I'm not sure how I..." I looked around me. Urs and Gus were asleep on their own pallets, and I'd traveled a good distance in my sleep, to crawl all over Lothar. "...got here."

"No?" he asked, his voice all sleep roughened.

I hated how much I liked that. "I mean, I occasionally sleepwalk." I chewed my lip, and Loth's gaze dipped to my mouth. "I must have..."

"I was on watch," he said.

"Okay."

"You stood up, eyes rolled back in your head like you were fucking possessed, strode over, shoved me to my back, and crawled on top of me."

My face exploded into flames. "Right." When was the last time I blushed? I had no idea, but I was now, so hot I had to squint from the heat waves coming off my own face.

I gave him one of my bubbly giggles. "I must've been cold or something."

"Or something," he muttered.

Oh, sweet Lucifer, no. My fake smile froze on my face "What else did I do?"

I felt him more than saw him shrug beneath me, then he flashed me his fangs. "Let's just say, I'm happy to be your scratching post any time, kitten."

My world spun, my heart stopped, then my soul left my body and shattered into a million pieces. *Kitten?* There's no way he'd know that name. No fucking way. Then the rest of what he'd said registered, hitting me like a six-ton elephant. "Your scratching post?"

His nostrils flared, and he nodded.

My swallow was audible. "Are you saying..." Oh my gods. *Oh my gods.* "Are you saying that I...that I..."

"Dry humped me?" He winked and lifted his hand, his thumb and finger a centimeter apart. "Little bit."

"What?" I shrieked. "Why didn't you shove me off?"

He chuckled. "You held a blade to my throat."

"I did not," I burst out.

He tilted his head to the side and there was a faint red mark. His grin broadened. "I didn't dare move."

"And you find that funny?" I yelled as I scrambled off his massive body. "I held you at knifepoint and dry humped all over you in my sleep, Lothar! That is not funny!"

"You did," he said, still lying there as if the most humiliating thing ever to happen to me hadn't just happened.

"I sexually assaulted you!"

He laughed then, that deep, rumbling laugh that made my toes curl. "If I really thought you'd take my head, I would have overpowered you." He sat up, his stomach flexing as he did. "You obviously needed to let off some steam, and it wasn't like I had to do anything. I was playing solitaire on my phone through most of it."

I screamed in horror, and Ursula jumped to her feet, her knife already in her hand, searching for danger. Gus only a second behind her, jumping to his feet, fists clenched.

"Stand down," Lothar said. "There's no danger." His gaze slid to me. "You good?"

"No." I spun to Ursula. "I had a nightmare," I said through clenched teeth, my eyes widening as if I could communicate the horrific thing I'd just done with one look. "I really wish you'd woken me before you went to sleep, like I asked you to."

"You were out cold," she said. "I thought you were good."

"I wasn't. I wasn't good, Urs."

"Shit," she muttered.

"Let's just pack up and get the hell going," I said too loudly as I shoved everything back in my pack. "We have a full day's travel to get to the keep."

When we'd eaten and were packed up, Gus shifted into his beast and I strode toward him, cutting off Ursula again.

"You don't wanna ride me, Rox?" Lothar asked, laughter in his voice.

I flipped him off, and he was still laughing when he shifted. I'd never heard a hound laugh in his beast's form before, but I was pretty sure I had now. I ignored the question in Ursula's eyes and quickly climbed onto Gus.

What the hell was I going to do when Urs and Gus left? I couldn't be trusted alone with him. Definitely no more freaking sleep tincture for me.

CHAPTER
FIVE

Lothar

MUSIC THROBBED through the night as we strode up to Asmodeus's keep. There was a party in full swing by the sounds. From what I'd heard, there weren't many nights that he didn't have a party.

As we reached the wide doors, Roxy handed me her pack, pulled the tie from her braid, and shook out her long, dark hair.

I frowned. "What are you doing?"

Rox ignored me.

"Just watch our little master at work," Ursula said. "Give her thirty seconds and Asmodeus will be putty in her hands."

Roxy gripped the door handles, plastered on a wide smile, and shoved the double doors wide. "Call this a party!"

Urs chuckled beside me as the demons in the room

turned to her and erupted, cheering and greeting her like a rock star.

"Will me and Loth be welcome here?" Gus asked, scanning the room heaving with demons.

"You'll be fine," Urs said.

My lips peeled back, a rumbling growl shaking my chest. The beast didn't like this, not at all. "What the fuck is this?"

Ursula smirked at me. "Asmodeus is hard to deal with, arrogant, reckless, an all-round giant fuck-stick, so Lucifer sent Roxy in to win his trust. She succeeded, epically. Now she keeps an eye on things in his quadrant and uses her charms to keep the lord in check."

"Her charms?" I snarled. "Lucifer fucking pimped her out?"

Ursula's green gaze sliced to me, and the promise of pain burned from her eyes. "Roxy is a warrior. She could slit your throat and slice off your junk before you realized you were wearing your own balls as earrings. You ever imply otherwise again, and you'll be choking on your severed tongue before you finish the sentence."

No one could make you feel more like a fucking asshole than Urs. "Didn't mean anything by it."

She huffed a harsh laugh. "Sure, you didn't. Now, how about you stay out of the way and let her get the info we need."

"Roxy, baby!" A booming voice echoed through the room a moment before the lord of lust, chaos, and destruction strode into the room, arms spread wide. He was wearing leather pants and boots, no shirt. His face was all sharp angles, long nose, square chin, and cheekbones like blades. A wide smile spread across his face, flashing a row of pointed teeth, while light from the wall sconces glinted off the ram's horns that curled back from his broad forehead.

Roxy squealed and ran at him, jumping into his arms and giving him a tight hug before pressing a smacking kiss to the leathery gray skin of his cheek. His hand dropped to her ass, and he squeezed it, hard. I stepped forward, a growl rolling from me before I knew it was coming—Ursula's hand slammed into my chest, stopping me from taking another.

"Slow your roll, Loth, seriously. She doesn't need your protection. Let her do her thing. You need to find Beelzebub, and if Asmodeus knows something, Roxy will as well by the end of the night."

I shook my head. "I'm not fucking okay with this."

"You don't have to be. You just have to suck it up and let her work."

A demon approached, carrying glasses of pomegranate moonshine, and handed them over. Urs gave me and Gus a shove toward a table at the end of a raised stage, where barely dressed female demons danced.

We sat and I scanned the room, keeping my eye on Roxy and the slimy motherfucker with his hands all over her. Asmodeus was a piece of shit and wasn't good enough to look at Rox let alone anything else. A demon sauntered up to me, and she was obviously terrified, which was to be expected. Demons had a natural fear of hellhounds, but still, despite that, she tried to get on my lap.

I waved her away, and she changed direction and approached Gus, who immediately sat back and let her climb up. "I won't hurt you," I heard him say to her. His eagerness and obvious inexperience instantly put the demon at ease, and she actually smiled. Fucking hell, the pup looked like the cat that got the cream.

The song that was thumping through the speakers stopped suddenly, and a moment later, the opening notes of a new song started. The room erupted, and they started chanting Roxy's name. Rox laughed, protesting as several demons tried to pull her toward the stage. I stood. Ursula grabbed my wrist, shaking her head at me.

Fuck. I dropped back in my seat and watched as Roxy, still shaking her head, laughed. They got her to the edge of the stage, and she tossed her hair, then jumped up and threw her hands in the air.

The cheering erupted and the feet stomping got louder as they continued to chant for her.

Rox strutted to the middle of the platform, then stilled, her head lowering, her hair covering her face. The cheers were deafening. On the next beat, she tossed all that long dark hair back, shoved her leather jacket off one shoulder, and shimmied it in time with the music.

Ursula threw her head back and laughed, then jumped to her feet, calling Roxy's name with everyone else in the room.

What the fuck was going on?

Roxy spun, then, tugging off her jacket completely and flung it at me. I snatched it out of the air and sat there stunned, watching as she strutted and shimmied and clapped, hyping up her audience.

She threw out an arm and a bottle of moonshine was tossed at her from somewhere in the crowd. She snatched it out of the air as a flaming wooden torch flew at her from someone else on the opposite side of the stage. She caught it with ease, spinning it expertly. Then swigging a mouthful of moonshine, she held the flaming torch in front of her and blew out the liquor, spraying fire in a huge arch.

Holy fuck. I shot to my feet. The song they were blasting was "Fire Woman" by The Cult, and now I understood why.

The demons and Asmodeus were eating it up, watching rapt as she danced, spinning the torch like a pro before slugging more moonshine and spitting fire. She flipped like a fucking circus performer, doing a routine that looked like something that would need years to perfect, and I couldn't look away, just as rapt as everyone else in the room.

The part of the song where the heavy bass eased up and the guitar took lead echoed through the speakers. Roxy strutted toward me, spilling moonshine along one side of the stage as she walked, winked at me, then strode back, pouring more of the strong alcohol along the other side as she strode away, ass swaying.

She spun back, took another swig, and spat more fire, setting the stage alight on either side of her.

My fucking jaw dropped when she lowered to her hands and knees and started crawling toward me, flames dancing beside her on both sides, as the lead singer sung about a female coming close, that he could feel her getting close to him, and my heart pounded while the beast rumbled in my chest nonstop.

Roxy arched her back and flung her hair, then she was right in front of me. She reached out, grabbed the front of my shirt, and tugged me forward, coming so close I felt her warm breath tickle my lips—then she shoved me back, her eyes bright, fucking glowing.

I dropped into my seat, and fuck, in that moment, I was as seduced by her as everyone else in the room.

She shot back to her feet then and shook her ass, hair flying everywhere, jumping around and shaking her tits, looking so fucking gorgeous and sexy that I had to adjust my dick, which was now threatening to burst through the zipper of my jeans. What the actual fuck was wrong with me? This was Roxy. I wasn't attracted to Roxy. Yes, she was gorgeous and sweet and hot, but she'd never made my fucking dick hard before this trip.

Right then, my dick was so fucking hard I could hammer nails.

Finally, she spun around as the song ended, taking her bow while everyone cheered.

She jumped down from the stage and strode back to Asmodeus, who ate up the sight of her as she approached, a huge smile on his face, laughing, fucking delighted as she took a seat beside him at his table.

He slid a drink her way—

"You're staring," Urs said. "Fucking stop it. She has a job to do."

Logically, I knew what the handmaids were. They'd been trained fighters, fucking assassins, warriors, whatever Lucifer needed them to be. Some were experts in diplomacy, in torture, and yes, some in seduction, but seeing them in action like this—seeing Roxy in action like this, fuck, I didn't like it.

"What's Roxy's specialty?" I asked, because I had no idea. How was it that I'd known her so long and I didn't know that?

"Roxy is what's special," Urs said and sipped her moonshine. "Her sweet nature makes her seem naive to some, and because of that, they underestimate her, and while they're underestimating her, she's manipulating their false idea of her, twisting her prey's will, until they're on their knees, willing to do anything for her that she asks, willing to tell her anything she wants to know. That would be specialty enough for any handmaid, but not Rox. When she fights, it's like watching a dance, so fluid and natural, and it's always been that way. She can murder an entire hoard of feral demons on her own, without breaking a sweat, and her skills in the art of seduction are second to none. Rox is one of Lucifer's favorites for a reason, she doesn't have one specialty, she is highly skilled in all areas." Urs winked at me. "Our sweet Roxy is irreplaceable."

I swallowed thickly, a weird feeling swirling inside me. My chest ached and the blood in my veins felt scalding hot. "I didn't know."

She snorted. "Because you underestimate her like everyone else." She shot the rest of her drink. "Roxy is my sister, and I know her vulnerable spots, because you and I know, despite all I just told you, she has them." She refilled her glass, took three vials from her bag, and added a drop from each to her drink. "If anyone manages to find one of those spots and hurts her, every handmaid in Hell, including me, will be after blood. Roxy is not just irreplaceable to Lucifer, she is our sister and we will carve up any motherfucker who causes her harm."

She held my gaze.

"You think I'd hurt her?" I growled. "I'd never fucking do that."

"You might not mean to, Lothar."

"I would never do that, Urs."

One of her shoulders lifted and dropped. "I hope not. I'd really hate to have to slice you up."

We stared at each other for long moments, and though there was no way in fucking hell I would hurt Rox, for some reason Ursula thought it was a possibility and I didn't know how to convince her otherwise. So I gave her the reassurance she needed. "I give you my word."

"I'll hold you to that." She swirled her finger in her glass, mixing it, then sucked off the liquid.

"What did you put in your drink?"

"Poison," she said and downed it in one.

"The fuck?"

She grinned. "That's my specialty." She winked. "Among others."

Well, fuck me. Again, I'd had no idea. "You're Lucifer's taster?"

"I am, and if you tell anyone, I'll have to kill you."

I watched as she repeated the process with three different vials. Micro dosing herself with different poisons, maintaining her immunity to them. "How do you detect the poison if you're immune to it?"

"I can taste the smallest dose no matter how diluted. If any of Lucifer's enemies slipped poison into his food or drink or any other way, I'd know."

"What does he do while you're away?"

"He stays close to home. Only handmaids will prepare and serve his food. My services are mainly required when we travel out of his quadrant anyway. He surrounds himself with only those he trusts implicitly. We also keep an eye on everyone who has access to Lucifer, until we're positive of their loyalty."

Roxy's laughter reached me from across the room, and my gaze slid back to her. She was on Asmodeus's lap now, her arm thrown around his thick neck, while she ran the fingers of her other hand along one of his horns.

Another growl rolled out of me, and I had no fucking clue where it came from. It was as if the beast in me was acting alone. That wasn't how it was for a hound, there was no separation between beast and man.

I was the beast, and the beast was me, but right now, the animal part of me was reacting in ways I had no fucking control over.

CHAPTER
SIX

Roxy

Asmodeus pressed his mouth to my ear. "How long do I have you, my dear?"

I cupped his face. "Just tonight. I'm needed elsewhere."

He nodded, but looked disappointed. "That is a shame."

"I'll be back before you know it."

He pressed a kiss to my temple. "I do hope so, Roxy. I honestly do."

"You know Luci keeps me busy."

He made a grumbling sound. "Since I only have you for one night, will you join me in my bed this evening?" He trailed his fingers along my spine. "It has been too long since I've held you in my arms, my sweetest one."

My stomach tightened. Lucifer had instructed me to seduce Asmodeus and gain his favor a very long time ago. It had never bothered me before, sex was just another weapon in my arsenal, but with Lothar here, with his glowing golden gaze burning into me like I felt him doing now, I wasn't sure I could bring myself to do what I needed to.

Get it together.

This was my job, my purpose. I was created to protect my king. Lucifer was all that mattered. His throne was on the line, it didn't matter that Lothar was here, or what he thought. The feelings trying to bloom brighter weren't of consequence, not when Lucifer's life could be at stake.

I smiled. "Of course, where else would I be tonight?"

Ursula strode over then and Asmodeus turned to her with a smile, pulling her in for a hug. Urs slipped something into my hand as she hugged him back, a small vial. The sleep tincture. Ursula knew me like no one else. She hadn't missed my reluctance. It was risky, giving this to Az, especially in his own quadrant, but I didn't think he'd suspect me of dosing him. I'd built trust with him over more years than I could remember.

"So why the hounds?" Asmodeus asked her. "Why are they with you?"

"Lucifer has us on a hunt," Urs said and winked, then called out for more moonshine.

"What are you hunting?" he asked me, when Urs strode off into the crowd.

I sighed. "I don't want to upset you, Az. Let's not talk business."

"You could never upset me, my sweetling."

I subtly searched the room, but not so subtle that Asmodeus didn't notice, then leaned in close. "Luci has us searching for Beelzebub. We're on our way to Mammon's stronghold, someone said they saw him there. Lucifer thinks Mammon could be hiding him." That was a complete lie.

Asmodeus scoffed. "B would never go to Mammon for help. That's the last place he'd go." He shook his head. "Lucifer is so out of touch with his lords, no wonder one of us finally rebelled."

I bit my lip and gave him a huge dose of wide-eyed innocence. "I don't like to talk badly about Luci, Az, you know that..."

"I sense a *but* coming?" he said as he tucked my hair behind my ear.

"Okay, yeah, he is a little out of touch, I guess. He means well...but sometimes he gets it wrong. Beelzebub was obviously really hurt to do what he did," I said, sighing. "I hate when everyone fights." I inwardly shook my damn head. Fighting wasn't what happened, Beelzebub committed treason, but there was no way I was using that word right now, not when I needed Az to spill what he knew.

"I know you do, sweetling, but Luci has taken us for granted too many times. B was just the first of us to be pushed past his limits."

He'd just confirmed that he knew about Beelzebub's plan without even realizing it. "Do you think he'll come back, so we can talk about this? So he and Luci can clear the air and move forward?"

Az shook his head. "He's not coming back, not yet anyway."

In other words, not until he has the means to overthrow Lucifer. "That makes me sad, Az. Hell doesn't feel the same with one of us gone."

Asmodeus swirled the moonshine in his glass and nodded. "I agree. It definitely feels wrong with only six lords here. I feel his absence strongly, as do the others."

And finally, he'd just confirmed that Beelzebub was no longer in Hell. As Lucifer suspected. I rubbed the back of his neck. "I'm sorry, my darling, that you're in pain. You must miss your brother terribly. I hope he's okay?"

Az lifted his red gaze to mine, and it gentled. "You have the softest heart of any being in Hell, Roxy, it astounds me that it hasn't been blackened like the rest of us."

"I love you all, Az, you know I do. I worry about my family."

He gently took my jaw in his gray fingers. "He is well, sweetling. I promise, he's thriving in fact."

Az could never resist my little *miss innocent* act. He hated seeing me worried. He underestimated me like most, and thought me naive, that I was ruled by my soft heart.

I smiled wide, and pressed a kiss to his black lips. For Beelzebub to thrive, he'd need to be somewhere you could look the way he did, and not draw notice.

"I want you, Roxy," he said roughly.

"Then take me to bed," I said and wrapped my arms around his neck when he stood.

I looked over his shoulder before he carried me from the room. Lothar was standing, lips peeled back, fangs fully extended.

Then we rounded the corner, and I lost sight of him.

I rolled an unconscious Asmodeus off me, and checked he was still breathing. The tincture wouldn't kill him, even if his heart did stall out, but if that happened, he'd know I'd drugged him when he woke and realized he had serious bodily damage. Hopefully, I'd gotten the dose right.

Usually, I endured fucking the lord. I did what Lucifer needed me to. Urs hadn't missed my reluctance, but thankfully, Az had. I'd slipped a few drops of her concoction in his wine when we got to his room. I'd gotten away with a quick make-out session and some wandering hands before he passed out on top of me.

He shouldn't wake after the amount I'd given him, at least not for a good eight hours.

We'd been on the road for a couple days, so I took advantage of his excellent shower, then grabbed some fresh clothes from my bag, dressed, braided my still damp hair, checked on Az one more time, then slipped out of his quarters, carefully pulling the door closed behind me.

I turned, and jumped, my hand moving before my brain registered who it was. My blade was about to fly, about to imbed itself in Lothar's skull, right between his glowing eyes.

"What the actual fuck, Lothar? I almost scrambled your brains." I slid the blade back into the sheath at my hip, looking back up at him when he didn't reply. "Well, what do you want?" I said, and couldn't shake the unease that was suddenly crawling all over me.

Lothar shook his head, like a wild lion. "I was making sure you were okay," he said, his fangs fully extended, his voice a deep rumble.

I straightened, this wasn't right. Why the hell was he out here? "Why wouldn't I be?"

He shrugged a massive shoulder. "I don't like that Lucifer uses you this way, Rox. It's not right."

My heart thumped hard in my chest, as anger pulsed through my veins in an instant. "What did you say?"

He growled. "You are family, Rox—"

"I'm not your family."

His eyes flashed brighter, glowing in the shadowed hall. "Yeah, you fucking are. I've known you longer than I can remember. You take care of all of us...when Relic was born, you—"

"Relic was an innocent pup with no one to care for him. I was only one of many handmaids to look after him." My head spun. Where was he going with this?

He frowned. "I know that. What I'm saying is, you take care of everyone, Rox, and for once, I wanted to do that for you."

I huffed a laugh. "By standing outside Asmodeus's room while he *used* me?"

His chest heaved with his rough breaths. Why was he breathing so hard? As in control as he sounded, his body was giving away how he was truly feeling. He wanted to fuck someone up, and I got the feeling that someone was Asmodeus.

"Like I said, I don't like that Lucifer makes you his—"

I closed the space between us in an instant and pressed my finger to his lips. "Whore?" I held his stare. It cost me, but I refused to look away.

He grabbed my hand, taking my finger from his lips. "I never said that."

"Maybe not in those exact words, but yes, you did. I know you, Lothar. I know exactly what you're thinking."

"No, you don't."

"You think Lucifer is pimping me out, using poor, innocent, naive little Roxy to get what he wants."

His eyes flashed again, and that jaw was granite.

I laughed, and it wasn't nice, then lifted my chin. "I am Roxana the Blade, handmaid to Lucifer. Warrior, torturer, seductress. Yes, I love deeply, and I look for the best in people, but I also have more kills under my belt than you ever will in your entire immortal life." I grinned. "I take immense pleasure in hearing the screams of those I take to my chamber of pain to extract the information we need." I pressed closer, lowering my voice, letting it go a little husky, sexy. "And if it benefits Lucifer *or me*, I can fuck like no other. I can make any male I set my sights on scream my name, then walk away while he's begging me for more. Without regret, and without emotion. So no, I don't need you to follow me about to make sure I'm okay. I don't need anything from you, Lothar. Understand?"

He dragged in a rough breath.

"Do you understand?" I repeated, adding a growl of my own.

"I understand," he said.

I stepped back, putting some much-needed space between us. "Good."

"I don't doubt you are all of those things, Rox, and more, but just so you know, that will never stop me from looking out for you. The way I see it, I owe you."

My heart seized. "For what?"

"Relic."

The frozen organ in my chest burst back into action. "I told you—"

"I don't buy that bullshit. You protected and loved my pup as if he were your own, Rox. I fucking saw it with my own eyes. I wasn't able to give him what War does Violet, and what Dirk does Brick. I couldn't give Relic what my brothers can give their pups, something that took me seeing them as fathers to realize the importance of. I wished I could've loved him then, that I could love him now. You gave him that, what he needed, what I couldn't. You showed him love, and yeah, maybe the other hand-maids helped out occasionally, but not like you. You were the constant he needed, that I now know all pups need. So yeah, even as emotionally devoid as I am, I know that, I understand that. You made him the good, loving male, the devoted mate he is now, and I will forever be thankful to you for it."

Why was he saying all of this now? I couldn't take it. "I love pups. It wasn't about you, it was about me," I said, curling my fingers into tight fists, though that was a lie, wasn't it? Deep in my heart, I'd thought of Relic as mine. I'd wanted him to be mine. The pup Lothar and I would never have together.

"Either way, I'm eternally in your debt."

That's all I needed. "You owe me nothing," I said and started down the wide stone hall. The sound of his heavy boots following me, echoed off the walls. I stopped. "Are you following me?"

He shrugged a big shoulder again. "Yeah, but not intentionally. This is the way back to the main room."

I huffed, turned, and marched ahead. And bit my lip as every thud of those big boots seemed to slam through me. What the hell was I doing? Every time I told myself to act normal, to rein the emotion back in, I lost my shit even more. I couldn't believe what I'd just said to him back there.

This wasn't me. I felt as if I'd been possessed by some unstable imposter, and as hard as I tried, I couldn't exorcise the demented, demonic bitch.

CHAPTER
SEVEN

Lothar

I WAS CREATED IN HELL, spent centuries there before we ever came aboveground, but as we stepped through the gateway and onto a Roxburgh pavement, something inside me shifted, spreading through me, and although I had limited emotions, Lucifer had made sure we understood them, and I was positive what I was experiencing was relief. But why?

Roxy and Ursula strode ahead, while I trailed behind them on my own, since Maddox had ordered Gus to stay in Hell, much to the pup's disappointment. Tonight, we would part ways with Urs as well, and it'd be just me and Rox. Lucifer had assigned Urs a mission of her own, and she'd been told to come to some bar in the city for further instructions. Apparently, we were tagging along before we headed to our next destination, one Roxy hadn't filled me in on yet. She was leading this search, and all I could do was follow.

Right now, that was all she was letting me do.

My gaze slid over the petite handmaid striding along in front of me, and I rubbed at my chest. There was a strange sensation behind my ribs, and this one I wasn't able to identify, no matter how hard I tried.

Something was seriously off, and like this constant sensation in my chest, I couldn't name it. All I knew was I'd felt this way since I stepped through the gateway into Hell to meet with Rox a couple days ago, but most worrying of all? The beast that all hounds carried inside them, our animal side, had been stirring restlessly inside me, in a way that didn't make sense, and absolutely everything about that concerned the fuck out of me.

But even more confusing? The beast was like a fucking pointer dog, nose aimed right at Roxy.

I didn't get it. All I knew was the female had me all fucked up. It was starting to feel like I had split personalities—the beast was all about her, wanted to protect her, be near her, while I continued to struggle with the sensation of wrongness whenever she was close for too long. My dick got hard around her, even while her scent filled me with a sense of dread, and with every inhale, the urge to get the fuck away from her increased—but as soon as I put space between us, the beast tried to take me back to her.

I'd known Roxy for centuries. Why was I feeling these things now?

Urs pushed open the door to a dive bar, and we walked in.

I scanned the room. It wasn't full, not yet anyway, but there were several other handmaids here, and they rushed over to Ursula and Roxy when we walked in. Since I had no idea how long we'd be here, I got a beer and took a seat at one of the tables.

As the night went on, more handmaids arrived, and I watched them dance, do a fuck ton of shots, sing karaoke, and on more than one occasion throw hands when someone pissed them off. Shit was getting rowdy, and Rox and Urs were right in the middle of it. When these females cut loose, everyone needed to stand the fuck back and leave them to it.

The seat beside me scraped as it was pulled out, and I turned as Silas dropped into it.

"Lothar," he said, his silver eyes hitting mine.

I hadn't seen the fallen angel in a while. He spent most of his time with the knights of Hell. "What brings you here, brother?"

Silas had been punished, his wings taken from him a few years ago, and right now he looked wary as fuck. The big male shoved his fingers through his gold-and-black-streaked hair, crossed his heavily tattooed arms over his chest and jerked his head toward Ursula. "I wish I could say pleasure, but I have a feeling the next few weeks are going to be far from that."

Urs had said someone would be here with further instructions for the mission Lucifer was sending her on. Looked like that someone was Silas.

The chair beside Silas slid out and Zenon, a knight of Hell, and Lucifer's grandson, sat. He put his beer on the table in front of him and slid one to Silas. He gave me a chin lift. "Loth."

"Zen, brother." I frowned. "You both here for Ursula?"

"Lucifer has me playing delivery boy," he said without heat. Zenon and Lucifer were tight. The king of Hell had pics all over his quarters of Zen; his mate, Mia; and their toddler, Zephyr.

"And you?" I said to Silas.

"A lot more than that," he said, and he sounded pained.

"Urs never said it was you she was meeting."

"She doesn't know." Silas's jaw looked tight as hell. "I'm not Ursula's favorite person. When she realizes what's up..." He blew out a breath and rubbed his temple, looking more than a little stressed. "Let's just say, she won't be happy."

"Best you try harder to make amends, my man," Zenon said to him. "Lucifer said she's still seriously pissed with you."

"What did you do to piss her off?" I asked, already feeling sorry for him. Ursula did not forgive easily.

He tilted his head toward the other side of the room, to Ursula's twin, Uma.

Oh shit. I'd heard he and Ursula had hooked up a while back, that things had ended badly. "Fuck, man."

"You could say that." His gaze slid back to the dance floor as he took a sip of his beer, and I knew the moment Urs spotted him, because the fallen angel actually flinched.

"Lucifer must have something pretty good on you to get you on board with this."

He tore his gaze from her. "Nah, the knights are my family. Lucifer approached me through Zen. He needed someone with my...special abilities, and since Heaven has locked me out, I don't owe them one fucking thing, certainly not my loyalty."

"You think our missions are connected?" I asked Silas glancing back at Roxy, who was still dancing. Her black hair was wild around her heart-shaped face and her big blue eyes fucking glowed under the lights.

"I think it's highly likely, given the timing."

Silas was right. As usual, Lucifer was keeping shit to himself. Did Roxy know more than she was letting on?

Probably. Especially with how tight she and Lucifer were. I curled my fingers around my glass. If they wanted me to do my damn job, they needed to fill me the fuck in. I needed to know everything they did. "So this thing you have for Urs, why did it have to be Zenon that gives it to her?"

"Lucifer said something about him not being able to leave Hell and bloodlines. Cryptic as usual," Zenon said.

The song changed, a gritty, guitar riff echoing over the speakers. Ursula was by the jukebox, and she turned to Silas and flipped him off as the opening lyrics to "Why'd Ya Do It?" by Marianne Faithfull filled the room.

Silas stiffened beside me, while the handmaids danced, crowding the floor as they sang along to the gritty song about a male cheating on his female. I didn't envy Silas. Ursula was a strong female, a vicious warrior, and she didn't let many get behind that tough exterior. Silas had obviously managed it, before he'd fucked everything up.

Urs stepped away from her sisters on the dance floor, her sight set on Silas and strode toward our table. The male made a low sound and shifted in his seat but didn't stand as Ursula closed in. She shoved the table aside, and Zen and I snatched up our glasses before they ended up on the floor.

Silas's fingers curled into fists as she flicked back her red hair, kicked her leg up, resting it on his shoulder, and leaned in, getting in close as she sang along to the part about betrayal, and oysters, and before she said the word *bitch*, she spun to Uma, who was avidly watching, and said it directly to her twin.

Uma surged forward with a shriek but was held back by several handmaids. Urs laughed and turned back to Silas, trailing her fingers down the side of his face, then gripped his throat.

He was like fucking granite. "I never fucked your sister,"

he ground out. "I've told you a fucking thousand times, we only kissed, *once*, because I thought she was you."

Ursula bared her teeth and gripped his throat tighter, then leaned in again. "Do you really think I give a shit whose mouth you stick your tongue in?"

"You played the song, Ursula. You walked over here fucking singing it," he said. "What else am I supposed to think?"

Her lips curled up and she chuckled. "Jesus, you're too fucking easy, Si. I think playing with you has become my new favorite thing to do." She licked her lips. "I bet if I checked, you'd be hard as fuck right now." Silas's nostrils flared, and Ursula laughed. "You really are pathetic."

"Back the fuck up," Silas said.

She smirked and pushed away. "I take it since you're sitting here like a stalker, you're my travel buddy?" He dipped his chin, grinding his teeth, and her smile widened. "Oh goodie. We're going to have so much fun."

Zenon called her name. She turned, and he tossed her something.

She caught it, and her eyes widened momentarily.

"From Lucifer," Zenon said and got the hell out of here. I didn't blame him.

She looked down at whatever it was he'd given her, then grinned. "About fucking time."

Roxy

Ursula spun away from Silas, a smirk on her face, but as soon as she was sure Uma couldn't see her, her expression shifted to fury. She grabbed my hand and led me from the room, down a short hall to the bathrooms.

She shut us in, locked the door, then snarled in rage, slamming her fist into the wall.

"What's going on, Urs?"

She held up her hand, showing me the jagged stone key.

"Holy shit." I'd only ever seen one like it, but that had been centuries ago. Now I knew why Zenon was here. The invitation had to be delivered by the leader of the realm you were representing, or someone from their bloodline. That didn't explain Silas's appearance though.

"What the actual fuck is Lucifer playing at?"

I frowned. "Urs—"

"First, he sends you off with Lothar and now me and *fucking Silas?*"

Shit.

She shook her head, pacing. "I've been wanting to represent Hell in The Tartarean for centuries, and he's forcing me to do it with Silas? I'm not doing it. No fucking way."

Ursula did not show vulnerability, and she didn't let people in. Even with me it was rare for her to admit how she was feeling, and this show of anger, of reluctance, told me just how much she still cared for the fallen angel. She'd wanted to take part in The Tartarean—a brutal tournament —for so long, but not like this.

She'd let Silas in, allowed herself to care for him, which was why what happened with Uma had cut her so deep. Uma and Ursula loathed each other at the best of times. Urs had good reason, and mistake or not, that made Silas's betrayal that much more cutting.

"You don't have a choice," I said gently.

She shook her head, still pacing. "I will never forgive Lucifer for this, for making me do this. Never."

"You don't mean that," I said and closed the space between us. "If I can forgive him, then so can you."

She spun to me. "And have you? Forgiven him for making you spend every moment with Lothar for the foreseeable future? The male you once loved with your whole heart? A male who doesn't remember that once upon a time he loved you too?"

It felt as if the oxygen had been punched from my lungs. No, I hadn't forgiven him. I wanted to, but I couldn't, not yet, not when I was still in this, living this, and Lothar was just outside those doors, waiting for me in the bar.

"Exactly," she spit out. "He says he loves us, then personally tears open our wounds, not caring if we fucking bleed out."

"You've wanted this for so long, and this time your skills will be invaluable. You have to do this—"

"I know," she snapped. "I know I have to do this, but it doesn't mean I'll forgive him."

I squeezed her hand. "It'll be okay."

Her vibrant green eyes held mine. "Do you really believe that?"

"I have to," I choked out. The alternative wasn't something I could contemplate.

Someone banged on the door.

"I hope you're right," she said, then yanked the door open and strode back out to the bar.

I followed her past the crowded dance floor and toward the table Lothar and Silas still sat at. The fallen angel looked as if he'd be more at home in Hell than Heaven. He kind of looked like a huge goth, all inked up, that black and gold hair, and those lashes that were so dark and thick they could be mistaken for eyeliner. He also had intense silver eyes, that made you think he saw too much.

Both males stood as we neared, but I purposely didn't look at Lothar, my emotions were too close to the surface right then, and if I looked at him, I was afraid of what he might see in my eyes.

Silas stood almost as tall as Loth, and as we closed in, he unfolded his tattooed arms and let his hands hang loose at his sides, as if he were braced for attack. I understood why. Ursula wouldn't make this mission easy on him, not for one moment.

She hooked her arm over my shoulder and pulled me in for a tight hug. "We got this," she said against my ear.

I nodded, then she released me, and Urs and Silas strode out of the bar.

I hoped she was right. I really did. "I guess we should make tracks as well," I said to Lothar.

"Ready when you are."

We grabbed our bags, I waved to my sisters still partying, and together we walked out onto the street. Ursula and Silas had already disappeared. I had no idea where they were going, the location of the tournament was different every time, or how dangerous it would be. No one was allowed to speak about it afterward.

"Urs will be fine," Lothar said.

I glanced his way and found him studying me. I quickly looked away. "I know."

He was quiet for several beats. "Where to next?"

I pointed ahead and started down the street.

Lothar growled.

I turned back. "What?"

"I was created by Lucifer just like you were, Roxy. I'm loyal to him, and I've proven it, time and again, so knowing you're keeping shit from me when it comes to this hunt is pissing me the fuck off."

I stopped in my tracks. "I'm not keeping anything from you."

"No?"

I scowled, even as guilt slammed through me. It wasn't info about the hunt I was omitting. "No."

He shoved his fingers through his hair. "Look, I honestly don't know why you can't stand the fucking sight of me anymore. Yeah, you've given me reasons for the animosity, but honestly, Rox, I don't believe you. I don't know this... this version of you, but we still have to get this done. So stop treating me like a fucking idiot."

I froze in place. "You're being ridiculous."

"You're hiding something."

"I'm not."

He bared his teeth. "Roxy—"

"I'm not," I said more forcefully.

He planted his hands on his hips. "You don't want to share, fine. But you need to realize that we're in this together. You may be Lucifer's favorite, but you're not my fucking superior. If we're going to find Beelzebub, you're gonna need my help, so how about you start by telling me where the fuck we're going and the information Asmodeus shared with you?"

He was right, of course. I was acting like someone else. He was a hound, he sensed things, even if he didn't understand it all. Emotions were confusing for him to read, even if Lucifer had given him and his brothers the ability to identify them, and my attitude and all the volatile things I was feeling had to be fucking with him. I was the one making this situation more difficult, not him.

I blew out a steadying breath, forcing myself to release some of the tension I'd been carrying the last few days. "I'm sorry," I forced out. "You've done nothing wrong. The weirdness you're feeling from me, it's not about you."

He frowned. "So what is it?"

"I don't want to talk about it, okay?" I lied. "But I promise I'll stop taking my shit out on you from now on and be my normal self again."

The muscle in his jaw ticced, but thankfully he didn't force the issue and, instead, nodded.

I hitched my bag higher and plastered a smile on my face, giving him the Roxy he wanted, instead of the psycho he'd been traveling with since we set off. "Okay, so our next stop is Limbo."

His head jerked back. "You think B's in Limbo?"

"No, but I think he passed through on his way to another realm." We started off down the street again. "I'm hoping once we get there, you'll be able to sense him and track him to wherever he went next."

"Asmodeus told you that?"

"Not in so many words. But he did let slip that Hell didn't feel the same with Beelzebub gone. He also said B was thriving. With the way he looks, hiding here in Roxburgh is out of the question. Beelzebub is drawn to death, and pain. Limbo is the quickest route to several realms that fit that bill, and he's been to Limbo before as Lucifer's envoy in the past."

Lothar nodded. "I agree. Good work."

I gave him another bright smile. Maybe if I did it often

enough, it would stop being an act, and I'd start feeling like myself again. "I thought since you're tight with Death's mate, you'd be able to call Zinnia and get us entrance?"

Lothar slid his phone from his pocket. "No problem. I'll call her now."

EIGHT

Roxy

"Zinnia says she'll be waiting for us."

"Excellent," I said as Lothar slid his phone back in his pocket. Especially since we were already on our way there.

The only way for us to enter Limbo was through the gateway located in Oldwood Forest, which was currently dark, and I'd tripped over my own feet several times already. I didn't do that. Ever. I'd once walked a tightrope across the burning river, during vysan mating season. They'd been bursting out of the water one after the other, snapping their jaws, and I hadn't missed a step. I was seriously off my game. "Good thing you're tight with Zinnia. It's been a long time since I stepped foot in Limbo. I wasn't sure Death would be very welcoming."

Demons had been following us since we started through the forest, watching from a safe distance because there was no way they'd come anywhere near Lothar. But I was a female, and these pricks were forever on the hunt for breeders. Apparently, they had no idea who I was, or that I was capable of turning them into mincemeat in record time. I turned when one particularly heavy one collided with a tree and yelped, or at least it sounded like it.

"What did that tree ever do to you?" I called.

Lothar's white teeth flashed in the shadows. He was grinning, amused by my outburst. It was something that still took me some getting used to.

"You've been to Limbo before?" he asked when I quickly looked away from him.

"Yup, I actually accompanied Beelzebub on one of his envoys. Luci likes one of us to go on any official get-togethers, to ensure his best interests are being represented."

"What's it like?"

I glanced back his way and caught his gaze dipping to my mouth again. He'd done it several times tonight, and it was...disconcerting. "Well, the last time I went, Death didn't have Zinnia. He was moody, dark, and inhospitable, and so was Limbo. His castle was cold and unpleasant like its master. So I'm not sure what to expect this time."

My phone vibrated in my pocket and I slid it free. I was expecting a text from Urs. A delighted laugh escaped my lips instead.

"What's going on?"

Smiling wide, I held up my phone, showing him the picture. "My grandbabies sent me pics of their babies. I'm their lovey, that's what they call me. They're so precious, Loth. I already can't wait to get back so I can snuggle them again."

His brows shot up. "Grandbabies?"

I chuckled. "Well, many, *many* times great, but yeah. They're my sweet girls, my twin granddaughters."

"You have grandchildren?" Lothar blinked over at me. "You had your own children?"

The penny had finally dropped, and there was no missing his surprise. "I had a daughter, yes. It was a *very* long time ago. Before people lived on Earth, before Lucifer created you or the other hounds, before a lot of things."

"Who sired her?" The question was fired at me like a gunshot.

His eyes changed color, glowing a bright gold, his hound in his eyes now. Was he aware of it? "Lucifer tried, but it didn't take, so one of his demons, a male I was quite fond of sired my daughter."

Lothar's eyes flashed from gold to red. "Lucifer tried?" Disgust curled his lips. "Are you saying that you and him—"

"I've been alive thousands of years, Lothar. You thought me and Lucifer had never had sex?"

A rumbling sound vibrated from his chest and there was more of that disgust on his face. "I thought he was like a father to you."

"Lucifer is many things to me." My anger rose at his judgement, and it was hard to control, but I wrestled it back down. "Sex is just two bodies giving and receiving pleasure, Lothar. I'm sure you've had plenty of experience with that."

His gaze was dark as it sliced from me. He stared ahead. "Right."

"Anyway, he wanted the handmaids to have children, to increase our numbers, and I volunteered. I wanted a baby, but he wasn't able to impregnate any of us, so we used demons."

More lip curling. "What happened to your daughter?"

A familiar bittersweet feeling filled me. "It turns out, only handmaids directly created by Lucifer are immortal.

Our children were long-lived, but they didn't survive. Cassandra, my baby girl, was...she was so beautiful, Loth. She eventually mated, had children of her own, then eventually grew old. I held her in my arms when she passed away. I've followed her line through the centuries, and I felt when the twins, her descendants, Kyler and Eve, were born. They're demi-demon and were too vulnerable, too powerful together. The demons living aboveground would have sensed them if I hadn't separated them. Now they're both mated to knights, and immortal because of it. I never have to lose them. I love them, Lothar, so much it takes my breath away."

"I never knew," he said, but he still wasn't looking at me. "I'm happy for you."

"I'm happy for me too," I said, stepping over a fallen branch.

We carried on walking, this time in silence. In fact, it was deafening.

The tension rolling off Lothar was thick, but I said nothing. Whatever was going on in his head had nothing to do with me.

"You and Lucifer, do you still fuck?"

Or maybe it did. "What?"

"Does he fuck all of you?" Lothar asked, and there was accusation, along with more of that disgust on his face.

My anger shot to new heights, but again I refused to let it show. "You're judging me."

There was a flash of his white fangs in the shadows. "No, I just—"

"I've heard of hounds sharing females, of hounds occasionally enjoying each other while the sharing is going on. I don't judge you or your brothers. Why would I?"

"That's different."

"How?"

"Lucifer created you, so there's a power imbalance. He's taking advantage of—"

"Stop, right there." This time the anger was clear in my voice. "He has never taken advantage of any of us. We are free to do whatever we want. Yes, we have been many things to each other over the centuries, but what you have to understand is the relationship between us, between Luci and all of his handmaids, is..." I struggled for words. "Unlike any other. Jealousy, greed, resentment, none of those things exist." Well, that last one had recently made an appearance, but I had a good reason for feeling that way, and he was currently staring at me like I'd grown a second head. "Lucifer is everything to us. So sure, in the early days, I occasionally shared his bed, but only because the love I felt for him was...was so all-encompassing, so vast, that sex was just another way of showing him. Over time, things have changed, grown, reshaped. What we have now, it's deeper than what we ever had. It's pure."

He scoffed.

"You're starting to piss me off, Lothar, and I promised I wouldn't take my bad mood out on you, but you're not making that very easy."

"You said, in the early days? So you don't sleep with him anymore?" Of course he'd ignore everything else I'd said. And there was still a growl in his voice.

I took a fortifying breath. "Not that it's any of your business, but no. Our connection is so much more, it's moved beyond the flesh. It wouldn't feel right to do that now."

He grunted.

I wasn't sure how we ended up talking about this, but I didn't want to anymore.

"Love of any kind is dangerous," he muttered. "Especially the way you describe your feelings for Lucifer."

I bit my lips together. *Don't say anything.* "You may not understand love, or even recognize it, but your loyalty to your pack, your devotion to Warrick, is love, you just don't know it." Okay, apparently, I couldn't stop myself.

Another grunt. "Loyalty is loyalty."

"Loyalty is a product of love. Of course there are different forms of love, but loyalty is earned through a connection with someone else, and a connection comes from a relationship that is cultivated over time, over someone showing you they can be trusted. It's cultivated by them choosing you over and over again."

He turned his scowling face on me. "You're trying to confuse me."

"I'm doing no such thing." I hitched my bag higher on my shoulder and gripped the straps tighter. "You're being closed-minded."

"I'm being logical."

"Logic has no place in love."

"Which is why I'm glad I don't feel it," he said dismissively.

I rolled my eyes. "What about your brothers? You'd risk your life for them, wouldn't you? You have, many times. Why do you think that is?"

"You can try to convince me all you like, but the reason we feel loyalty for each other is because Lucifer created us that way. End of story."

Gods, he was a stubborn ass. Nothing new there. He always had been. "So you don't want what War and Jag have, or Dirk and Relic? You don't want a...a mate, and more pups that you can form a true bond with?"

Shut the hell up! What is wrong with me?

Asking that question was cruel and selfish. He would never have a mate, or more pups, and he had me to thank for that.

"No. Why would I want that?"

My fingers ached from gripping my bag so tight, and my heart felt as if it were ten times too big for my chest. "I get you're freaking clueless, Lothar, but even you must be able to see how happy your brothers are now?" And still I couldn't shut my damned mouth. I had wondered, though, many times over the years, if he thought about a mate for himself. If he wanted what some of his brothers had. Obviously not. That was a good thing. It should make me happy. I didn't want him to pine for something he'd never have.

It was stupid to feel sad about that or hurt. In fact, it was masochistic. A form of self-mutilation. I wanted it this way, right? I'd made a decision a long time ago, and I had to live with it. I had been living with it, for hundreds of years. I'd made peace with it, or at least I thought I had.

I glanced his way. "Let's change th—"

Lothar dived at me without warning, hooking me around the chest and throwing us to the ground mere moments before an axe whistled a centimeter past my face.

What the fuck? How had I missed that?

I tried to get up, but he held me down, pressing a finger to his lips.

If I wanted to, I could move him easily. I could flip him, hurt him in multiple ways that would make him get off me, but I indulged him for a moment. I let him take the role of protector as hounds often needed to do, and if having him pressed against me was nice, I wasn't going to dwell on that.

But more than those things, I was seriously shaken that

85

I'd allowed myself to be distracted enough by him that I hadn't seen that axe coming.

He reached up, tugging the axe from where it was buried in a tree trunk, and inspected it, causing his hard body to press more firmly against mine. I curled my fingers into tight fists so I didn't run my hand up his back, seeking more of the heat radiating from his skin, and forced myself to study the weapon. It was intricately carved. I touched the side of the blade with the tip of my finger and hissed. It was made of an ancient steel, the kind capable of killing immortals. I'd had up-close-and-personal time with a weapon made from the same steel a long time ago and was lucky to survive it. The memory was still so raw after all this time, just touching the weapon made my scar ache like some kind of phantom reminder. How did some asshole in Oldwood Forest have one of these?

"Can you see how many?" I whispered, taking the axe from him and sliding it into my bag.

He shook his head.

"We need to move," I mouthed.

He nodded, lifted his head again, then ducked back. "Hang on."

I frowned. "To what?"

A split second later, Lothar tossed me over his monster shoulder, bounded to his feet, and exploded into the forest.

I hung there, utterly stunned for several seconds, while I flopped around like a dying fish. "Lothar?" I ground out. "Why are you carrying me?"

He didn't answer, too focused on running like hell through the trees, determined to *save* me. *Me*, a being more than twice his freaking age, a warrior who had literally been given the name, *The Blade*, because of my expert skills with a knife.

"Put me down," I ordered. "Now."

Lothar continued to ignore me, still running so fast, the forest was a blur around us.

"Put me down," I said more forcefully.

Still nothing.

We were being pursued. Our assailants were camouflaged, blending with the shadows, but they were closing in. I could see the trees moving, the undergrowth being crushed as they moved at a rapid speed after us.

Any moment now they were going to attack, and I refused to be dangling here over Lothar's shoulder like an idiot when they did. Straightening my back, I hooked my arm around Lothar's neck, shoved my feet into his hips, forcing his arm from around the backs of my thighs, and flipped, pulling one of my blades free as I did. As soon as I landed on my feet, I let it fly. Nothing, not a scream, no scent of blood. What the hell? I never missed.

Shit.

I shoved Lothar, as I took off. "Keep running, big guy. And, hey, your mouth is hanging open."

"What the fuck, Roxy?" he snarled, bursting into action again to catch up with me.

"I needed to know what we're dealing with. If they bleed, we can kill them. And I could say the same thing to you," I fired at him as we burst through the trees, finally reaching a clearing.

The rocks that would form a gateway into Limbo were just ahead.

We just had to reach them before the immortal killers hot on our tails reached us.

"And do they?" Lothar asked. "Bleed?"

"No."

"Fuck."

Fuck, indeed.

CHAPTER
NINE

Lothar

WE SPRINTED to the pile of stones at the far end of the field, and I spun around, facing the enemy, covering Roxy. Demons wouldn't dare attack me, and they sure as fuck wouldn't have weapons, not like that. I had no idea who was pursuing us, or what they were, but they weren't getting through me.

"What the hell are you doing?" Roxy fired at me.

I couldn't think, not with the buzzing in my head and the constant roar of the beast to protect, to kill.

"Are you using your body to freaking shield me right now?"

Honestly, I didn't know what I was doing. Logically I knew this was fucked, but the beast wouldn't have it any other way. Growling, I shook my head, trying to clear it, trying to wrestle back control.

Roxy cursed. "The gate needs *your* blood, Lothar." She grabbed my hand, yanking me back.

I snarled, fighting the beast, fighting myself to do what I needed to, to open the fucking gate. Zinnia had arranged everything with Death, but in my panic I'd somehow forgotten that the stones needed my blood to open.

Roxy stepped in front of me and shoved me back farther. It was a struggle, but I let her. "Open the damned gate, Lothar. Now."

Then she spun away, using her body to *protect me*. That's when the beast lost it. It was as if the animal part of me was a separate entity, one I didn't fucking recognize. I gripped my head when another roar echoed through my skull.

"Lothar!" Roxy yelled. "Do it."

She'd pulled a knife free as figures with no distinguishable features and moving like shadows gathered on the opposite side of the field.

"Not good," Roxy muttered.

I blinked. They were getting closer, their weapons glinting in their hands.

"Lothar!" Roxy yelled again. "Fucking do it."

Gritting my teeth, I managed to wrestle the beast back long enough to slice my hand and let my blood pour onto the stones. Roxy backed up, a string of curses flying from her, until she bumped into my side, knives in both hands. Without thought, I hooked my arm around her waist as the ground rumbled, ready to pull her behind me again if I had to and out of harm's way.

Her scent drifted around me, fucking with me like it always did, sending shudders down my spine, telling me to get the fuck away from her, while the beast roared again and forced me to pull her closer, to protect her at all costs.

Something was wrong with me. This wasn't normal.

"They're getting closer," she said under her breath.

The gate needed to open, right the fuck now. I threw up a hand and sent a blast of power rippling across the field. It didn't touch them. "How the fuck do you kill a shadow?"

"You can't."

The rocks and boulders finally rumbled into action, rolling, shifting, reforming into a gateway. Hellfire ignited across my palm, and I blasted it in a wide arc around us, scorching the ground and creating a wall of flames, not knowing what else to do.

The gateway opened, and we were finally looking through to the other side, to where Zinnia stood on the skull pathway waiting for us. The shadowed assassins swarmed us then, closing in quickly.

I tightened my arm around Roxy just as she threw both knives, sending them spinning through the air, and dove through the gateway.

"Close it!" I roared.

Zinnia didn't hesitate. She slashed her hand through the air and the stones instantly collapsed, the gateway vanishing, locking the shadows out.

Zinnia rushed forward. "What's going on?"

Zinnia Thornheart was a powerful witch and Death's consort.

I shoved my fingers through my hair, trying to get my shit together. "We were being chased by...fuck, shadows? I don't even know?" I growled.

Zinnia blinked at us, her gaze sliding down to my arm still locked around Roxy, and then back up.

Roxy shoved out of my hold and strode to Zinny, pulling her in for a tight hug. "Hey, Zinny," she said, then shook her head. "Not shadows. Wraiths. And someone's armed them with the kind of weapons that can kill an immortal."

"Wraiths?" I snarled.

"Yes." Roxy planted her hands on her hips. "I haven't seen any for a really long time though."

"They're impossible to kill."

"Mors might be able to help," Zinny said, calling her mate by his true name. "I had Egon prepare rooms for you both. Come to the castle and rest, then hopefully we'll get you the information you need in the morning."

I didn't want to rest. I wanted to find out who the fuck had sent wraiths after us and cleave their head in two, but this was Death we were talking about. You didn't demand shit from him, which meant we'd have to cool our heels until morning.

Zinnia led us back to the castle. It was huge, made of black stone, and looked as if it had burst through the ground fully formed on its own. We took the wide steps up to the massive arched doors, and they instantly swung open.

A horned demon with leathery, mottled green skin and scarlet eyes greeted us.

"Hey, Egon!" Roxy said, beaming. "It's been a while."

He inclined his head, his lips curling up. "Miss Roxana. It is a pleasure to see you again. It has indeed been a long time." His gaze slid to me and back to Roxy. "I have rooms all ready for you," he said. "Would you like me to bring a tray up once you're settled? You must be hungry after your journey."

"That would be much appreciated, Egon. I'm starved," Rox said and gave his arm an affectionate squeeze.

I lifted my chin when his gaze came back to me.

Egon headed off, and I took in the massive room we'd

walked into. I never thought I'd ever step foot in Limbo, or I fucking hoped I wouldn't, not the way a hound would usually end up here, let alone come to Death's castle.

Zinny cheerfully carried on, leading us up a wide staircase and along a dark hall with walls that seemed to whisper and move.

Roxy's room was right beside mine, and when I shut my door, I could hear Zinnia and Roxy talking through the wall —well, not what they were saying, just their muffled voices.

Roxy laughed, and before I knew what I was doing, I'd stepped closer to the wall separating us and had pressed my ear to it.

I jerked back. *The fuck?*

What was wrong with me? I was starting to get seriously worried.

Ignoring the beast who wanted me to stay right where I was, cheek pressed to the fucking wall, I strode to the bathroom and stripped off. I didn't understand any of this. The beast being at odds with me, *not feeling like part of me*, was messing me up big-time. We weren't two separate entities. I was the beast, and the beast was me—or that's how it had been. How was this even possible, this separation? Why was it happening now?

I gripped the edge of the bathroom counter and stared into my own eyes. They flashed red without me even sensing it, as if my beast was looking back at me and he was pissed. I knew what he wanted. To get closer to Roxy. If Roxy told me to drop to my knees, I had a feeling he'd force me to do that as well.

The beast was acting as if...as if Roxy was something more to me—to *him*. Fuck. How was there a *him*?

I rubbed my hands over my face. I'd know if there was

93

more between me and Rox, if there was a...a special connection. My brothers told me how it felt when they found their females, and this wasn't it.

I stepped into the shower, and the cool water felt good on my overheated skin. Okay, yes, Jagger missed the signs for a while there, but that was different. There were reasons for that. I'd known Roxy for centuries, if there was anything more between us—the kind predestined by fate, because I couldn't even bring myself to think the word—I would have worked it out a long time ago. Her scent sure as fuck wouldn't repel me or, on the odd occasion, make my skin crawl when she was too close for too long.

The water ran down my chest, and I dipped my head under the stream. I lathered up, rinsed off, and—what the actual fuck?—I couldn't help wondering if Roxy was doing the same thing.

Images of her naked and soaping up were quickly followed by ones of her bare skin covered in blood, the way I'd seen her in Skull Forest right after she'd taken out those demons. She'd looked wild. Shit, she'd been spectacular like that—vicious, ruthless, a fierce little warrior. I squeezed my eyes closed. I shouldn't be thinking about her like that. It wasn't right.

None of this made sense, but I'd gotten hard for her, more times than I could count since we took off on this hunt for Beelzebub.

Seeing her mutilate a group of demons naked wasn't the only thing that had happened in that forest though. I'd locked it away, right after it happened, because, motherfucker, it had been exquisite torture—and it had been messed up for me to enjoy what happened as much as I had.

A groan slipped free as the memory pushed forward, of

Roxy, all warm and sleepy, crawling on top of me while I lay by the campfire, of her soft moans as she'd rocked her hips, fucking riding my thigh in her sleep.

I shook my head, trying to shake the memory loose, but it was no good, and before I realized what I was doing, my hand had slid down my chest, over my stomach, and was gliding up my rock-hard cock.

A growl slipped from me, and I slapped my other hand to the marble wall and squeezed my dick more firmly. She'd been so hot; the smell of her slick pussy had covered her usual offensive scent and I'd lain there fucking mesmerized as she'd gotten herself off. I acted like it didn't affect me, as if I'd barely noticed when Rox had woken up, teasing her. I'd lied.

While she'd rocked against me, I'd imagined freeing my aching dick, shoving down her pants, and letting her hot little pussy take what it needed. I'd actually contemplated waking her up and offering her my cock instead of my thigh.

I groaned again, my strokes quickening even as I tried to force the images of Roxy out of my head. It was impossible, though, especially when the beast took over, feeding me more scenarios, ones where I tossed her onto all fours and fucked her from behind in front of that fire, ones where I buried my face in her pussy and used my beast's tongue on her until she came, shaking and screaming.

I leaned forward, resting my forehead on the cool marble, hissing through my teeth as my cock throbbed like never before. It felt tight, molten hot, like it was confined, like it was being strangled—like there was something more I needed, badly, but it was just out of reach. Still, I couldn't stop stroking, my hips thrusting into my fist. It was agony and bliss all at once.

When I finally blew, spurting all over the wall like a high-pressure fucking hose, I had to lock my knees. The release was so great that as soon as I was spent, they did give out, and there was no stopping it. I hit the floor, then fell forward on my hands and knees, panting, struggling to catch my breath. I actually looked down at my spent cock dangling between my legs to make sure it hadn't been rent in two from the force of whatever the fuck had just happened.

I stayed where I was, needing far longer to recover than I should. Finally, when I was able to, I dragged my ass out of the shower, slung a towel around my hips, and walked back into the room—and pulled up short when I found Roxy sitting on my bed, scrolling on her phone.

Had she heard me? How much noise had I made? I had no fucking clue. I felt as if I'd fucking blacked out, honestly.

She glanced up from her phone, a wide smile on her face, like the old Roxy, not the attitude-filled version she'd been giving me for a while now. "Egon brought up our trays. I thought we could discuss our game plan for tomorrow while we eat." She jumped off the bed and strode over to the small table now covered in food. "You know, since you got all pissed at me for 'keeping secrets,'" she said, making air quotes.

Her hair was damp. She'd showered as well. I swallowed thickly and nodded, struggling to find my voice. It felt rough as hell after the way I'd just gotten off. Had I been growling? Shit, had I said her name when I'd come all over the shower wall?

Swiping a pair of jeans from my bag, I turned my back on her, dropped my towel, and shoved them on. Hounds didn't hide their nudity, and Roxy had seen me naked more times than I could count, but in a room like this, just the two of us, it was bad manners to flash your dick at someone. And after what had just happened and where my mind went while it was happening, I was worried I'd get hard again—and that was most definitely bad manners.

I did up my pants and joined her at the table, taking in the spread. "Looks good," I said, finally managing fucking words, then lifted my gaze, searching her face for any sign that she'd heard me beating off to thoughts of her.

She popped a piece of cheese in her mouth, that sweet smile with zero calculation or hint of teasing still on her face. "Egon knows I have a big appetite," she said.

What she said could have a double meaning, but there was nothing sly or knowing in her delivery either. She couldn't have heard anything. She'd give me shit if she had. I was sure of it.

I loaded up my plate. "So where are we going tomorrow?"

"I was thinking Ferine," she said.

I froze. "The Savage Realm?"

"It's dangerous, I know. But Beelzebub has friends there. He can also blend in easily."

"Dangerous? They fucking eat their own." If you broke their laws, you were sentenced to the pot.

"I know, and it's fucked up, but remember, Az said, wherever he was, he was thriving. And Beelzebub would fit in there like a house on fire."

At the mention of Asmodeus, the beast snarled. I ignored it and tried to focus on what she was saying.

"He'd definitely thrive there." She gave a nod of certainty, then popped a little pastry of some kind in her mouth. "You game?"

What choice did I have? "Lucifer wants us to bring the traitor back. If that's where you think he is, then that's where we'll go, but we'll need to be prepared and better armed. I'll try to track him tonight, and if that doesn't work, I'll go for a run in the morning and see what I can pick up."

She nodded as she sucked on a piece of melon, sliding it between her lips, then licked the juice from her fingers. "Sounds good. Hopefully, Death can help us with that, well, if he's feeling generous. He and Luci aren't the best of friends."

I shifted in my seat as she did it again, licking melon juice from her fingers after slipping another piece past her full lips. I cleared my throat. "We better hope Zinnia can convince him to help us or we're fucked. Going to Ferine unprepared would be suicide."

"The place is definitely wild, but I've given Luci an update, and he's on board."

A snarl tried to crawl up my throat. "He's not worried about you?"

Her smile dropped and she simultaneously shook her head and rolled her eyes. "Why would he be? He knows what I can do and trusts my abilities."

I bit my tongue, because she was right, and the shit swirling in my head, what I wanted to say, like, *I'll protect you,* and *I'll kill anyone who tries to hurt you,* made no fucking sense and would only piss her off.

I got into bed, but my mind wouldn't quiet. I needed to talk to War, or maybe Lucifer, about what was going on with me, because something was really wrong. Even now, the beast snarled and writhed beneath my skin, trying to force me to go to the wall between my room and Roxy's and press my fucking ear to it—but better yet, to go to her door and let myself into her room, her bed.

I shoved that out of my head.

Then an image of her with Relic when he was tiny, the way she'd loved and cared for my pup, filled my mind. She'd had her own child once, a daughter she'd been forced to watch age and die. Now I understood why she was so loving, so fiercely protective of any pups, even the older ones like Gus and Brick. She missed Cassandra, she understood what it was to be a parent and lose your child.

There was so much more to Roxy than she let people see.

The female had hidden depths, and every layer that she revealed only made me more curious.

I dragged my hands over my face.

Get your head back in the game. You're here to do a job, not obsess over Roxy.

If only it were that easy.

CHAPTER
TEN

Roxy

Lothar stood by a tree, one hand gripped Beelzebub's shirt while he ran the other over the rough bark, his eyes closed, reaching inward, searching. A shiver shimmied up my spine as I watched him from a distance.

I'd woken when his bedroom door had opened and closed early this morning, and I'd quickly dressed and followed. If Loth picked up Beelzebub's trail, I didn't want to miss any details. And if he sensed he was being watched, or followed, he hadn't let on. But then, I'd purposely stayed back so as not to get in his way while he worked.

My gaze trailed down his large, muscled and tattooed body and I bit my lip. He was in only a pair of running shorts, the rest of him bare, even his feet. His long hair was roughly braided, and as he tilted his head back, drawing in a deep breath that expanded his ribs and tightened his abs, I had to bite back a whimper.

It was no use, the memory slammed into me and was so visceral, my fingers curled into a tight fist.

"Your hair's softer than mine," I said as I sectioned his hair off. "It's really not fair."

"Kitten, your hair is the softest silk. I think about burying my face in it at least ten times a day," he rumbled.

"You do?" He turned to me as I tied off his braid, then slid my hand over his beard. It needed a trim but was soft as well. I loved stroking it.

"You doubt me?" His voice was so low and gritty, tingles slid over my skin.

"Never," I said.

I leaned in, kissing him, then he hooked his arm around my waist with a growl, tossing me back on the bed.

I opened my arms for him as he came down on top of me....

No. I viciously shoved the memory down right as Lothar lowered his chin and opened his eyes. They were glowing red, all hound, and, gods, they drilled into me. It was as if he could see into my mind, to all the secrets I was keeping. If I could, I would tear them from my mind, I would shred them so I never had to relive this pain ever again.

His nostrils flared as if he were scenting me, and as soon as he did, he kind of flinched and the red bled away, leaving only deep gold.

I forced myself to move. "Anything?" I said, striding over to him, acting as if I wasn't as close to spiraling and crashing as I had been in a very long time.

He nodded slowly, his big shoulders kind of heaving with each breath.

The look in his eyes was disconcerting, and it took everything in me not to squirm. Thankfully, I was a good actress. If I wasn't, I wouldn't have been able to pretend I hadn't heard him getting off in the shower last night...

vigorously. I'd honestly never heard anything like it. When I walked in and realized what I was hearing, I meant to leave. I truly had. But I couldn't make my feet carry me back out. His hisses and gasps were a potent mix of pleasure and pain, and his deep groans had me transfixed. Then everything had gone silent, except for his desperate panted breaths. I'd ended up outside the bathroom door, with my hand pressed to it. I'd never wanted to walk through a door more in my life.

Then I'd heard him coming, and there'd been no time to get out, so I'd dived across the room, landed on his bed, and yanked my phone out, pretending I was busy scrolling, just as he'd opened the door.

I had to be more careful. If I let myself fly too close to the sun with him, I'd end up with fourth-degree burns, suffering and scarred for eternity. There was no cure for that kind of pain, and I knew deep in my heart there'd be no getting through that hell twice. I'd be stripped back to muscle and bone, and he'd walk away unaware and unscathed.

Lothar still hadn't said anything, and I resisted shuffling my damned feet under that unnerving stare. What was his problem? His jaw was tight and his eyes flashed red again, then back. "Are you okay?"

He dragged in a sharp breath, a growl rattling his chest on the exhale, then his eyes seemed to clear again, and his shoulders lost some of the tension. He jerked his chin up. "Yeah. Just took a lot to find him."

He held a knife, one he never seemed to be without, and every time I saw it in his hand, my heart crashed against my ribs. He used it to slice a small piece of bark from the tree, slid it between his lips, chewed, then spat it out and nodded, as if confirming something to himself.

Lothar was the best tracker in his pack. The depth of his power, his connection to it, was extraordinary. I winked because all this felt way too intense. "This is why Luci pays you the big bucks," I said, hoping to ease the tension flowing from him.

Lothar didn't crack a smile. "B was definitely here. He passed through Limbo."

"Best we go talk to Death, then. See what he's willing to tell us."

When we walked into the castle, laughter came from an adjoining room, and we headed toward the happy sounds in the dining room.

Death sat at the head of a long table, Zinnia at his side, and Marigold, Zinny and Death's daughter, was next to her. Egon's son, Ryker, sat next to Marigold, and Death's brother, Somnus, sat on the opposite side, with his mate, Pascal, next to him, both smiling in welcome when they saw us.

"Come, have some breakfast. You must be hungry," Zinnia said, her smile just as welcoming.

"Thanks," I said and took a seat next to Ryker.

Lothar rounded the table, sitting beside Pascal. His gaze slid to Death. "Beelzebub passed through Limbo—"

"Not here," Death said, his voice resonating through the room and lifting goose bumps all over my skin. "After breakfast." He took Zinnia's hand and brought it to his lips, kissing it, a not so subtle way of letting us know he was only indulging us because his wife had asked him to.

The muscle in Lothar's clenched jaw jumped, but he said nothing, just inclined his head and got busy loading his plate with food.

"Do you like my new doll?" Marigold asked me, holding it up. "Aunty Jazzy gave it to me."

"She's beautiful," I said, smiling at Zinnia's little one. "Do you have many dolls?"

She nodded. "I love them. Me and Ryk made a town for them in the music room. We're playing in there after breakfast if you want to join us?"

"Thank you for the lovely invitation," I said. "As long as Ryker doesn't mind me playing as well?"

Ryker looked at Lothar, and his cheeks turned pink. He was Egon's son, but his mother must be more humanoid in looks. He had his father's horns but not his skin color or red eyes, or at least not all the time. "I don't care. I hate playing dolls. They're dumb. I'll be a warrior when I'm older. Warriors don't play dolls," he said, still watching Lothar.

Mari's eyes widened with outrage and hurt. "You do not hate playing dolls."

He looked down. "Yeah, I do," he muttered.

Mari turned her back on him, and Ryker huffed, but his gaze was locked on his best friend, and I could see he regretted his words. He looked back at Lothar and realized the big hound wasn't paying him any attention, focused on eating his breakfast, and didn't care one way or the other.

"I'm sorry, Mari," Ryker said, swallowing thickly. "I didn't mean it."

"You shouldn't say things if you don't mean them." She huffed. "I'm going to play...*by myself.*" Then she stormed off.

Ryker jumped off his chair and, calling her name, ran after her.

Zinnia sighed.

I stared after them. "Friendships can be complicated."

"You're not wrong. Especially BFFs," she said and chuckled.

I glanced across the table, and Lothar's stare locked on mine. He was getting impatient but said nothing as Death took the last bite of his breakfast, then drained his mug of coffee.

Finally, he stood, and his dark stare slid to Lothar, then to me. "We can talk in the library," he said in that soul-shaking voice. When he spoke it felt as if he reached inside your body and sent ice through your bones.

Zinnia stood, and he took her hand in his.

Loth and I stood as well, I said my goodbyes to Somnus and Pascal, then we headed upstairs to the library.

The library was all dark leather and deep mahogany furniture. A fire blazed in the ornate fireplace and the walls were lined with ancient leather-bound books. Death stood to one side of the room, in front of a wide window that looked down to the grounds and the forest beyond. Everything we could see, and so much we couldn't, had been created by Death thousands of years ago, including the sky and the stars, that he'd mirrored, mostly, after the ones we saw on Earth.

"You are here in my realm because Zinnia asked it of me. I have no time for Lucifer or his games. If one of his lords has trespassed, and if he still hides here, he will receive no mercy from me. If I find him first, I will slice him in two and send Lucifer the pieces. I don't give a single fuck what the king of Hell wants or thinks about that." His gaze slid from me to Lothar. "Just to be clear."

"Totally understandable," I said. "Beelzebub is no longer in Lucifer's favor. He has committed treason and is possibly still attempting to take Lucifer's throne, so the lord of Hell is no longer any friend of ours...*but* we need to take him back alive. There are more pieces to this treasonous puzzle, and B can provide us with those missing pieces."

"I can't promise you anything," Death said, his voice

void of emotion. "And I have no intention of doing so. If I see him first, he's dead."

Lothar made a rough sound. "What do you know about wraiths?"

"They are creatures without souls, they have no mercy, no conscience. They live for the hunt, to inflict pain." He looked at Zinnia. "Did you see them?"

She shook her head. "No, but I trust Roxy. If she says that's what they were, then I believe her."

Death cursed.

"What is it?" Lothar said.

Death crossed his tattooed arms over his wide chest. "They have been locked away for a very long time. It took some doing. I was part of the alliance, as was Lucifer and several other powerful beings. We fought them, contained them, then locked them away. Whoever freed them has to be of the same ilk, or have some very powerful friends."

"Beelzebub is powerful, but not like that," Lothar said. "And they had weapons, the kinds that can kill immortals."

I bit my lip, because the more Death and Lothar talked, the more the unsettled feeling grew inside me. I'd tried to tell myself I was wrong after seeing that weapon, but I wasn't so sure anymore.

Death's gaze came to me then, slicing into the deepest part of me. "Do you have any idea who it could be, Roxana?"

He knew. He knew everything I was hiding. I could say the name swimming around in my head, lacerating my mind with memories I wished I could forget, and maybe he would take pity on us and be more inclined to help, or maybe he wouldn't. I should say something, but I couldn't do it, I couldn't bring myself to speak that name.

My heart thudded with force against my ribs. "No. No

idea." I was also terrified that if I said it out loud in front of Lothar, his own memories would be shaken loose, along with a whole lot of awful things that were better left locked away.

Lothar turned to me and frowned. "What's going on?"

He could sense my distress, of course he could. "Nothing. I'm just frustrated, you know? I want this over with like you do."

He nodded, but his gaze remained on me for several long seconds, as if he didn't believe a word I'd said. He always did have good instincts. "Do we have your permission to pass through your realm to Ferine, then return?"

Death inclined his head. "You may pass through, but we won't be making a habit of this, understand?"

"Completely," I said, then turned to Lothar. "Let's get our stuff. Time's a-wasting." I wanted him away from Death pronto. We were here because of Zinnia, but Death didn't owe me shit. He definitely didn't have to keep my secrets for me.

As soon as I shut myself in my room a few minutes later, I pulled the axe from my pack and inspected it. My blood turned to ice when I caught the worn insignia carved into the side, that I'd missed in the darkness of the forest. I slid my thumb over it, and a shiver rolled through me. No. It couldn't be. My side burned, a deep ache throbbing beneath my scar.

Quickly taking my phone from my pocket, I snapped a pic of the insignia and sent it to Lucifer, then shoved my phone back in my pocket. There could be several reasons for this weapon being in the wraiths' possession. There was no need to panic. Not yet.

I packed my things, forcing myself to breathe evenly and not jump to conclusions.

When I walked out a few minutes later, I heard low voices coming from the library. Lothar and Death. I heard my name and walked up as silently as I could.

"What's Roxy hiding?" Lothar said, his hound in his voice making it nothing but a growl. "She knows something, something she's not telling me."

Death was silent several beats. "Whatever Roxana knows or doesn't know is not for me to say. Only she or Lucifer can give you the answers you want."

Fuck.

Lothar's boots pounded on the carpet, and I rushed back to my room, walking out as if I hadn't been eavesdropping. "Ready?" I said, trying to slow my racing pulse.

Lothar held my gaze for several painfully tense seconds, then dipped his chin and carried on walking. "Let's get the fuck out of here."

CHAPTER
ELEVEN

Roxy

In a way, Limbo was like a floating island. The realm was connected to nothing because it was Death's own creation, which meant you could open a gateway to other realms—if not directly, then pretty freaking close—rather than pass through a whole bunch of other territories to get to the one you wanted, which made things a lot easier and faster. Well, it would be if Death allowed it. We got lucky, thanks to Zinnia. He refused entrance to everyone else, which meant Beelzebub most likely had someone here in Limbo willing to help him. Something I'm sure Death had considered. I could guarantee he'd started hunting down the weak link before we'd even left.

"You didn't ask for weapons?" I said to break the silence.

"He said knives, claws, and fangs were all we needed in the Savage Realm," Lothar said, striding beside me. His shoulders were stiff, and he'd been distant, okay, straight-up pissed off, since we'd left the castle.

"I've journeyed through Ferine before. We'll be fine," I said, trying to get him to stop frowning. He was in his head; I knew that look well. But it wasn't the talk of weapons making him tense. No, he was still convinced I was keeping things from him, information that would help us find Beelzebub. What I was hiding wouldn't help our cause, if only I could convince him of that.

"So today you've decided to go with the old, upbeat Roxy, huh?" His gaze slid to me. "Why is that?"

I threw up my hands. "You wanted the old Roxy, so that's what I'm giving you. Now that's pissing you off as well?" *Shut up. Do not goad him.* "What the hell do you want from me, Lothar?"

He snorted like an enraged bull. "We're about to enter a realm that is notoriously dangerous. We need to be on the same fucking page."

"We are!"

"Bullshit."

I drew in a sharp breath. "We're going to need to have each other's backs in there. Are you saying you don't trust me to do that?"

"Honestly?" He glanced over at me. "No."

Heat spread through me like wildfire. "No?" I fired back at him. "Are you freaking serious right now?"

"Deadly." He kept his gaze straight ahead, as if he couldn't bear the sight of me anymore. "You will always put Lucifer's interests ahead of anyone and anything. I'm his loyal servant, and I have been for a thousand fucking years, but I would never shit on one of my brothers to please him—"

"You're not one of my sisters, Lothar."

"No shit, but I can't do my job if you don't trust me, and especially if you're keeping important fucking information from me."

"Not this again," I said, even as my face heated.

"Yeah, this again. You're keeping something from me, female. Something big. I can feel it, fucking smell it on you. Death saw it as well. Yet you continue to deny it. So no, I don't trust you, not in this."

My nails dug sharply into the flesh of my palms. We needed to work efficiently together. This situation we found ourselves in was my fault. I'd lost control of my emotions, I'd let them get the better of me, and he hadn't missed it. I had to fix this, or at least try. I had to tell him something, and I had to be honest, at least for some of it, so he'd sense that as well. "Okay, fine." I shook out my hands. "There are things I'm keeping from you—"

He cursed.

"Hold up, it's not what you think. It's nothing important to this mission, anyway. And FYI, it's not a lie, it's an omission. The two are completely different."

He growled deeply. "What the fuck does that mean?"

"It means, you need to drop this. There are some things I have no intention of sharing with you. The fact that you can sense it can't be helped, but you don't need to know what those things are, they have nothing to do with finding Beelzebub." For both of our sakes, my secrets needed to stay that way. "No matter how much you grumble, I'm not going to tell you, and you need to be all right with that, okay?"

His frown stayed firmly in place. "No, not okay. I have no idea what the fuck you're talking about."

"And that's totally fine. Like I said, it has nothing to do with finding B. It's personal."

"Female, you are talking in riddles."

"My secret does not have anything to do with this mission, is that clear enough for you?" I was itching to strangle him.

"But it has something to do with me?"

I pushed a branch out of my way. "I never said that."

"I fucking know it does."

"I have no control over what you believe to be true, Lothar. Whether it does or doesn't have anything to do with you is something you're just going to have to learn to live with."

He looked ready to self-combust. "How the fuck am I supposed to do that?"

"Easy. Stop talking about it. Better yet, stop thinking about it."

"Roxy," he growled.

"On the subject of hunting down B..." I quickly said to keep the conversation moving, but in a slightly different direction. "There is one thing I have been considering, something I haven't shared with you yet." My belly quivered and my heart felt like a frozen lump in my chest. As much as I didn't want to mention this, I had no choice, because he was right, when it came to finding Beelzebub, or anyone else who could be involved, I had to be fully transparent. I just hoped that Lucifer's block was still unbreakably strong in Lothar's mind, because once I said what I was about to say, and where it might lead us, I couldn't take it back.

"I'm listening, Roxy," he said when I didn't immediately carry on.

I cleared my tight throat. "The weapons, the ones the wraiths attacked us with, I'm pretty sure I've seen something like it before." Gods, my voice sounded strained.

"Pretty sure?"

Fuck. "I'm positive."

His eyes flashed. "Where?"

I gripped the straps of my bag tighter. "Lucifer has a battle-axe made of the same steel that he keeps under lock and key. It was gifted to him before he fell..."

Lothar's brows shot up. "You think angels are behind this?"

"Fallen angels, but yes, I think that's a very real possibility." I swallowed thickly. "The wraiths had weapons made of the same steel, and like Death said, the power it would take to release them from their prison would have to be great...so yeah, I think we could be looking for one or more power-hungry fallen angels."

He stopped suddenly, hands planted on his hips. "Why the fuck didn't you tell me this before?"

"I didn't know, not for sure. But when Death was talking about the wraiths, the idea wouldn't leave me, and I guess it makes sense. When Poe and Tarrant were working for Beelzebub, trying to help him take over...the forgotten prophecy was mentioned."

"Yeah, I remember."

"It seemed impossible, something so out of reach it was ridiculous to even consider, but with angels involved?" I shook my head. "It's not so ridiculous. I think they're trying to change fate, setting us on a new path, one that would be devastating to all of us."

He looked away, jaw tight, staring into the trees. "How easy would it be for a fallen to move between realms?"

My stomach knotted. "Fairly easy."

"Fuck."

"We're going to have to be really careful, Loth."

He stared down at me. "Who do you think's behind it? You must know which of them has it out for Lucifer."

I couldn't say her name with him looking right into my eyes like that. I couldn't do it.

He kind of leaned forward, getting more into my space. "You have an idea, I can see it on your face. Who?"

Could he sense the rising alarm inside me? His frown was back. If I didn't say it, he'd think I was hiding things from him again, but he was right, we needed to be able to trust each other. I needed him to trust me, especially when we entered Ferine. "Nathaniel has always been jealous of Lucifer's power...and ah..." I held his gaze, my mouth going bone dry. "Seraphina." There was no flinch, not even a twitch of recognition. "In the past, she's made no secret of how unhappy she is with the status quo." He hadn't reacted to hearing her name, still, I felt the blood drain from my face and I broke out in a cold sweat.

"Okay." He nodded. "That's a good start. Do you think Silas could help? He might have an idea where they are?"

I felt like my ribs were playing air-hockey with my heart. I knew where Sera and Nathaniel should be, but Lucifer hadn't texted me back confirming it yet. "It could be worth a try. I'll text Urs and ask if Silas knows anything."

"Sounds good," he said, then started walking again.

My legs shook as the rush of adrenaline drained away. I blew a breath past my trembling lips.

Lothar stopped suddenly. "Seraphina?"

I stopped abruptly, and my adrenaline spiked back up again. "Mmm-hmm." It was hard, but I kept my breathing even.

"Took me a minute, but yeah, I remember her."

I swallowed thickly. "You do?"

He turned. "It's been a long time, but I've met her more

than once. Lucifer had me act as an envoy between him and her. Can't remember what for though." His brow scrunched as he tried to remember the details.

I quickly started walking again, and he did the same. "I doubt she or Nathaniel will make an appearance, even if they are behind this. They have the wraiths to do their dirty work, and obviously B had gotten to a few demons when he was still in Hell. The ones who attacked me had to be doing it on his orders." Although Sera would really love to see me dead, if only to hurt Lucifer, and if she'd broken free from her prison, I'd be at the top of her hit list. "So let's just focus on Beelzebub for now."

He nodded, but it was slow, and that thoughtful look was still on his face, like he was searching the deep recesses of his mind.

I gripped the straps of my bag tighter and sent a prayer to all the gods I could think of.

Don't let him remember what I did. Please, don't let him remember.

Lothar

Roxy stood, legs slightly apart and head tilted back, as she muttered the words needed to open the gateway, then she sliced her palm and stepped forward.

She lifted her hand but turned back to me before she held it over one of the stones. "Be ready. Anything could be on the other side."

Sliding the knife from my boot, I strode up behind her and braced.

She curled her fingers into a tight fist and held it over one of the porous stones. Her blood dripped from her palm, landing on the rough surface, and was instantly absorbed. Much like the gateway into Limbo, the stones around us began to roll and reform.

Roxy pulled knives from the sheaths on each hip, twirling them slowly.

"How is it you have a never-ending supply of knives?" I muttered as the last few stones rolled into place.

"I'm Roxana the Blade," she said, and winked. "It's magic."

The gateway finished forming, and Limbo's forest, still visible through the stone archway in front of us, vanished, replaced by darkness and a cool blast of air that carried on it the fetid stench of rot and the distant calls of creatures I'd never heard in my life.

"Let's go," Roxy said and stepped through into the Savage Realm.

I followed and my boots sunk into mud and rotting vegetation. The gateway closed behind us and I took in our immediate vicinity. We were deep in a forest of shadowy trees. Everything was dark and murky, except for what looked like odd-shaped sticks poking from the mud here and there. They were the only things not in shades of gloom.

Roxy reached back and grabbed my wrist, pulling me closer.

I dipped my head.

"Watch out for the bones, they're old and brittle," she whispered, her lips so close they brushed my ear, and goose bumps shot up all over me. "You stand on one and you'll give us away."

Bones? I scanned the ground again. Fuck. Not sticks. I cursed under my breath.

We picked our way through the shadowed forest, watching our steps as we weaved around black slime-covered trees.

"You hear that? That hissing sound?" I said low, searching the ground.

Roxy pointed to a cluster of deep purple flowers. "They spit acid."

As she said it, the petals jerked wide and spewed out something thick and gray. The ground where the substance landed sent out a trail of noxious smoke.

"Watch out for the—"

The ground vanished from beneath her feet.

Roxy gasped as she slid several feet away, then continued to sink. The mud was already at chest level.

"Fuck. Don't move." Struggling would only make her sink faster. Though the way she remained utterly frozen, she didn't need me to tell her that. I grabbed for the tree closest, but my hand slipped off its slimy trunk.

"Quickly, Lothar," she gasped out, now submerged up to her chin.

Yanking off my shirt, I wrapped it around a branch, quickly testing its strength, then wrapped the shirt around my fist and leaned out over the bog. Roxy's fingers brushed mine, but I couldn't grab hold of her. Gritting my teeth, I fucking prayed the branch would hold as I tested it to its limits and stretched out as far as I could. She made a desperate dive for my hand, and I grabbed her, griping her tight. She clung on, wrapping her other hand around my wrist, and with a growl, I hauled her out.

As soon as her feet hit solid ground, she bent over at the waist, sucking in desperate breaths. "Holy fuck."

That was too fucking close. "You good?"

She nodded, but I could see that she was shaken in a way I'd never seen this female before. She never let you see her truly vulnerable. Yeah, until recently, she'd been sweet and bouncy and loving, but not vulnerable, never that. Lucifer's right hand had never shown an ounce of fear as long as I'd known her.

I grabbed her hand to pull her close, but she slid it free instantly and straightened, squaring her shoulders. The beast snarled, roaring at me to pick her up and run, to take her to safety. I ignored the fucker inside me, who seemed to have gone completely fucking rogue, and searched the ground. There was deep purple and gray fungus that looked like spindly mushrooms scattered around the quagmire. "I think if we look out for that fungus, we can avoid any more bogs like this one."

She nodded. "I can't believe I missed them." Then she led the way around it, something else the beast didn't fucking like.

A bubble rose up beside us, making a plopping sound as it burst on the surface. Then another rose up, and another.

"Lothar..."

"I see it."

Something was coming.

A huge, misshapen form rose slowly from the mire. It was so caked in mud I didn't know what I was looking at. Then it's mouth opened wide, gnashing long sharp teeth.

"Run," Roxy hissed.

Snatching up her hand, I gripped it tight, refusing to let her pull away this time, because there was no fucking way I was risking losing her in this fucking realm of rot and death, and broke into a sprint. We rounded trees and swamps, jumped fallen logs, and slipped on rotting vegetation. The crash and roar of the bog creature making chase echoed behind us. It was fast and gaining, more familiar with the treacherous terrain than we were.

Another roar came from somewhere else close by. I wasn't sure we could outrun these swamp fuckers. A huge tree was just ahead. It had thick gnarled roots thrust into the ground, and some of the earth under it had dropped away, leaving a dark, open space.

I glanced back at the mud-slicked mire monster crashing toward us. We needed to do something. Now. I didn't have time to tell Roxy my plan. "Hold on to me," I said as I hauled her off her feet, darted one way toward a thicker cluster of trees, leading the creature there and giving us cover, before I veered back and dove for the ground.

We slid in the mud and sludge, across the forest floor and between the huge tree's roots, stopping when we hit the wall of dirt and roots underneath. Roxy smashed into my front and blinked up at me, eyes huge. She opened her mouth to speak, and I clamped my hand over it.

If the creature had eyes, I didn't see any. It seemed to me it was using sound and probably scent, and I was banking on the mud now coving us both to disguise us.

Roxy's stunning blue eyes stayed on me, widening even more when the heavy thud of the creature's feet squelching in the mud grew closer. It slowed, and I could hear it scenting the air. It paced back and forth, then roared, before it took off running deeper into the forest in search of us.

We were both breathing hard now, and her soft, little body was pressed tight against mine. I could feel every soft curve, and for once her scent wasn't a problem, because the mud was disguising it from me. Nothing inside me was demanding I get the fuck away from her, and for the first time since we started this hunt, my beast sunk back into me, with me again in all ways, as it should be. It was a good feeling.

Roxy's fingers curled around my hand, her movements slow, careful, as she eased it away from her mouth. Her lips looked darker, a little fuller, from my rough skin pressed against them. I scented her experimentally, and my beast rumbled in my chest when I smelled my own scent now on those plump pretty lips.

I slid my hand up her back and into her hair, and the beast growled again from the softness of it. Hounds loved certain textures, soft, silky things drew us, and we loved touch, hugs especially. My senses were in pleasure overload, and I didn't even try to stop myself from leaning in so I could press my nose, my lips, to her neck, so I could slide them up her silky skin, the only part of her not smeared with mud. The vibrations in my chest increased.

Roxy's breathing quickened, her fingers against my side digging in and making me moan.

"Lothar?" she whispered. "What are you doing?"

I wasn't sure. All I knew was I didn't want to let her go. I wanted to get closer, I wanted more, needed more. Lifting my head, I took her chin in my hand and slid my thumb over the plump warmth of her tempting lower lip. "You're so fucking beautiful, Roxy." I shook my head. "Fucking gorgeous. Have I ever told you that?" I had, hadn't I? I couldn't remember saying it before, but I was positive I had.

Her throat worked, and she blinked up at me. "We can't...we shouldn't—"

"Why shouldn't we?" It felt right to have Roxy in my

arms. The beast purred from just how right this felt. Why hadn't I done this before?

"It's not a good idea," she said, her voice husky and sexy.

I pressed my forehead to hers and nodded. "Yeah, it is."

Her breath shook. "Please."

The plea was soft, barely there, and I wasn't sure if she was begging me to kiss her or asking me to release her, but instinct took over and I curled my fingers around the side of her lovely face and pressed my lips to hers.

If Roxy wanted me to stop, she could easily make me. She could gut me in three seconds flat. Another growl left me, as I opened my mouth over hers. My tongue delved into that silken heat and took my first drugging taste of her. Motherfucker, I knew her taste. I'd dreamed about it. I was positive I had. Something wild ignited inside me.

Her fingers dug into my sides, hard enough that her nails would leave indents in my skin. She stilled, and I braced for her to shove me away, but then she hooked both arms around my neck, and with her considerable strength, she pulled me closer and kissed me back. I groaned when she slid her sweet, little tongue against mine, as if she were as desperate for a taste of me as I was her.

I shoved my hand up under her shirt, my fingers sliding across the scar on her side, then up over her ribs. Fuck me, it was like sparks arced between us wherever I touched. She gasped like she could feel it too.

Her hands slipped from around my neck and traveled lightly down my chest.

Yes. Touch me.

She shoved, hard, breaking the kiss.

I snarled, and we stared at each other, panting. I went for those lips again, fucking hungry for more, but she slapped her hand over my mouth this time and shook her head.

The rumbling in my chest intensified, a throbbing purr and low growl rolling from me. The beast wanted more, right the fuck now.

She kept her hand over my mouth and lifted her finger to her lips, telling me to be quiet. That's when I heard the snuffling and heavy footsteps squelching through mud nearby.

We were about to be discovered.

I untangled myself from Rox, and she grabbed my arm, alarm in her eyes.

Be ready, I mouthed.

I needed to incapacitate the creature, do enough damage that we'd have time to get away.

She shook her head and held my arm in a tighter grip.

Covering her hand with mine, I shook my head and carefully pulled away, then crawled between the twisted roots. I looked back and held up two fingers, hoping she understood what I was telling her. *Give me two minutes, then come.*

Her chin was stubborn, and fire blazed in those pretty blue eyes.

This had to be done, so I turned away and waited.

The monster returned half a minute later, its mud-slicked body hunched over, walking on all fours now. Its eyeless head pressed to the mud and rot, using the two holes in the center of its face to search for our scent. Finally, it turned its back on me.

I didn't hesitate, I burst from our hiding spot, shifting as I went—and attacked.

CHAPTER
TWELVE

Roxy

LIKE HELL WAS I going to cower under this tree and leave Lothar to fight alone, not even for two minutes. In two minutes, I'd once slaughtered eight rebel demons I'd found munching on humans, and had time to clean off my blades. He'd lost his damned mind if he thought I was waiting.

Sliding my knives free, I followed him.

He'd fully shifted, and the huge hound tore at the swamp creature. Still, it was almost twice his size. With a battle cry, I ran and jumped, landing on its slimy back, and stabbed and hacked at it. It shrieked, black sludge oozing from the tears Lothar had made with his fangs and claws and the deep cuts I'd made with my knives.

It jerked from side to side, then reached back, digging its claws into my shoulder and tore me from its back. I was tossed with such force that I was airborne for several seconds, stopped only by the huge tree I slammed into. I dropped, hitting the ground hard enough to rattle my freaking bones.

Shaking it off, I bounded to my feet and sprinted back.

The slimy beast swiped its claws across Lothar's skin again and again, leaving his fur matted with blood. With a scream of rage, I leaped up, using my blades in its flesh like ice picks, then, gripping its thick head, I buried my blade into the opposite side of its throat and cried out as I dragged it across with all my strength, slicing its throat open.

Its roars and shrieks turned to gurgles before it finally stumbled to the side and went down, taking me with it. We hit the ground hard, and its dead weight pinned my legs beneath it.

Lothar shifted with a hiss and stood over me, naked and teeth bared. He was covered in blood and mud, and his chest heaved with his panted breaths.

"A little help?"

He cursed viciously, then shoved his shoulder into the dead bog monster, pushing it off long enough for me to roll out from under it. Yanking my blades free of its rancid flesh, I jumped to my feet. "Thanks."

His face contorted. "I told you to wait."

I wiped my blades across my thighs and slid them back in their sheaths. "No, you held up two fingers."

"Which meant"—he pointed at me—"you wait."

"You point at me again, I'll cut that finger off and add it to my collection from other males who've tried to pull that shit with me. And in case that isn't clear enough, I don't follow orders from you."

He growled, his fangs still extended. "You could have gotten yourself killed."

"The only one of us who could have been killed is you. If

I hadn't followed, that giant bog monster would have shredded you. As it is, your back is sliced to shit and we're going to have to clean out those wounds before infection sets in."

"I had things under control. I protect you, it's my job to—"

"I am not your job, or yours to protect," I bit out, pain and anger resurfacing again. It never truly left, even when I tried to tell myself I had control over my emotions. I felt bad for him, I did, hounds protected, that's who they were. But I didn't need that from him, and he knew that, of course he did, and no matter how hard it was for him to see me fight, that was *who I was*. Getting in my way all the time was just making things harder for both of us. "I'm older than you, Lothar. I have fought in more battles, have more kills, and possess skills you could only fucking dream of. Do not try to play the protector with me again. I'm not a help-less female. You pull that shit again, you won't like what happens. We clear?"

His beast was rolling under his skin, his body moving in an odd way. He was fighting the shift. His lips curled back, and his chest vibrated again. "Yeah, we're clear." The gold of his eyes shifted to red. "What about before the fighting? Can I pull that shit again, Rox?" he said, a rumbling purr in his voice.

I sucked in a sharp breath and my anger shot higher. "You kiss me again, I'll cut out your fucking tongue," I fired at him and started walking. I could not think about what happened under that tree—how right it felt, how wonderful it was to be close to him like that, to have his arms around me. It couldn't happen again. I couldn't let it.

He strode up beside me, still naked. "You didn't seem to have any complaints when it was happening."

His voice had gone impossibly deep. I forced myself to glance at him. "I was curious."

"And?"

"Once was enough."

He scowled. "Bullshit."

What the fuck was happening? Even more concerning, what did Lothar *think* was happening? No, he had no memory of our past, but he was clearly feeling a certain type of way toward me, and that was much more dangerous than just me pining after him, stuck for centuries in this agonizing cycle of unrequited love and unbearable pain and anger. I was strong, I could take it, I had been taking it for a long fucking time, but I wasn't sure how long I could resist him, especially if he decided to put all his effort into getting what he wanted.

"You kissed me back, Rox, and you fucking liked it," he muttered.

"Not enough to repeat the experience," I lied, even as my belly swooped and heated. "Now shut up about the damned kiss, and let's get the hell out of here. There's a small village a few miles away. We can clean up and ask around, see if anyone's seen B. They have an inn beside the tavern." I glanced his way again. "You might want to put some pants on before we get there."

·)〉〉·●·〈〈·

"We only have one room available," the birdlike innkeeper said, looking down her long nose at us. Not surprising since we were both covered in mud and blood. On the plus side, we didn't look very appetizing.

"Are you sure you don't have another room?" I asked with a good dose of desperation in my voice.

Lothar snorted. "Afraid you can't keep your hands to yourself?"

My face heated, because, yes, that was exactly what I was afraid of.

"Yes, I'm sure," the innkeeper said, her answer more than a little snappish. She gave us another unhappy perusal. "We don't want any trouble here."

"You won't get any trouble from us. We're just passing through." I slid my phone from my pocket and pulled up a picture of Beelzebub. "We're actually looking for a friend of ours. You haven't seen him around the village, have you?" I held up the picture of B. I'd taken it several months ago at Nixie's birthday party. The lords had been invited, like they were to all handmaid parties, and he'd rolled up with Asmodeus.

She leaned in, scanned the picture, shook her head, then tossed the room key on the counter like she wanted to avoid touching either of us, and again I got it. We were disgusting. "Room 13, top of the stairs, fourth door on the right."

I thanked her, and we trudged up the stairs. Lothar was in front of me, and I winced at the sight of the gouges in his back. Most had already healed, trapping mud, rotting leaves, and whatever other filth was on that creature's claws under his skin.

"Your back's a mess. I'm going to have to reopen those wounds to flush them out," I said as we reached the top of the stairs.

"You'd just love that, wouldn't you?" he said, a smirk on his handsome face, his eyes darkening. "Getting to carve me up with one of those pointy little blades of yours."

How the hell had he made *that* sound sexual? Heat washed over me as we reached the door to our room, and I quickly pushed in front of him, giving him my back so I could unlock the door. But then, it wasn't what he'd said but how he'd said it. I knew all too well how Lothar sounded when he was in the mood to get frisky. "It'd be a dream come true," I said deadpan as I shoved the door open.

The room was a floral explosion, or nightmare, depending on your tastes, but it smelled fresh, and I knew from my last stay here that all the rooms were kept to a high standard of cleanliness.

Studiously ignoring the chintz-covered bed overflowing with throw pillows, I dumped my bag on the luggage stand against the wall, kicked off my boots, and rummaged around for clean clothes. "I'm taking first shower, then we'll deal with your back. Put our boots outside the door, would you? They have a service for that here since this realm is a muddy cesspool."

He grunted, and I didn't give him a chance to say more. I quickly hit the bathroom and locked myself in.

Clumps of mud fell out of my hair when I dipped my head under the hot spray. I had to wash it three times to get all the crap out of it. As much as I was enjoying the hot water and the break from Lothar, I didn't drag it out. I needed to see to his back. The longer we left it, the deeper I'd have to cut and the more painful it was going to be for him.

As I was drying off, I glanced up and caught sight of myself. My skin was bruised. There was a big one on my shoulder, and when I turned, there were more across my back, and my thighs as well. No doubt from being tossed into a tree, then pinned under that creature. That was an hour ago, though. I should be healed by now.

My gaze dipped to my side, to my scar, and I sucked in a breath. It was pink, irritated. That was not normal.

It had taken years for the wound to heal, but it had. This morning, it had been pale, silvery—now it looked like something had aggravated it. The mud? The creature? Maybe I was having an allergic reaction of some kind to one of them?

The nerves were dead around the scar tissue, maybe the tree got me there and I didn't notice? But if that were the case, wouldn't it be bruised as well.

Chewing my lip, I dug my phone out of my discarded jeans and checked for any word from Lucifer. The uneasy feeling, since I'd seen the sigil on that axe, increased. Still nothing from Luci. I cursed and fired off another text, but with so many of us—handmaids, hounds, the lords, and high-ranking demons—his phone was always blowing up. He tended to only reply when he had the answers we wanted.

I quickly dressed, and when I walked out, Lothar was standing at the window, his eyes closed.

"Any luck?"

He turned to me. "He definitely passed through this town."

Excellent. We were in the right place at least.

Lothar hit the shower after that, and when he walked out, I was at the little desk by the window, sterilizing one of my blades over a candle flame. His gaze dipped to the blade, then up to me. I grinned and winked. "Time to slice and dice, big guy."

He huffed out a rough breath and shook his head.

The clean jeans he'd put on clung to his monster thighs. He was shirtless, and his damp wavy hair hung loose down his back. I tried not to, but it was impossible not to eat up his thick, muscled torso and huge biceps when he rummaged in his bag and grabbed a hair tie. My stupid mouth literally watered, watching the way his muscles moved as he gathered up his hair and knotted it messily, getting it out of the way.

"Where do you want me?" he said when he was done.

I quickly slammed my damn mouth closed, kicked the stool out from under the desk, then grabbed the ice bucket I'd acquired while he was in the shower, and went to fill it with warm water, grabbing a few towels as well.

"You done this before?" he asked when I walked back into the room.

I rolled my eyes. "Well, obviously. Like I said, I've fought alongside my sisters in a lot of battles, Lothar. We're fast healers, like you hounds. Stuff like this happens a lot." Well, I was usually a fast healer. I wasn't sure what was going on right now. Maybe it was just this realm?

"You ever fought any angels?" he asked as he sat.

My stomach cramped instantly and a humorless laugh slipped free. "I've got the scars to prove it." *Why did I say that?*

He froze and twisted on the stool to face me. "The one on your side? An angel did that?"

"A fallen, but yes." *Why was I telling him this?* Being in close quarters with him, just the two of us forced together all the time, was making me act stupid.

Just shut the hell up, Roxy.

I poured gin that I'd found in the mini bar on my blade. It was the best I could do, but hounds weren't prone to infection.

"So what happened—"

I sliced into his skin, and Lothar hissed. "Sorry."

130

"A little warning before you cut into me would be cool, yeah?"

There were dark lines visible under his skin, the mud and other crap showing me where I needed to cut. "Brace," I said, then continued to follow the jagged line with the tip of my blade. His body went rock solid, but he didn't move or make a sound this time. Stubborn male.

Grabbing a towel, I dipped it in the water and ran it down the open wound, wiping away the dirt and grime, then did it again to make sure I got every trace. It was a painful process, but it was the fastest and best way to make sure I got everything out. Then I repeated it over and over until every trace of mud was gone.

"I've got some balm that Willow gave me. It'll make sure there's no nasties left in your skin so you should heal up without any problem." I got it from my bag and carefully smeared it along the first slice I'd reopened.

He said nothing, sitting there patiently as I carefully smeared the powerful healing balm over his wounds. As the minutes ticked by, I became ultra-aware of his closeness, of the sound of his slow, even breaths, of the goose bumps I could see breaking out along his shoulders with every gentle swipe of my finger.

I cleared my throat. "Okay?"

"Mmm-hmm."

The rough throaty sound had me breaking out in goose bumps as well. I quickly smeared balm on the last slice and stepped back. "All done."

He rolled his wide shoulders and stretched before he stood. "Thanks."

I busied myself with cleaning everything up, and not looking at him. "No problem. You wanna head down to the tavern, get some dinner, and ask around? Beelzebub isn't hard to miss. We know he passed through here now, so someone had to have seen him, and there's no way B would pass a tavern and not go in."

"Sounds good."

Loth tugged on a shirt, and we grabbed our now clean boots from outside our door and headed out.

As we walked, I refused to think about coming back to this room alone with him later, or the one and only bed we'd be sleeping in...

CHAPTER
THIRTEEN

Roxy

The tavern was full. Apparently, one of the locals had just mated, and the village was celebrating. I guess that explained the "only one room at the inn" situation I found myself in. We grabbed drinks and passed on the carvery dinner, since it was a good chance the menu tonight was Ferinian, and opted for buttered bread. We found a standing table to eat and watched the festivities.

"A lot of these people have probably traveled here for the celebration. That's going to make things more difficult," Lothar said and took a bite of bread.

He was right. It was going to be a lot harder to pick the locals out of this crowd.

The newly mated couple hit the dance floor, and everyone surrounded them, cheering as they danced and seriously made out. I sipped my drink, not daring to look Lothar's way, but I felt his eyes burning into me.

He shouldn't want to look at me, and he sure as hell shouldn't want to kiss me.

"I'm gonna go ask around," I said and rushed off, disappearing into the crowd.

I worked my way around the tavern, showing B's photo to everyone, but no one had seen him, or if they had, they weren't talking. Gods, I could still feel Lothar's gaze on me, following me around the room. As the night wore on, and no one admitted to having seen B, I was becoming more on edge, and honestly, I was having trouble holding it together.

"I've been watching you flit around the room all night, beautiful. I was hoping you'd come my way," a deep voice said.

I turned and looked up. A tall male with shiny black horns and pointed ears grinned down at me. He was handsome, leanly muscled, had black nails, and wore a lot of piercings and silver rings. He had bad boy written all over him, and was totally Ursula's type. My gaze dipped to his plate, though the half-gnawed-on roasted foot with charred toenails was a major turnoff.

I grinned back at him, holding his vibrant green eyes. "I promise I was making my way over to you. You're hard to miss," I said and leaned against the wall facing him. "Are you from here?"

He grinned back, flashing white teeth. "Yeah, born and raised. You're not, though, are you, gorgeous."

"Nope, just passing through." I pouted a little. "I'm looking for a friend of mine actually." I knew exactly what this male liked, it was part of my skill set. I knew how to give a person exactly what they wanted. I could offer the personality traits they found most attractive and reel them in. My new friend here liked sweet and a little ditsy.

"Yeah?" He sipped his drink and leaned in. "I might be able to help."

I widened my eyes and tugged on the front of his shirt. "Could you really? That would be *amazing*. I'd be so grateful."

His gaze darkened and slid down my body, and I giggled and preened.

"You got a picture of your friend?"

I nodded enthusiastically and pulled out my phone, opening to the picture of Beelzebub. "This is him."

His gaze slid up from the picture. "Is he your mate?"

"Nope, I'm not mated. He's just a good friend. We've been really worried."

"We?"

A heavy arm landed on my shoulders. "That's right, we." Lothar's eyes were burning red as he leaned in. "So you seen him or not?"

Fucking hell.

"Nah," the male said, his lips curling in distaste. "Never seen him before in my life." Then he glanced down at me, his displeasure still there, and strode off.

I shoved at Lothar's chest, pushing him away. "What the hell was that?"

"What?" he asked as if butter wouldn't melt.

"You know what you did," I fumed. "We may as well leave. No one will talk to us now. You made me look like a manipulative asshole. You piss off the locals, everyone else will clam the hell up. Goddammit, Lothar." I strode off, through the crowd and out onto the street.

He followed, seeming unruffled, pleased with himself in fact, and that just infuriated me more.

"You're acting like a crazy person. You see that, right?" I fired at him.

"He didn't know shit. He just wanted in your pants, and you were fucking falling for it," he said, looking arrogant as hell.

"I wasn't falling for anything! He had a freaking *foot* on his plate, Lothar. I was using his attraction to me against him. That's literally what I do. You know this, we've already had this argument."

His eyes were still red and showed no sign of changing. "I don't like it, Roxy. I don't like males using you that way, and you can't make me believe different."

"Dickhead." I stormed off, because I was out of fight right then. We'd argued our way across three realms, and I was fucking exhausted.

He said nothing else, just followed me to the inn and up to our room. I didn't talk to him as I grabbed my things and changed in the bathroom, and I continued to say nothing when I walked out and found him bare-chested and lying in bed with his hands behind his head.

Flicking off the light with more force than was necessary, I got in beside him and thumped my arm down on the covers between us several times, creating an invisible boundary, then squeezed my eyes closed.

We lay there in silence for several long minutes, and every second that passed, the tension in the room grew. Maybe it was just me, but I was positive I could feel a restlessness rolling off Lothar, as if he were coiling tighter and tighter, about to burst out of bed—or something.

I jumped when he suddenly did just that. He shoved the covers back, bounded out, stalked to the window, and shoved it open. He dragged in a deep breath, then another.

"What are you doing? It's cold."

"I need it open," he grumbled.

"Well, I need it closed. This realm drops in temperature overnight. We'll freeze."

"You'll be fine," he said and strode to the wardrobe, opened it, dragged down another comforter, then threw it on top of me before getting back in bed.

I lay there, confused and now cold. "I can feel a draft. I'll get frostbite on the end of my nose at this rate," I said, tugging the covers higher. "What's the problem? It's not like it's hot in here."

"Drop it," he said and tucked his hands behind his head again.

"Drop what? Your weird need to turn me into an ice statue?"

He said nothing.

"Is it the cleaning products they use?" I breathed deep. "It just smells fresh to me."

He continued to say nothing.

"So it is the smell?"

"Drop it, Roxy," he said again.

"Is it me?" I said, joking, and made a show of smelling my pits, and as expected, they were fine.

He was back to not answering.

I froze. "Lothar?"

Silence.

No. No freaking way. "Is it me?" I said again. "Do you think I smell?"

He cursed. "No, not smell exactly."

"What!" I shot up. "You think I stink?" I couldn't believe it.

"Fucking hell," he muttered. "It's not that you stink, it's more that your scent, well, it kind of...repels me."

"What!" I shrieked again. "I'm repellent?"

"You're making it sound worse than it is," he said.

"How is that possible? It sounds pretty horrific any way you put it." I spun to him. "You truly think I stink? Oh gods, do all the hounds think I smell?"

"Roxy—"

"Lothar, tell me."

"No...just me."

I gripped the covers more tightly. "So right now, you want to—"

"Roxy, fuck. It's fine most of the time, but in an enclosed space like this—"

"Oh gods, you want to throw up and run the fuck away, don't you?"

"I don't want to throw up," he said roughly.

He wanted to get as far away from me as fast as he could. "Is it helping with the window open?"

"Yeah."

My face was burning with humiliation, and I quickly rolled away from him. I couldn't believe this. What the hell was going on? Why would I smell bad to Lothar—

It hit me like I'd run headfirst into a brick wall. *I was going to kill Lucifer!*

"We good?" Lothar muttered sleepily.

"Yep. Fine." I would never be fine again.

Lothar's breathing evened out, asleep in minutes, and as soon as I was sure he wasn't going to wake up, I snatched up my phone from the bedside table.

Roxy: You made me stink!

Luci: I did no such thing.

An actual answer from him. At least that was something.

Roxy: Lothar said I stink.

Luci: Ahh, then yes, I did do that.

I bit back my scream of rage.

Roxy: Why would you do that?

Luci: Better to be safe than sorry.

My repellent stench to Lothar was a safety measure?

Roxy: Are you saying there's a chance he could remember everything?

Luci: A small one.

If I wasn't already lying down, I would have fallen on my ass. I'd been worried it would happen, but told myself I was overreacting. Now I knew it was a real risk. As much as I wanted to yell at Luci, it wouldn't do any good. It wouldn't change anything. The only way to make sure everything didn't unravel around me was to find Beelzebub ASAP and put some serious distance between me and Lothar.

Roxy: Any info on the fallen?

I couldn't bring myself to say that bitch's name.

Luci: I'm working on it. The angels are forcing me to barter for the information. We're still in negotiations.

Shit. Lucifer wanted B found, badly. Whatever the angels wanted in exchange for the info must be big.

Roxy: Let me know as soon as you have anything.

I placed my phone back on the bedside table and rolled to my back, staring up at the ceiling.

What was I going to do? And where the hell was Beelzebub?

"That's it, kitten." His low, deep voice made me shiver. He made an mmmm *sound, but it was gritty and my belly fluttered. "Rock those hips...yeah, take my fingers deeper."*

I slid my hand over his shoulder and down his arm to his

wrist and gripped tight, holding him there. "I need you," I whimpered.

He growled low. "It won't be much longer. I promise, soon we'll be together like we were meant to be."

My eyes snapped open. It was still dark and my body was on fire. I was panting, sweating, a throbbing, aching need burning between my thighs from the dream.

Oh fuck.

I was draped over Lothar, again, straddling one of his huge thighs, and I was still freaking moving against it. Gasping, I tried to pull away, but one of Lothar's hot hands pressed against my lower back—or maybe it had been there the whole time?

"Don't stop. I got you, Rox." He lifted his knee, the muscle beneath my pussy flexing.

I shook my head, even as my inner muscles spasmed in protest. I was so close to coming, I was trembling.

His thigh flexed again. "Can smell that pussy, babe. Can feel how fucking hot and wet you are. You need it, take it."

I told myself to push away, but he was right. *I needed it.* More than food or water, more than air. So instead of getting off him, oh gods, I ground down harder and moaned. I shouldn't be doing this. I had to stop. Still, I showed no signs of stopping and fell forward, my mouth opening against his chest on another moan as I rocked faster. It wasn't enough. It would never be enough.

"Loth, please." Had I said that? Oh gods, I needed to shut up and get off him. Somewhere in the back of my mind I was screaming a warning, *stop this now, before it's too late.* But my body had taken over. The need inside me was too great to ignore. The longing to be close to him like this had been forced down for so long, I couldn't hold it in another moment.

What was Lothar thinking? Was he disgusted? My scent repelled him. He had to hate this.

"I'm sorry," I whimpered. "I'm so sorry." I wasn't only apologizing for this, for what I was doing to him in this moment, but for things he would never remember—for what I did to him, to us. For what I did to save my own devastated heart.

His hand slid up and down my back. "Nothing to be sorry for," he rasped. "You're so fucking hot, Roxy. So sexy, babe." He groaned. "Fuck, female, you're killing me."

"I'm sorry," I whimpered again, then groaned against his chest. "I'm repellent. You think I stink, you think—"

His fingers dug into my ass, hard enough to shut me up. "Baby, the last thing you're doing is repelling me. All I can smell right now is that hot-as-fuck pussy."

It was all my desperate, needy brain needed to hear to justify what I was doing. I reached back, grabbing his hand, and he didn't resist as I brought it around and shoved it between my legs. "Then touch me. Please, I need you to touch me."

"I'll touch you anywhere you want, sweetheart." His beast rattled in his chest as his hand slid down the front of my shorts. "This where you want me, Rox?"

"Yes, *oh gods, yes.*" His rough-skinned fingers slipped through my slick pussy, rubbing over my clit. He didn't let up, working me, teasing my opening, but not sinking in. With every swipe of those thick, talented fingers, I lost more of my control.

On the next swipe of his thumb over my clit, there was no holding back, and I sank my teeth into his pec on a muffled cry. Lothar hissed and his hips jerked up.

Oh gods, I'd missed him so fucking much.

I'd missed his gritty voice against my ear, his rough

hands against my skin—I'd missed just being near him. He'd destroyed me, but I'd torn us apart forever, shattering us beyond repair.

"More," I moaned against his chest, desperate to feel and not think, because I was barely holding back a sob.

Then finally, he slid a thick finger inside me, a guttural sound vibrating from him. "Fuck, Roxy, you feel so fucking good. You want more, baby?"

I nodded furiously, and he slid out that thick digit and pushed it back in, but this time with a second. I gripped his shoulders, unable to do anything but ride his fingers, chasing the pleasure unfurling inside me.

"You're all over my hand, Roxy. You're so wet, baby. I can feel how badly you need to come." He pressed his lips to my temple. "Let go, beautiful. Stop fighting it, and let go for me."

How did he know? How could he feel the battle going on inside me? I wanted to come so badly, but I also didn't deserve this with him. I didn't deserve it. "I c-can't," I whimpered.

He flipped me suddenly, so I was on my back, then he loomed over me. "Yeah, you can. You're gonna come for me, Rox. You're gonna give me what we both want."

The fingers of his other hand slid back into my hair, and he fisted lightly again while he thrust his fingers into me.

I closed my eyes and shook my head. "L-Lothar, I can't—"

"Yes, you can, but you gotta look at me," he growled.

I kept my eyes squeezed shut.

"Open your eyes," he demanded.

I tried, I really did, but I couldn't refuse him. I bit my lower lip when I blinked up at him and found his hound staring back. The beast was looking deep into my soul, as if that part of him knew the truth. As if the beast knew all my secrets but just didn't know how to share them with Lothar. That was a ridiculous thought. They were one, man and beast, but gods, staring into his glowing eyes now, I was positive I could see it all there in their depths, the secrets and lies, all the ugly truths.

"Let go," he growled, pure dominance in his voice as he slid his thumb over my clit and thrust his fingers inside me faster, deeper. "Let go for me, Roxy."

My hips jerked and my thighs spread wider, seeking more, because I was losing this battle. I'd regret this later, but in this moment, I wanted to lose.

He thrust his fingers deep again, and I arched against the bed, coming all over his thick fingers, crying out.

Lothar groaned above me, watching me, while my head spun and my body trembled from the power of my orgasm.

When I finally collapsed back on the mattress, I lay there with my eyes closed, too scared to move, too damn terrified to look up at him, to face what I'd done.

He brushed my hair back and pressed a soft kiss to my lips as he slid his fingers from me.

"Let me see you, Rox," he ordered roughly as if he knew what I was thinking.

I blinked up at him then, unable to hide any longer, unable to deny him, and watched as his gaze moved over my face, seemingly tracing every inch of it. I had no idea what he saw when he looked at me. Then my mind scrambled because he lifted the glistening fingers he'd had inside me and sucked them into his mouth with a moan.

A shiver rolled through me, seeing that pleasure move over his face, and I had to squeeze my thighs together.

"Delicious," he rumbled. "But I'm gonna need another taste." His hand moved to my belly, and he hooked his fingers in the waistband of my underwear. "You gonna give me another taste, Roxy?"

Right then I'd give him any-fucking-thing he wanted from me.

Was this truly happening? Maybe I could have this, have him? Maybe we could get a second chance after all. Maybe...

Someone banged on the door.

Lothar growled, then jumped off the bed and strode across the room. He was in only his boxer briefs and the male was *hard*. He yanked the door open and the innkeeper stood there, hair a mess, her robe wrapped tightly around her, and a harried look on her face. She held out a folded piece of paper. "I was told to give you this." Then she spun and rushed away.

Lothar shut the door and turned to me. I was already off the bed and crossing the floor. He handed it to me and I quickly unfolded it. "It's an anonymous tip. Has to be from someone at the bar." I scanned the message and my gaze shot up to Lothar. "Beelzebub's still here."

CHAPTER
FOURTEEN

Lothar

"Anything?" Roxy asked under her breath.

I followed a worn path around a cluster of gray slime-covered trees. "Still nothing." When we got to this realm, I felt his energy, which was what hounds used to track, but now the trail was cold. Beelzebub knew we were here and had found someone or some *place* that could block him from me.

"Well, if our informant's right, we're close. According to the map they sketched for us, Drake's place isn't far from here."

I grunted, unable to take my eyes off her as she strode ahead. I could still smell her pussy, still taste it on my tongue. I didn't understand what was going on. I'd never had the driving urge to fuck her, not like I was experiencing now. Her scent had made it impossible for me to spend any length of time with her, even if I had admired her ass from across the room a time or two, and yeah, how good she felt pressed up against me when she hugged me before her scent got too much and I had to retreat. Her scent was still an issue, but for some reason I was handling it a lot better.

My gaze slid down her back, over her ass, and down to her strong thighs capable of choking a male out if the mood struck her. My dick got hard again.

I clenched my teeth. What had changed? Why was making her come all I could think about? Why couldn't I get the sound of her voice begging me to touch her out of my head? This was Rox, I admired her. She was an exceptional female, a talented warrior, and good and loyal friend—but that's all she was. It was all I'd wanted from her, all I still wanted—a friend.

The beast, on the other hand, had gone full rogue. He was losing his shit around her more and more often, roaring at me to get closer to her, to touch, to scent, to fuck —to *bite*.

It was fucking with my head, confusing me. So when I woke to Roxy all over me, rubbing against my thigh, something flipped deep in my chest. There'd been other moments on this trip where the beast and I were in alignment—seeing her with Asmodeus was definitely one of them. And when we were under that tree and the need to kiss her, to taste her pretty lips, had taken over was another.

It was a head-fuck because, yes, her scent still made me want to retreat, but when I wasn't close enough to her, I didn't like that either. Maybe it was just a matter of us being stuck together?

Hounds were notoriously horny, and it had been a while since I'd done more with a female than gotten her off. We were big males, our cocks included, fucking wasn't always an option, especially with humans, but everything in me knew that Roxy wouldn't have an issue with my size. Like shifters and demons, she was made different.

So why fight it? Neither of us was against casual sex. We were both old as fuck and we'd tried everything. Beings like us didn't have hang-ups about that shit. There was an obvious attraction there. Pleasure was pleasure. I'd just never seen myself spending that kind of time with Rox.

If I wanted to calm down my beast, I needed to give us what we both wanted. "Rox, what happened earlier, back in the room?"

Her shoulders stiffened. "Mmm-hmm."

"The way I see it. You want me, and I want you. You wanna stop playing and do this? I want more of you, babe, and I think you do too."

She was silent for several very long seconds as she side-stepped spitting flowers and dodged fallen branches and brittle bones sticking out of the mud. "What exactly are you asking for, Loth?" she finally said, not looking back.

I shrugged, even though she couldn't see me. "Let's fuck, at least while we're away from home. Get that shit out of our systems. No point going to bed each night wanting more when we could have it."

She huffed out a laugh and shook her head. "As easy as that, huh?"

I ducked under a moss-covered branch. "Seems logical to me."

"Things could get complicated," she said.

She still hadn't looked back at me. I didn't like that. "How?" I licked my lips and bit back my groan when I tasted her again. "Already made you come, Rox, why stop now?"

"What about Asher?"

My head jerked back. "Like I told Gus, me and Ash don't fuck. We hang, we ride our bikes, nothing more."

Roxy stumbled but caught herself. "The amount of time you spend together...I thought you two were an item."

I was getting sick of people saying that shit. I was betting Ash was as well. "Ash had a mate, the male died, she's not looking for anything other than an occasional fuck with someone random, which means she's got no interest seeing them again after, that counts me out."

"How disappointing for you," Roxy said, kind of stomping around another tree.

I frowned. "I'm not disappointed. I'm sure if Ash and I fucked, it'd be good, but not any more than any other female, and if I'm that hard up, I can get laid whenever I want." No, I hadn't been with anyone in a while, because it had felt like too much effort. But Asher's pack mates came to our bar, Hell Fire, all the time, and they liked to fuck as much as we did. Or I could go to Hell. Some demons loved the danger of being with us, following us around like fucking groupies.

Roxy finally glanced back at me. "Is that right?"

I shrugged. "Well, yeah."

She spun around. "Well, don't let me get in the way of you hooking up with someone else."

"What are you talking about?" She stalked off, and I quickly strode after her, not sure what just happened. "I could, but I don't want any other female. Despite your offensive scent, and all the fire and attitude you've thrown at me lately...shit, maybe it's because of the attitude? I honestly don't know, but right now the only female I want to fuck is you."

She rubbed her temples and released a long breath. "Wow, with lines like that, you should still be a virgin."

This conversation was confusing me, and I got pissed off when I was confused. "I don't know what you're talking about. And I don't know what you want me to say. Your pussy was dripping all over my fingers a few hours ago, now you're pissed off because I said we should get each other off while we're here?"

She blew out a long breath. "There you go again, you charmer, you."

My anger shot higher, and the beast made his displeasure felt, showing me images of Roxy and a particular lord, while pushing against my skin and snarling in my skull. "Sorry if I'm not fucking Asmodeus. Seems he's the only male who has the ability to charm you out of your clothes."

"You did not just say that to me," she fired back.

I scowled, not sure what the hell I'd done wrong.

"Gods, you're an asshole." She strode ahead again.

Now I was an asshole? What the fuck did she want from me? "Whatever, Roxy. Forget I said anything. This is way too much trouble just to get off." As soon as the words left me, I regretted them. I was confused and angry, but how much I wanted her had not lessened in the slightest.

She spun back to me, her eyes flaring. "Awesome. Perfect. Sounds good to me. I'd hate to cause you any *trouble*. And it suits me just fine, since no one can get me off like I can," she said, then stormed off. Again.

Motherfucker. Why did she have to go and say that? Now the beast was filling my head with images of Roxy doing just that. My brothers apologized to their mates when they said things to piss them off. Roxy wasn't my mate, but I did want her in my bed, so if I apologized, maybe she'd stop arguing with me and let me give her what I knew she wanted as well.

I rushed after her, rounding a cluster of trees, and found

her behind some kind of thicket made up of deep purple leaves. She turned to me, one finger to her lips.

Slowing my roll, I stopped beside her. There was a house just ahead. "You been here before?" I asked low.

"No, Drake is super paranoid about his private residence and doesn't invite just anyone here."

The ruler of the Ferine lived in a strange house that was all sharp angles. It was black with pointed turrets on both sides and pointed stone windows. It was surrounded by a black iron fence, and the yard around the house had a bunch of hideous concrete statues covered in moss and other creeping plants.

"You know this guy," I said. "How do you think we should approach this?"

She nibbled on her lip, and my stomach fucking clenched when a look came over her, one that had her pouty lips curling up in a sultry smile.

"We're going to fake it." She pulled her bag off her back and rummaged around inside. "Drake doesn't know that we know that Beelzebub is here, and even if he thinks we know, he can't let on that he knows that we know, because that would be admitting he's turned his back on Lucifer and provided his enemy with a place to hide out."

I had no idea what the fuck she'd just said.

She winked. "So we're going to walk on in. I'll say Lucifer's sent me as his ambassador on a...a friendship tour to strengthen our alliances." She pulled a red leather box triumphantly from her bag. "I'll give him this, say it's a gift from Luci, and thank him for his continued loyalty. Drake will assume Lucifer gave us his location. No way he can turn us away then."

I frowned. "What's in the box?"

Roxy flipped it open. A large ring with a huge stone sat inside.

It was ugly as fuck. "Where did that come from? Is it real?"

"It's just a cheap novelty."

She pressed something on the side, and the stone snapped open. There were a couple of little green pills inside. "What the fuck are those?"

"It was a parting gift from Urs. She said to use it if..." Her eyes darted up to mine, then back down. "If I needed to take down...something large." She tipped the pills into her hand and slid them in her pocket. "I'm betting Drake won't think to question the authenticity of the ring. Hopefully, he won't look too closely at it until we're gone." Her grin turned wicked. "Preferably with an unconscious Beelzebub in tow."

"If you think it'll work, I trust you," I said, and meant it. Roxy had more experience with people like Drake and other high-ranking fuckwits than I did.

Her smile brightened. "Well, isn't that a nice change."

I ignored the barb, and she thankfully let it drop, even though I deserved it after telling her I didn't trust her. "Ready when you are."

She shoved the red box in her pocket, slid her bag back on, and straightened her shoulders. Then she glanced back at me. "How are your acting skills? Any good at improvisation."

I stiffened. "I think you know the answer to that."

She pressed her hand to my chest, looking up at me, and my heart slammed against it. "Fine. You can play my strong and silent boy toy. Do you think you can handle that?"

"Boy toy?"

"My much younger, sexual plaything," she said, and smiled sweetly.

"You just said you didn't want that." But hope throbbed through me. She rubbed at her temples again, something she'd done several times during our conversations recently. I assumed it was frustration she was feeling, that's what my instincts told me. I didn't understand why she was frustrated though. "What?"

"We're just acting, remember? Also Drake knows I don't need a guard. He'll be suspicious of you anyway, which is why we need a decent cover story. The only logical reason I'd be traveling with a hound would be for your tracking abilities. So we need to make sure you're here with me for another reason. Capisce?"

"And that reason is sex?" I said, my voice back to being rough as fuck.

"Yup." She nodded. "A boy toy, since you're my junior by a good number of years."

When you were as old as us, that shit meant nothing. She was purposely trying to piss me off. "If you introduce me to that asshole as your boy toy, I won't be happy."

"What about sex puppet?"

I growled.

"Fuck buddy?" Her brows lifted, her blue eyes wide and innocent. "That's a nicer one, right? I mean it's all right there in the name."

"Do not call me your fucking fuck buddy, Roxy. I'm warning you."

She tapped her lower lip. "Manstress?"

I snarled a warning.

She threw up her hands. "Fine. What about paramour? Surely even you can't be offended by that one."

I hated it, but I guess it was the best of her suggestions so far. "Fine."

"The moment we walk through those gates, you need to be on. They'll be watching us," she said, then tossing her long dark hair back, she transformed in front of my eyes, becoming the warrior she was. Roxy carried herself with the bearing of a general as she strode right through the iron gates and along the cobbled path, weaving through statues, and up to the front door.

CHAPTER
FIFTEEN

Lothar

I FOLLOWED Roxy and did my best not to scowl. That was as far as my acting skills went. I sure as hell didn't know how to play the part of besotted fool.

She turned to me, a frown creasing her brow. "Well, knock."

In other words, she didn't lift a finger, that's what her *paramour* was for—besides other things, obviously. I pounded on the door and stood back, barely swallowing the growls building in my chest. I didn't like going into situations blind. Every instinct I possessed told me this place was dangerous.

Someone approached at a fast clip on the other side of the door, and my arm snapped out like I was fucking possessed, and hooked around Roxy's waist, pulling her back against me.

I had no idea what was coming, but I would be prepared. My other hand slid to the hilt of my knife.

Roxy's gaze sliced up to mine, her eyes sharp, but she laughed, the sound musical and completely fake. "You need to chill, lover. You'll have me all to yourself again soon enough."

This was her acting, and I didn't like the part she was playing. It only took a split second to see that this Roxy was calculated, not warm, not loving and sweet. She was who she needed to be in this pit of vipers.

The door opened and she smiled. "Grimmel! It's been forever," she said to the dour-faced male holding the door open a foot and peering out.

"Miss, Roxana." He wasn't happy. "My master wasn't expecting you."

"No, and that's my bad. Luci has me traveling all over the place. A tour, if you will, visiting all our friends as a gesture of goodwill, to show them how much we appreciate them." She slid the small red box from her pocket and held it up. "I have a gift for Drake, chosen especially for him by Lucifer."

The lies rolled off her tongue with practiced ease.

Grimmel's gaze slid from her to me, then back. "And your companion?"

"Oh! This is my paramour, Lothar." She giggled. "I can't bear to leave home without him, especially on such a long journey." She slid her arm around mine. "Isn't that right, Cookie Monster?"

Cookie Monster? *What the fuck?* "Yeah, that's right..." I searched my mind for a name, and it popped up out of nowhere. "Kitten."

Roxy's head snapped back, the smile still plastered on

her face, but she'd stiffened against me, and her eyes looked a little wild.

Grimmel didn't seem to notice the change, but I did. I noticed every tiny thing about Roxy lately.

"I'll check with the master, and see if he's free."

Roxy's smile shifted, not nice, not sweet or friendly. "Of course, though I'm sure he can find time for me. Lucifer would be so disappointed if I wasn't able to personally deliver his very thoughtful gift."

The threat was veiled, but there was no missing it. If you want to keep Lucifer as an ally, then let us in or you won't like the consequences.

And sure enough, three minutes after Grimmel left us waiting at the door, he was back, welcoming us into the house.

The tall male was spindly, like skin stretched over bone. I didn't like the way he looked at Roxy, as if she were a snack he wanted to take a bite out of, and honestly, I didn't fucking like the way he looked at me either.

"The master will see you at dinner. Until then, I'll show you to your room." He looked down his long nose. "And you can freshen up."

We followed the walking corpse up stairs that were uneven in depth and height to the second floor, then down a hall that wasn't even close to straight. The whole place was misshapen and uneven. Grimmel opened the door with a flourish. "Your room. I trust you'll find your accommodations acceptable?"

Roxy patted his arm as we walked by. "This will do nicely."

He bowed a little and stepped back. "Dinner will be in an hour. The master requires formal attire. If you don't have anything appropriate, I'm sure you will find something suitable in one of the closets." His beady gaze slid over me, before darting back to Roxy. "There are fresh towels in the bathroom." Then he backed out completely, and shut us in.

I spun to Roxy. "What the fuck was that?"

She screwed up her face and strode to the window, shoving open the drapes. "Grimmel has been with Drake for so long I don't remember one without the other."

"I don't trust him." Roxy opened the window, no doubt for me. My gut tightened. I didn't like that she knew how her scent affected me, my rogue beast hated that I'd said something and was pissed off that I'd caused her distress. I was starting to agree. I wished I could take it back.

"You shouldn't," she said, turning back to me. "You shouldn't trust anything or anyone in this house."

We held each other's gaze. Was that another dig at me? Then she cleared her throat, breaking the weird vibe that had surrounded us and scanned the room.

"You think they're watching us?"

"In here? I don't think so. Pissing me off would mean pissing off Lucifer, and that's not something Drake would risk. It's the only reason we were granted admittance. But let's stay cautious."

I nodded and closed the space between us, dropping my hands to her waist, wanting her to know that her scent wasn't bothering me, that she didn't repel me, at least not right then, and that I did trust her. And yeah, I wanted to know if she'd let me touch her, or if she'd deny me and push me away.

She stilled, standing there like one of the statues outside, but she didn't shove me back. Pushing my luck, I leaned in, and her eyes widened before I pressed my mouth to her ear. "Just in case they are listening, we should probably continue to play our roles."

Rox released a shaky little breath that lifted the hair on my neck. "You're probably right."

"Yeah?"

Her hands lifted to my biceps and she squeezed. "What do you suggest?"

You on all fours, pussy wet, ass up. I wasn't sure if the voice in my head was mine or my rogue beast, but we were both on board with that idea. I didn't think Roxy would go for that though. Even I knew that was too much too fast. She'd denied me only a short time ago, but now she seemed to have had a change of heart, and not just for appearances. Despite my excuse to get closer to her, no one was in this room but us, and she still hadn't shoved me away.

I lifted my head, my gaze dipping to her lovely mouth, then back up. "We got interrupted earlier, right before you were gonna give me another taste of that pussy. How about we pick up where we left off?" Pink hit her cheeks. The fact that someone like Roxy could still blush did something to me. "I promise you'll love it."

Her fingers stilled on my arms, then flexed. "But why would you want that? If I'm remembering correctly, and I know I am...you said, and I quote, 'This is way too much trouble just to get off.' I wouldn't want to cause you any trouble, Lothar," she said and batted her long lashes.

My gut gripped tight. "I regretted those words the moment I said them, Rox. I'm sorry I said that shit, baby." I ran my hands up and down her small waist, squeezing gently. "I want to make you feel good, female, so fucking badly. Please. Please let me make you feel good."

"You're truly sorry?"

"Yes. I can guarantee that right in this moment, I regret it more than fucking anything."

Her lips curled up. "You really think this is a good idea?"

Something was holding her back, but I could see how much she wanted it. It was all there in her pretty, expressive eyes. I got the feeling she wanted me to talk her into it, but that wasn't something I could do. The decision had to be hers. I could only tell her the truth. "All I know is, I fucking want more of you, Rox. I don't know why now, I just know it's all the beast...all *I* can think about." I tucked her hair behind her ear. "You wanna take this slow, we can do that, but, baby, I really need to make you come. I need to hear you crying out in pleasure, and I can do that without using my dick, if you're not on board with us fucking yet."

Her eyes drifted shut, and I searched her face, the subtle shift, the slight parting of her lips, the trembling of her lashes, the quickening of her breath.

I waited, my own breath trapped in my lungs.

Finally, her eyes opened, and I was fucking dazzled by their beauty. They seemed brighter somehow, like liquid sapphires.

"Okay," she whispered. "Let's see how this goes."

"Yeah?" Truthfully, I expected her to say no fucking way.

She nodded.

I bared my teeth, cock hard in an instant as pleasure throbbed through me. "Get on the bed."

More pink hit her cheeks. "Let me shower first."

I shook my head. "I like you like this." I breathed deep. "All I can smell right now is how wet you are, and you're making my fucking mouth water." I tugged the button of her jeans open. "Take these off, Rox. Now."

She stepped back, nibbling on that lush lower lip again, and slid off her jacket. She was wearing an oversized T-shirt under it, some band I'd never heard of emblazoned on the front. She left the T-shirt on, and instead kicked off her boots, stripping down so all she had on was that shirt. How was that so unbearably sexy?

"You want me on the bed?" she asked.

"Yes."

She backed up, and I took a step toward her. One of her hands lifted, and she shook her head, telling me to stay where I was. I did, but fuck it was hard with all that smooth bare skin on display for me. My fucking mouth was watering as my gaze slid up her strong, muscled legs to the bottom of that shirt that was covering everything I wanted to get my hands on, my mouth on, so fucking badly.

Roxy got up into the middle of the bed, her gaze not leaving me as she slid her hands back so she was leaning on them. Her legs were out in front of her, her delicate feet crossed at the ankle. "Like this?" she asked, her head tilting to the side, the move was coy and sexy as hell.

"No." I took another step forward, but again she shook her head.

"Stay where you are, Cookie Monster."

My nostrils flared, every muscle tight as fuck. "Female, do not fuck with me—"

Her knees still pressed together, she slid her feet up, so they were resting on the edge of the mattress. "Better?"

"No..." The beast interrupted me, emitting a hungry, desperate sound that had nothing to do with me. It was the first time that rogue motherfucker had taken control of my vocal cords. I gritted my teeth, forcing the beast back when he tried to take control again. *What the actual fuck?*

She opened her knees, just an inch. "Now?"

I growled, the beast and me in unison this time.

Then fuck, Roxy let her knees fall open, which forced her shirt up to her hips and bared her pretty pussy to me, spreading it wide. It was smooth and blush colored and glistening from her juices.

"What about now?" she asked huskily.

"Roxy," I growled.

She licked her lower lip, then dragged her teeth over it. "Well? What are you waiting for? Come get your cookie," she said.

With a snarl, my boots ate up the floor between us and I sank to my knees beside the bed. Then hooking my hands under her thighs, I dragged her ass to the edge. The beast rumbled as I slid my mouth along her inner thigh, breathing her in, then finally, fucking finally, I licked her. Some of us older hounds could partially shift, and we were more adept at making smooth changes. It could make it far more pleasurable for females when we went down on them.

The beast surged forward, merging with me again, the way it should be, the way it always had been, and my tongue shifted, widening and lengthening. Like this, I had more control over the various muscles, and my chest vibrated as I lashed hungrily through her slick pussy and up to her clit. I worked her with the tip, while the rest undulated against her, keeping her pussy spread wide and massaging her tight little opening.

Roxy groaned, her fingers thrusting into my hair as she lifted her hips and ground up against my mouth. She was gasping and panting, but she didn't have to beg me for more. I knew exactly what she needed. Covering her pussy with my mouth, I slid just the tip of my tongue down to her tight opening, slipping it in and out, teasing her, over and over again.

"Lothar, please," she all but sobbed and lifted those churning hips, opening her thighs wider. "Please, I need—"

I pushed the tip in, and kept going. In one smooth movement, filling her with the full width and length of my beast's tongue, then rolled it in a wave of hot flesh, moving inside her.

Roxy cried out, shuddering, writhing against the mattress, not holding back this time. No, she fucking lost it, arching and jerking and calling out my name as her inner muscles clamped down, pulsing deeply before she came all over my rolling, thrusting tongue.

When she slumped against the bed, gasping for breath, I carefully slid my tongue out and stood. She blinked up at me drowsily as I retracted it, shifting the muscle back to its human form.

Her eyes were all innocence as they lifted from my mouth and caught mine. "See? Total Cookie Monster," she said, and her lips twitched.

Fuck me, she was cute, and so sexy I'd been close to coming in my jeans getting a taste of her. I reached back, grabbed my shirt, tugged it off, and tossed it aside. Her gaze slid down my bare chest, following my hands as I undid my pants and fucking finally freed my achingly hard cock.

I grinned, flashing my fangs. "Your turn, kitten," I said, teasing her, using the stupid pet name I'd come up with when we'd gotten here, since she was using the one she'd given me.

"Is that right?" She swallowed thickly, then licked her lips.

"Oh yeah, the only question is, where should I put it?" With how hard she'd gotten me, I'd take her fucking hand at this point. I leaned over her, planting a fist in the mattress. "Just warning you though, you stay lying there like that, legs spread wide for me, I'll start to think you don't want to take it slow anymore."

CHAPTER
SIXTEEN

Roxy

MY BELLY SQUIRMED as I looked up at him, his eyes were glowing gold, and that perfect mouth, those lips that I'd wanted to spend an eternity kissing were curved up slightly, giving me a glimpse of the tips of his fangs.

I drew in a deep breath to try to settle the flurries in my belly. Gods, he was so beautiful like this.

But then, to me, Lothar was beautiful all the time.

I should never have let it get this far, I should have said no. I'd told him nothing more would happen, I'd told myself the same thing, but as soon as the door closed and the space evaporated between us—when he touched me and told me he wanted more of me—my will to fight this dissolved to dust.

Getting out of this bed and putting some space between us was what I should do. I needed to end this before it spiraled out of control and I said or did something that was dangerous, for both of us—but I couldn't. How could I do that when he was all I'd ever wanted? I'd dreamed about being with him like this for so long, of having him back, having my Lothar again, and there was nothing that could tear me from this bed.

Smiling up at him, I swallowed down the emotion gripping my throat. I pressed my hand to his chest. His skin was hot, his heart thudding rapidly against my palm. He wanted this, me, badly. Still only a fraction as much as I wanted him.

There was a line we couldn't cross though. But what I could do was make him feel good, make him come so hard he lost his mind.

"On your back, big guy," I said, and I liked how my voice was still raspy after he'd made me scream his name.

His grin widened, then he dropped to the bed beside me and propped his hands behind his head. His biceps twitched and his abs tightened as he watched me, waiting for what I was going to do.

His jeans were still on, just shoved down, so I tugged them off the rest of the way, removing his boots as well. He tracked me the entire time, and his nostrils flared as I crawled back onto the bed and straddled his ribs. "We don't have much time before we're expected at dinner." I slowly dragged my nails down his chest. "So we're going to have to be quick. You might want to hold on tight there, Cookie Monster."

He chuckled. "You think you can get me off that fast, kitten?"

My nails dug a little deeper into his skin. He was teasing me, using that name, like I was him, but he had no idea what it was doing to me, that every time he called me that, in his deep, rough voice, I was thrown back to the past so fast my head spun, and honestly, it was killing me. I couldn't let him see it, though, so I grinned and leaned in, letting my hair fall around us, and pressed my lips to his ear. "Oh, I know I can." I nipped his earlobe and kissed his throat, taking my time, something he loved, something he only learned he loved when he was with me.

I slid my hands over his shoulders and felt the goose bumps he'd always gotten when I did this. "Feels good, doesn't it?" I said against his ear, then kissed my way down his chest.

His fingers slid into my hair, and I felt his stomach tremble under my pussy. "Yeah. Fuck. Really good."

I continued to use my nails, dragging them over his skin, then following with more sucking kisses as I went. His fingers tightened in my hair, and I doubted he knew he'd done it. Everything fell away when we were together like this, it always had. When the head of his cock bumped against my ass, I lifted myself over it and sat on the tops of his thighs, then wriggled lower. He looked down at me as I took him in hand, then holding his darkened gaze, I sucked the head into my mouth.

His hips shot up with a growl, my name following, rolling from him all blended with his beast, so deep and raw.

Yeah, I knew how he *thought* he liked his cock sucked, but that wasn't what I was going to do. Instead, I planned to do what I knew got him off so good, it made him fucking feral. Again, something he'd only discovered with me.

I teased the ridge with my tongue, working it, then sucked it into my mouth. I couldn't get enough, and I did it over and over again, until he was panting hard and every muscle on his body was rock solid.

He hissed and groaned. "Roxy..."

Slipping a hand down to his balls, I massaged them, the way he loved. His abs trembled, and he cursed. But I wasn't finished. Dragging my other hand down my body, I slipped my fingers between my thighs, sliding them through my pussy and slicking them up really well. Then I slid them between his sexy, muscled ass cheeks.

On a deep growl, he widened his legs for me. I fought back my grin as I ran the tip of my finger over his ass, then finally, when he was shaking with need and growling constantly, I pushed one in, but just the tip for now, teasing him like he had me.

"Roxy," he gasped, then groaned. "Fuck, kitten...don't stop."

This time kitten had just rolled off his tongue without thought, as if he'd been calling me that for years. My heart squeezed in my chest and I sucked him deeper, stretching my mouth to its limits, and instead of massaging his balls, I gripped his thick length and stroked what I couldn't fit into my mouth, which was a whole hell of a lot.

"Fuck...*fuck*, Rox. Slow down, baby."

I wasn't going to do that. The longer I was with him like this, the more I tried to convince myself that we could be together again, for real, that we could put the past behind us, that I could pretend that it never happened—and that I could finally have my happy ending with the male I loved.

As if all the awful, hurtful, heartbreaking things that came before had never happened.

"Roxy," he choked out. "Baby...*fuck*. Slow down," he said again.

I slid my finger in his ass nice and deep and found my target.

Lothar snarled, and his cock jerked in my mouth, then

throbbed a moment before he shot his seed down my throat. He groaned and hissed and growled as I swallowed it down greedily, not letting up, not for a second, not until the pulsing of his cock slowed and his punishing grip on my hair eased.

I dragged my mouth up his length, sucking gently now, and released him with a delicate pop as I carefully slid my finger from his ass.

His gaze hit mine and locked on, while he panted hard, his chest heaving.

My heart was thudding hard in my chest, but I couldn't show him how affected I was after what we'd done, so I smiled up at him and licked my lips. "Tasty," I said, then quickly looked away and bounded off the bed.

He was silent as I flung one of the closets open and pretended I was busy looking for something to wear, pretended that I wasn't completely tuned in to him, to every panted breath he took or every rustle of the sheets as he moved, then got off the bed, because I couldn't be near him right then. Not with that look in his eyes that felt like so much more than it was—so much more than it could be.

He was grateful for the best orgasm he could remember having, that's all that look was, and I had to remember that. I forced myself not to stiffen when he came up behind me and wrapped his arms around my waist, then dipped his head, burying his face in the crook of my neck.

"Fucking hell, female, you've ruined me," he rumbled roughly against my skin.

I rested my hands over his. "You think so?"

"I know so. Never come that hard before, baby. Not too proud to say that was some out-of-body shit you performed right there."

I chuckled. "And you doubted me."

"Fuck, never again."

I leaned against him, letting his warmth soak into me, letting my guard down a little more. Letting myself have this, just for a moment. "I...I like being with you like this, Loth," I confessed.

He pressed a kiss to my throat. "Me too, baby, and if you're on board, I'd like to explore this some more? This thing between us."

"I'd like that." I felt him smile against my skin. *You're being a stupid, reckless idiot.* I ignored the voice in my head because I didn't want to hear the truth. "Right, we better get dressed and go down to dinner." I stepped out of his arms, and he let me, then I glanced at the clock on the wall. "Shit, there's no time to shower."

Lothar's eyes glittered. "Good, I want you smelling of me. I want them to know what we've been doing up here in this room."

My mouth went dry and my swallow was audible. "Yeah...well, it definitely makes our story more believable."

He shrugged. "That too."

My heart flipped in my chest, then thumped hard.

Lothar wanted everyone to know I was his.

At least for now.

·))) ● (((·

Showtime. I tightened my hold on the small ring box as we took the stairs.

Lothar was beside me, looking ridiculously handsome. He'd opted to wear his own black jeans and a black shirt and dinner jacket that he'd found in the closet, the only items that fit him. His long, dark wavy hair was in a braid down his back, and he'd removed any visible traces of mud and dirt, but he'd refused to do any more than that.

I was trying not to think too much about why he wanted my scent on him, but it was hard not to let myself fall deeper into the fantasy of us being together again.

Was it even possible? Could I be with him again?

Could I hide the truth of our past from him, from everyone? What if we kept our relationship secret? Would Lothar agree to that? Could I convince him to without telling him why?

Stop.

I had to stop thinking like that.

If he was to ever learn the truth, the consequences would be dire. This can never be undone.

Lucifer's voice echoed through my mind. If Lucifer used the word dire, you knew it was really bad. Allowing myself to think there was hope for us was dangerous, for so many reasons. What we were doing now was bad enough, especially if I was right about who was behind the bid for Lucifer's throne.

"What is it?" Lothar said, his hands touching the small of my back, concern on his handsome face.

"It's fine," I said and forced a smile. "There's just a lot riding on tonight." I had to prepare myself to let him go again. I had to walk away. There was no other choice. It was impossible.

He nodded and his hand slid up and down my back. "I got you tonight, babe. Whatever you need."

Hounds liked certain textures, things that were soft and smooth especially. Lothar liked the silk of the long slip dress I'd selected. It had thin delicate straps, and the burgundy fabric fell over my curves like liquid. "I know. Thanks, Loth. I appreciate it."

His hand slid up my spine again, but this time his fingers curled around the back of my neck in a hold that was so utterly possessive, my breath caught.

"We're in this together, yeah? We're a team, so you don't need to thank me."

We hit the bottom of the stairs, and Grimmel materialized out of nowhere like a creepy spindly shadow.

"This way," he said and strode ahead toward a set of ornate double doors.

"Just an FYI regarding dinner," I said. "Lothar and I both have special dietary needs. Strictly no people meat."

Lothar's lips twitched, and my heart beat a little faster at the sight.

"Noted," Grimmel said, then gripped both handles and shoved the doors wide.

We followed him into the large room decorated in shades of burgundy like my dress and lit by candles in a large number of silver candelabras placed around the room. There was a long table in the middle and several people sat around it. Their gazes all slid to us.

It seemed Drake had other guests attending tonight, though the host himself wasn't here yet.

Grimmel cleared his throat. "May I introduce, Roxana the Blade, revered warrior and handmaiden to Lucifer, King of Hell."

There were rumblings from the table, and the bland expressions turned to interest.

"Accompanying our esteemed guest this evening is her paramour, low-ranking hellhound, Lothar."

Low ranking? It was a lie, of course. Lothar was one of the older hounds and one of War's most trusted inner circle. Grimmel was purposely trying to piss Loth off, who'd gone rock solid beside me. As unpredictable as hounds could be, I had no idea how he'd react to the insult. He could say nothing and brush it off, or he could turn around and tear Grimmel's head from his shoulders. Both were serious options.

I quickly slid my hand in Loth's and squeezed.

He glanced down at me, and I held his furious stare. *Ignore him. Don't react.* I hadn't said the words out loud, and he couldn't read my mind, but he saw something in me, because he calmed almost instantly.

Grimmel motioned me to my seat and strode ahead to pull out my chair for me. Lothar growled low and strode over, forcing him to step back, and slid it out instead. One of the guests laughed. I ignored them as I took my seat and Lothar did the same beside me. Tension still rolled off him, but he at least seemed to have a handle on his anger.

"You're very growly tonight," I said to him and laughed, since we had an audience and they weren't missing a thing.

His shoulders stiffened. "You know how I get, kitten," he said as he scanned the room with glowing red eyes. "I don't like it when other males ogle you." Then he dragged my chair closer to his and flung his arm around my shoulders.

Two of the three males at the table instantly dipped their gazes, the third smirked and sipped his wine, not sparing Lothar a glance, and kept his eyes on me. "You need to get that dog to heel, Roxana the warrior," he said, sarcasm dripping from his voice. "Drake doesn't stand for posturing in his home."

I sharpened my gaze on the male and squeezed Lothar's thigh under my hand when I felt it tense to stand. Not looking away from the prick across the table, I let my pleasant smile drop. I'd really love to carve some pretty slices into that smarmy face of his. "Lothar doesn't posture.

So perhaps you should mind your manners if you don't want to piss him off."

His smirk stayed firmly in place. "Ah, like that is it."

"Like what?"

"Grimmel announced you as 'the blade,' but it's clear that the little lady needs her attack dog."

Lothar growled, then drew in a breath, about to say something or perhaps roar in his face, but before he could, and with centuries of practiced speed, I slid a blade from the sheath strapped to my thigh and threw it.

The point of my blade sunk into the surface of the table, right in front of Smarmy, dead center, and only millimeters from the edge, and his soft belly.

The prick jerked back, eyes widening, alarm on his face. His gaze sliced back to me. "You could have stabbed me," he shrieked.

Again, with speed, I slid another blade free and fired it as well. It landed so close to the first, the sound of the steel blades sliding together rang out in the now silent room. His shocked gaze sliced between my knives and me, mouth gaping. I sat forward. "Um...sorry, I didn't get your name?"

He blustered, panting and sweating now. "Fennel."

The guy was named after a vegetable, and a shit-tasting one at that. "If I'd wanted to stab you, *Fennel*, you would already be dead. And FYI, an insult to me is an insult to Lucifer. Was it your intention to insult the king of Hell?"

"Now now," a cultured voice said, "behave yourselves."

I turned as Drake strode into the room. He was wearing black trousers and a red velvet dinner jacket with black lapels. Drake was average height, stocky. His hair was slicked back and his aqua eyes were striking as he smiled, flashing his short, pointed teeth.

He moved to his seat at the head of the table, and

Grimmel rushed to pull out his chair. Drake sat and took us all in with a congenial smile. "Fennel, my dear, Roxana has more than earned her moniker. She has bathed in the blood of more of Lucifer's enemies than all of your father's men put together. You must show her the respect she is owed. And despite how Grimmel announced her companion, Lothar is far from low ranking." His gaze slid to Lothar. "By all accounts, our new friend here is not someone to be trifled with." His lips curled up in a barely there smile, his gaze sharpening. "No wonder you make such good bedfellows." He waved Grimmel over to fill his glass. "Why one can positively smell it on you. Did Grimmel not provide you with clean towels?"

He thought he knew why we were here, but he wasn't sure, and he wasn't going to admit a thing.

"I like my scent on Roxy," Lothar said in his deep growly voice.

The woman across from Fennel jumped.

"He speaks," Drake said.

"When necessary," Lothar said.

Drake clasped his hands together on the table. "And you think it's necessary now?"

"Yes."

"Care to elaborate?"

"Was I not clear?"

"Apparently not."

"Roxy is mine." His gaze slid to Fennel. "Insult her, come anywhere near her, and die."

Oh dear.

Drake laughed, as if delighted, but he was furious. We were in his house, but we outranked him. This realm was small, without a proper army. He relied on Lucifer and his demons for protection. Us coming here had reiterated that, and in front of an audience as well. His gaze slid back to me. "Have you been introduced to everyone?"

"Only Fennel." Fennel looked at me as if he wanted to puke. I winked.

Drake made the introductions, but I barely registered their names. They weren't important.

"So, tell me, Roxana, what brings you here?" Drake said as Grimmel delivered the starters.

I smiled. "Didn't Grimmel tell you? Lucifer's sent me on a bit of a tour, visiting our allies, reconnecting." I placed the red box on the table and slid it toward him. "Lucifer wanted me to personally give you this small token of friendship."

"He did?" His eyes didn't leave mine.

"That's right."

He opened the box. Drake had a practiced eye for fine things. One glance and he'd know it was cheap rubbish. His gaze flicked back up to me, and there was alarm there. Lucifer would never give him something fake. I'd thought Drake knowing our real purpose here might work against us, now I realized it was the opposite.

He sat calmly, but his mind was racing, weighing what he should do.

"I must thank him." He slid his phone from his pocket.

"Right now?" I said.

Drake smiled wide. "But of course."

He decided to go straight to the source. If Lucifer knew nothing about my visit, I was working independently, and maybe he had a shot at getting out of this mess. If Lucifer went along with my obvious lie, he'd know he had limited and seriously unpleasant options. Either continue to lie and hope he got away with it, or hand over Beelzebub and beg for forgiveness. Both options came with consequences— some far more severe than others.

Lothar stilled beside me. We hadn't yet had a chance to tell Lucifer what was happening. It didn't matter though. However Lucifer reacted to this call, if he even answered, was the right way. That's how it worked with him.

Drake scrolled to Lucifer's number and hit call, putting it on speaker. Maybe he thought he was going to catch us out and turn the tables on us.

"Drake," Lucifer's deep, smooth voice echoed through the speaker. "How can I help you, old friend?"

Drake kept that aqua gaze locked on me. "I'm just calling to thank you for the gift."

"Of course," Lucifer said without missing a beat. "You are one of my most treasured friends and trusted allies. I hope you're treating my Roxy well."

At *my Roxy*, Lothar stiffened again. "Hi, Luci!" I called. He may have suspected, or already knew, we were there. Now he knew for sure. That's just how it was with Lucifer. Yes, he was a mystery, but I never doubted him.

Even if sometimes that was incredibly difficult. I gave Lothar's thigh another squeeze to get him to relax.

Lucifer chuckled. "There she is. If anything should ever happen to her..." Silence echoed through the phone. "Well, it doesn't bear thinking about, or the aftermath."

Drake shifted in his seat. "I assure you, Roxana and her paramour are being treated as honored guests, my lord."

"I hope you like your gift," Lucifer said without missing a beat. But I heard the change in his voice, subtle as it was, when Drake mentioned me having a paramour, because I knew Luci better than almost anyone, definitely anyone at this table. "We'll talk again soon, Drake," Lucifer said, then ended the call.

I widened my smile at a rattled-looking Drake. "Shall we eat? This looks delicious."

The blood had drained from Drake's face.

Ding. Ding. Ding. Give the man a prize. He'd worked out exactly how fucked he was.

Now we just had to wait and see what he chose. Give Beelzebub up.

Or continue to lie through his pointed teeth.

CHAPTER
SEVENTEEN

Roxy

DINNER HAD BEEN long and exhausting, but now I knew for sure that Drake, the idiot, had Lucifer's number one most wanted squirreled away somewhere in this creepy freaking house. Either he wised up and handed Beelzebub over, or we would tear this place apart until we found him.

I glanced over at Lothar again. He stood just inside the bathroom, holding Beelzebub's shirt again. His feet were bare and on the stone floor, and he was trying to tap into the house's vibrations and, hopefully, pinpoint where B was hiding. If we were going to take the lord of Hell by force, it would be handy to know where possible danger lurked, but more importantly, where our target was. Distance could make it more difficult, especially if someone was blocking him, but we were within the same walls, I was sure of it, and Lothar said if he was close, he might be able to break through whatever was surrounding B and pinpoint him. I really freaking hoped he was right.

Lothar's eyes were closed, his head tipped back, the same way I'd seen him standing in the forest when we were in Limbo. His throat, thick and corded, worked when he swallowed, and I did the same, my mouth suddenly going dry. His jaw was square, strong under his beard. I bit my lip. Yeah, I wanted to climb him like a tree and sink my teeth into him. I wanted to lick him, kiss him everywhere, wrap myself around him and cling to him like a freaking limpet and never let go...

Stop.

I dragged in a deep breath, pulling myself back from the edge, or at least tried to.

Lothar finally lowered his chin and opened his glowing, golden eyes. They looked distant, as if he wasn't here in this room with me but somewhere else. Until he blinked.

As soon as his focus was back, that gaze burned into me. My belly swirled. "Anything?"

He lifted a hand to the doorframe, and his bicep threatened the seams of his shirt. "Think I've found him. Unless Drake's playing some kind of game."

Shit. "Are you locked on to him?"

"Yeah."

I paced to the window and back. We needed a game plan, but our options were limited. "We have two choices: hunt him down in this house, whatever it takes, and drag him back to Hell...or give Drake some time, a chance to do the right thing."

"Drake betrayed Lucifer by hiding that fucker here, why give him an out?" Lothar screwed up his nose, then pressed it to his sleeve.

"I can't see Drake risking his alliance with Lucifer easily.

Maybe B has something over him? Or maybe he's just made a really stupid mistake. B could have convinced him he's not trying to overthrow Lucifer and Drake believed his friend?"

"Or maybe he's a traitorous fuck as well?"

He crossed his arms, and I was momentarily distracted by their bulging magnificence. He quirked a brow, waiting for me to say something, and I shook off my ever-growing lust. "Yes, you could be right, but all I know is, as soon as we take the choice from Drake, we're all but signing his death warrant. I've killed, many times, but in cases like this, I don't like to kill without just cause. At least if Drake hands over B himself, he could survive this." It would also make our task a hell of a lot easier, but more importantly, end it.

Lothar grunted, then scowled and sniffed the shirt again. His scowl deepened, and he literally tore it off and tossed it aside with obvious disgust.

I winced. "Sorry, is my stench all over it?"

Lothar's chin jerked back, his brows lowering. "No, it's not you." He shook his head. "Honestly, I think I'm starting to get used to your scent...you smell, I don't know, different now." He kicked the shirt he'd shredded into the corner. "It's Grimmel, the fucking weirdo kept touching us whenever he served our meals." Lothar seemed to be fighting his instincts again. He bared his teeth and his fangs elongated a moment before his eyes flashed red. "Fuck, I can smell you all over me—"

"Sorry—"

"No, I told you, that's not the problem. I want you all over me. I...fuck, I like it. A lot. What I don't like is Grimmel's scent on me as well, near yours. It's messing with the beast for some reason." He reached over and turned on the shower.

Holy shit. His back and shoulders rolled like waves. "Lothar? Are you okay?"

His chest vibrated, I could see it moving as a rumbling growl reverberated from him like rolling thunder. "If I don't get that fucker off me now, I might have to kill him."

I realized he was stone-cold serious when he quickly stripped off the rest of his clothes and, eyes still glowing red, got in the shower and started scrubbing the hell out of his skin and hair. It was as if he'd forgotten I was even there, so focused on washing Grimmel's scent off his skin.

I forced myself to leave him to shower alone. My ogling his magnificent body was not something I wanted to be caught doing.

Something wasn't right with him. I'd seem him struggling with his control several times now. He was constantly on the verge of shifting, snarling and growling all the time, and now suddenly my scent *wasn't* offensive anymore?

I sat on the edge of the bed and rubbed my hands over my face. This had to mean something, right? Luci said the scent thing was a safety measure to keep us apart. To keep Lothar away from me.

If I didn't smell bad to him anymore, did that mean...

A vicious snarl came from the bathroom. I jumped up, ran across the room and flew into the bathroom.

Holy fuck.

Lothar was in the throes of a fight, as what looked like *the wall* attacked him. The hard marble had sprouted arms and a face, and spindly arms were wrapped around Lothar from behind, hanging on desperately, while whatever it was said lewd things about me in a strange, distorted voice. Lothar jerked forward, and more of the face was revealed.

Holy fuck, it was Grimmel.

Drake's loyal sidekick lashed out his tongue and ran it

up the side of Lothar's neck. "Be a good boy and give her to me," he said to Lothar. "I'll take good care of her."

So focused on Lothar, he hadn't even seen or heard me enter the room. Lothar reached back, fisted Grimmel's hair, grabbed one of his arms, and with a vicious snarl tossed him across the room. Grimmel hit the wall, then landed on his back. He lay there panting, his skin still a deep green, the color of the wall. His dark eyes were locked on Lothar. His bony body naked and misshapen. His gaze finally sliced to me, and he hissed like a wild cat.

"What the fuck, Grimmel?"

His creepy gaze burned into me, then sliced back to Lothar. "I want her, you can't have her," he chanted in that strange singsong voice. Then he lurched forward a little and hissed again. "You can't have her. *She's mine.*"

"The fuck she is," Lothar snarled.

With another hiss, we watched in horror as Grimmel's arms and legs cracked and bent at weird angles, and his skin returned to its original shade of sickly white. He stopped contorting when he resembled a fleshy spider, then scuttled across the room.

Snapping out of my shock, I snatched a blade from the sheath at my hip and tossed it. It was too late, though, and the blade sunk into the wall where Grimmel had run right into, then disappeared.

"Motherfucker," Lothar snarled and stormed out of the shower. "I'm going to kill him, and fucking Drake as well."

Lothar was right about one thing. No more waiting. Drake's time was up. Still, none of what just happened made any sense. Why would Grimmel do that? If he was attracted to me, he had to know what he just did was point-less. There was no way he could overpower Lothar and take me.

"This is some kind of setup," I said as we strode out into the hall. "You were possessive over me at dinner and they're counting on you losing it and going after Grimmel."

"Agreed," Lothar said reluctantly and obviously still furious. "But if we stay where we are, we're sitting ducks. This house is messed up, dangerous. We need to get the hell out of here, but then we'll be walking into their trap."

He was right about that as well. "We'll just have to be prepared for anything." Lothar nodded, and we grabbed our bags and rushed from the room. "Be careful," I said as we jogged along the hall.

The floor jerked beneath my feet, and I was suddenly standing in front of a wall, the new configuration forcing us to turn a corner.

"How's Drake doing that?" Lothar bit out.

"He's powerful. He has to be to rule over his own realm, but I've never seen him do anything like this. His powers have to be connected to this house somehow."

Lothar grunted his agreement.

It happened again, and again, in quick succession, the walls shifting, the house configuration changing.

"He could have us running around in circles for eternity if he wanted. I'm starting to think this house is not just a house, that it's more a realm—"

"Within a realm," I finished.

Shit. He was right.

The ground beneath our feet jerked to the side again, and I almost collided with another wall. I sidestepped it and turned, heading down the next hallway, this one dark, eerie. None of them looked the same—different flooring, wallpaper, furniture, paintings. There were no doors off any of them, just long, shadowed corridors, one after the other, appearing in front of us, the floor shifting beneath our feet as we were sent down yet another, then another.

I glanced at Lothar. "He's forcing us to go where he wants."

His eyes flashed with fury. "Herding us like cattle."

The floor dropped out from under me, and if Lothar hadn't been quick and fisted the back of my jacket, I would have tumbled down a sharply angled set of stairs.

There was a wall in front of us now—and one behind. "He's not giving us any choice but to go down."

Lothar lifted me before I could take another step and put himself in front of me. I didn't argue, there was no point, his protective instincts had kicked in. Nothing else mattered, definitely not the fact that I was more than capable of taking point in wherever Drake was leading us.

Lothar's eyes glowed in the darkness as we headed down the steep stairs. Actually, it was probably a good thing Lothar had taken the lead because it was almost complete darkness down here, and Lothar had far better night vision than me. "Can you see anything?"

"Yes," he said gravely. "Grab on to the back of my shirt, baby, and don't veer off the path."

Baby. He'd said it before, but when we were giving each other pleasure. I quickly put it aside. This was not the time to start overthinking things. "There's a path?" My boots squelched with each step. "More mud?" Though it didn't smell like mud, it had a tinny scent, a scent I realized I knew all too well. Blood—gore. Then something revolting hit me, and I gagged. "What am I stepping in?"

"Corpses."

"If the path is rotting corpses, then what the hell is on either side?"

"Let's just worry about getting to wherever this fucker is sending us," he said, instead of answering.

Something seriously bad, then?

Every step we took released another waft of rotting flesh. My foot slipped on what I could only assume were limbs, but thankfully I managed to stay upright. The path seemed to be never ending, at least it felt that way when I could barely see a foot in front of me.

"Where do you think all these corpses came from?" Lothar asked.

"I don't know, we could be anywhere, and if this is some random realm we're in—or worse, one he's sent us to —almost anything could be possible."

Lothar stopped suddenly, one of his arms flying behind him to wrap around my waist.

He held me tight to his back. "What is it?" I whispered.

"Do you hear that?"

"No, what did you—" Something warm and smelling even more like death than the sea of corpses beneath our feet wafted over the side of my face.

"Roxy?" Lothar said.

A weird sound came from behind me, a repetitive, thumping rattle.

"I think I've got a problem back here."

Lothar's leather vest creaked as he slowly turned. "Don't move," he rushed out under his breath.

I jammed my mouth closed as something warm and slimy hit my arm, then *slowly* slid down it. Drool, I was sure of it. Drool from something vicious—and I was only guessing here, but the evidence pointed to me being correct—after some fresh meat to add to his rotting collection.

"He's focused on you, Rox, but I don't think it can hear. I

think the only thing it can sense is movement or it would have attacked already."

Oh fuck. It'd been stalking us, and as soon as we'd stopped, it'd lost sight of us.

I could tell it was big, and going by the amount of drool sliding over my shoulder and soaking my shirt—and now burning into my flesh—it had a big mouth and a mean set of teeth.

"I can see light ahead. It's faint, but I think we can make it if we run like hell."

My burning skin grew worse, and I was sure I could smell my own singed flesh. If we didn't move soon, I'd quickly be joining one of the decomposing corpses on the path below my feet.

Lothar's hand tightened on my waist, and I knew instantly what he planned. *Oh no, you don—*

One moment I was behind him, the next I was flying through the air. I hit the path a couple yards in front of him, landing on one knee, my hand deep in warm, wet gore. I heard Lothar's boots slapping as he barreled down on me. Jumping to my feet, I pumped my arms and sprinted toward the light up ahead.

The ground shook as the monster made chase, its roars causing my ears to ring and covering us in more toxic drool.

There was an open gateway just ahead. We were almost there. Lothar was right behind me.

Another roar followed, so close my drool-soaked hair was blasted over one shoulder.

Lothar barked a curse—then he was slamming into my back, knocking me to the ground.

My body crashed down onto severed limbs and blood and guts, and we slid along the path at break-neck speed as if we were on some gruesome slip 'n slide.

I turned back, and now that there was light spilling in from the gateway, I could finally see the monster clearly. It was huge, like a wingless pterodactyl with razor-sharp teeth, vicious claws, and a shorter beak, and all around it, bodies, corpses of all shapes and sizes, hung from spindly trees.

The monster was gaining on us, mouth opened, roaring. Lothar threw a hand out behind us and, with a roar, blasted it with a steady stream of hellfire. It shrieked and flailed but kept coming.

Lothar wrapped himself around me then, forcing me into a tight ball as we hurtled toward the gateway, and whatever fresh horrors waited for us on the other side.

EIGHTEEN

Lothar

THE MONSTER SLAMMED its now singed and blackened foot down, narrowly missing us as we hurtled toward who the fuck knew what, but whatever it was, I would not let it hurt Roxy.

Wrapping my arms around her bent knees, I lifted mine, cocooning her smaller frame with my own as we flew through the gateway, leaving the oppressive darkness and its gore-loving monster behind, and burst into blinding light.

I braced, tightening every muscle a moment before we crashed down on what felt like wood. We rolled, crashing against a wall with force. Still surrounded by me, Roxy cursed and turned her head in an effort to see where we were, to see if there was danger, and I did the same.

We appeared to be on our own. For now, anyway.

A bird squawked overhead, and I realized the ground beneath us was rocking slowly. I breathed deep and got a lungful of sea air. "We're on a ship."

"What?" Roxy pulled away from me, and I forced myself not to drag her back.

She bounded to her feet, a knife already in her blood- and gore-covered hand.

I listened intently for anything or anyone that might be nearby. The ship creaked, swaying, an enormous black sail puffed out catching the breeze, sailing us toward the setting sun. "Do you know what realm we're in?"

Roxy had her back to me, and I watched as she lifted her face to the sky and breathed in the sea air. "We're on the Night Sea," she said. "There are demons close by, can you feel them?"

I focused, and she was right. I could definitely sense them. "They feel different."

She pointed across the ocean. "That way is the Night Realm. Home of the goddess Nox, the personification of night, and also Death and Somnus's mother." She pointed toward the horizon, where we were headed. Black clouds had gathered in the distance, and forked lightning flashed through the sky. "We're sailing toward the Outer Realm."

I'd been alive a very long time, but I'd never traveled so far from home. I'd also never doubted my instincts before, but I was struggling with that now. So far from Hell, from my brothers and, fuck, so far from the beast—the part of me that had always steered me in the right direction. I couldn't trust what my gut was telling me anymore. I had this sensation of being untethered, as if the beast, who until recently had been one with me since my creation, was drifting farther and farther from me with every day that passed.

"Lothar?"

I shook off the unease. "I've heard of it, but I don't know anything about it." She stood to my side, the wind whipping her thick, wavy black hair around her face.

"It borders Limbo and should be a kind of no-man's-land between Death's realm and Nox's, but she's been stealing Outer Realm territory for herself over the centuries. There were demons and other creatures living there a short time ago, before Death and his mother finally had it out. Most of the demons are rogue, escapees from Hell, and I'm not sure how many are still there, or how much sway either of us will have over them once we reach land."

I rubbed my forehead, and my fingers slid in the blood covering me. "So Drake just decided to send us back home?"

She gripped the railing, staring out at the ocean. "I'm not sure. Nothing is ever simple with Drake."

"Let's search the ship." The ship's wheel held steady, the vessel appeared to be steering itself. "There wasn't a welcoming committee, and this ship doesn't seem to need a crew, but we might not be alone."

She nodded and finally turned to me. "You're right, let's—"

I snarled, my fucking heart stopping in my chest. She was injured, badly. I could see it even through all the blood and other shit covering her.

"I'll be fine," she said not missing my reaction. She strode across the deck and opened the door to the cabin under the helm. "Once we've searched the ship, I'll take care of it."

I wanted to snatch her off her feet and force her to let me tend her, but the stubborn look on her face told me that would be a serious mistake, which meant we needed to conduct this search as fast as possible because the beast went wild seeing Roxy like that. Over and over, he was slamming into my subconscious and writhing under my skin, trying to force me to shift. He wanted to lick her wounds and heal her, right the fuck now.

Striding ahead of her, I stormed the small cabin we'd walked into, opening and closing cupboards and looking under anything big enough to hide someone.

Roxy headed for the steep stairs that led below. I got in front of her again and went down first. She huffed but let me have my way. Thank fuck, because the beast was becoming more insistent. There were several smaller cabins below as well as the captain's quarters, and after a thorough search we were positive all of them were empty. We made our way to the galley next, where a fire in the stove blazed and a huge pot of water bubbled away on top and another with some kind of rich-smelling stew, but still no sign of life.

"Drake must be worried. He even provided dinner."

"No fucking way will I be eating that," I muttered.

We hit the cargo hold, but that was just as empty as the rest of the ship.

"Looks like it's just us," Roxy said. "I've been reaching out, and I can't feel anyone else here."

Neither could I. Good. I grabbed her hand and led her back up the stairs and down the narrow hall into the captain's quarters.

"What are you doing?" she asked, her big blue eyes narrowed.

"Strip, I'll get water." Not waiting for a reply, I strode back to the galley.

Quickly filling two buckets with boiling water, I strode back and tipped them into the small tub sitting on one side of the room, then strode back and did the same again. Then

I switched to cold, scooping it from a barrel of fresh water, to get the temperature just right. Roxy just stood there, not taking off her clothes. "Strip, Roxy. Now. You're injured and covered in blood."

"I can tend my own wounds, Lothar," she said. "You go and keep watch and I'll—"

"No." That was unacceptable to me, and to the beast. At least we agreed on that. I strode over and jerked her jacket down her arms.

"Lothar," she snapped. "Stop it."

The beast snarled, taking hold of my vocal cords for the second time. "We will tend you, female." I grabbed at my throat, clamping my jaw tight. It was my voice, but it was the beast's words.

Her gaze snapped up to me, wide, alarmed. "We? Lothar, what's going on?"

I ground my teeth, refusing to let him do it again. It should be impossible. The beast wasn't supposed to have autonomy. We were one being, of one mind, yet the animal in me was fracturing, splitting me in fucking two. I shook my head instead and tugged at the bottom of her shirt, trying to fucking plead with her, with just a look, because I needed this and the beast wasn't going to let me leave her here on her own.

Whatever it was, she saw it written on my face and relented, but there was a wary expression in her eyes. She finished stripping off, revealing the extent of her raw, angry skin that had been burned by the monster's toxic saliva. I snarled, and she got into the tub. There was soap and a washcloth beside it, and I handed them to her, unable to look away, to take one fucking step back until I saw her washing that filth off her skin.

She did so without argument, cleaning off every bit of

muck, then finally rinsed the blood from her hair before silently lifting the soap and cloth toward me. That's when I realized my flesh was burning as well. I'd been so focused on Roxy, I hadn't even noticed. Tugging off my gore-soaked shirt, I dipped the cloth in the bath water, lathered it with soap, then quickly ran it over my face, neck, chest, and shoulders. The relief was almost instant, as was the warm buzz over my skin, telling me my healing had kicked in and was already working to mend the damage.

Roxy's, on the other hand, would take longer. The saliva had soaked her thoroughly and had burned deeper. Tossing the cloth and soap in the tub, I reached into the water.

She grabbed my biceps. "I can get out on my own."

The beast's constant need to growl and snarl had me tightening my vocal cords and clamping my mouth closed again. I had no idea what would come out of my mouth, but with the shit the beast was thinking, I knew I didn't want to give him free rein to talk through me like I was his fucking puppet.

Ignoring her protest, I hauled her out of the water and carried her to the bed.

She sat silently watching me as I quickly stripped and washed as much blood and other shit from me as fast as I could. It wasn't the best job, but it would do. All I could think about was looking after Roxy, of tending to her wounds. When I was sure I wouldn't get her dirty again, I advanced on her, clearing my throat as I got on the bed with her.

"Lothar? What are you doing?"

I wrestled control back from the beast. "Need to lick you," I said. It was all I could manage to get out.

Her cheeks flushed and she blinked up at me, and I

knew what she was thinking. I didn't have time to correct her, though, and as much as I'd fucking love to go down on her and get another taste of her pussy, healing her was the driving force inside me right then. I leaned over her, and her arms came around me a moment before I dragged my tongue over her shoulder and up the side of her throat, right over the top of her burns. My eyes drifted closed at the taste of her blood on my tongue and the sweet warmth of her arms around me. She squirmed, and I licked again, gently, using my healing saliva to start work on the deepest wounds.

"You're healing me?" she said.

I nodded, and the beast growled his approval. Was that disappointment I heard in her voice? I hoped so because I planned on having her writhing against my tongue again very soon.

"You know I have accelerated healing as well, right?" she said in a soft, sweet voice that lifted goose bumps across my shoulders and tingled down my spine.

Maybe so, but not as fast as me. There were several bruises on her skin and it stressed the beast out to see them.

She tried to push me off, but the beast growled louder, and she sighed and gave up, giving me what I wanted. Good. She squirmed again and giggled.

"It's warm and it tingles," she rasped, then gasped and squirmed some more. "I can feel it working."

My chest expanded with relief and pleasure that I could do this for her, that she was experiencing a feeling that was good enough that it made her laugh, and my rogue beast agreed with me wholeheartedly.

In these moments with Roxy, when I gave in to the

beast's instincts, even if they confused me, he and I slipped back into alignment, and we were in perfect harmony. It was intoxicating and filled me with a sense of rightness. I wasn't sure if the feeling actually came from being with Roxy, or that I was again one with my beast.

The former confused me. This need to be close to the little handmaid made no sense. And the latter made me feel like a parasite. Honestly, I didn't understand what I was thinking or feeling, only that I needed to do this, to care for her, to tend her wounds.

She'd stopped squirming and laughing, but she wasn't trying to push me away either.

"I think I'm okay now," she said in a soft voice that made my skin tingle.

But I couldn't stop, not yet, not until I'd licked every bit of red, raw skin, not until I was sure I hadn't missed a spot. I lifted her, so she was sitting up, and again she let me. This way I could get better access to her shoulders and upper back. Gathering up her thick hair, I lifted it out of the way and got back to work.

That's when I spotted the vicious scar at her side. It was red and inflamed and had to be painful. "What happened here? Why does this look so fresh?"

"It's nothing. The mud in Ferine irritated it, that's all." She tried to pull away, and I pushed her back against the mattress and carefully dragged my tongue over it.

"Lothar...you don't have to—"

I swiped over it again, and she gasped softly, her fingers sliding into my hair.

This scar, I didn't like it. I wanted it gone. I wanted anything that caused her pain, now or in the past, fucking gone. When I licked the ragged scar for the last time, and I was certain I had tended to every single wound on her body, the knot in my gut finally loosened.

"You'll be okay now. You're okay." The words swimming around my head tumbled from my mouth. I wasn't sure if I was reassuring her, myself, or the beast when I'd uttered that, but again a wave of relief washed over me.

She stared up at me, a look in her eyes I didn't understand, while her hand touched my back, her smooth warm skin sliding over mine in a way that was gentle, soothing. "I'm okay, Lothar. Thank you."

The beast wanted to nuzzle, and I didn't resist. I let him have control and went with my animal instincts. A repetitive thumping sound rolled from my chest as I rubbed my face against her throat, as I branded her with my scent. That was very important, covering her with my scent again after washing it off. I needed everyone who came near her to smell my scent on her.

The beast was blissed out and taking me along for the ride. "Will you get on your hands and knees for me, female?" The beast growled, talking through me again, but I was totally on board with the request. I felt fucking dizzy with lust for her. I couldn't think straight, my mind wholly focused on mounting the curvy little female beneath me. I kissed her throat, her jaw. "Will you?" I asked against her skin, but this time it was all me.

She made a soft, desperate sound that had me lowering my body on top of hers, forcing her to fall back on the mattress. Hooking a hand under one of her legs, I spread her wide so I could grind my hard cock against the soft silkiness between her strong thighs. I kissed her cheek, the corner of her mouth. "Please, kitten."

Roxy stilled beneath me, sucking in a shaky breath. "Lothar—"

A light flashed so bright that when I spun toward it I had to lift my hand to shield my eyes. *The closet.* The light began to fade instantly, until all that remained was a soft glow from around the door.

The flash of light had come from inside.

I snarled, bounding off the bed.

Roxy followed. "I think we've got company."

NINETEEN

Roxy

A THUD CAME from behind the door, then another, followed by a muffled shout of fury. Sliding my knife from its sheath, I sidestepped Lothar's hand as he tried to stop me from moving closer, and yanked the door open.

Beelzebub was crammed into the small space, his hands and feet shackled, his mouth gagged. Rage-filled eyes stared back at me as he released a stifled roar.

I tutted. "Now, now, Bub. I think we both know you brought this on yourself." Lothar tried to get in my way again, but I shoved him back and spun on him. "You need to cool it with the overprotective bit, okay? It's getting out of hand." I motioned to Beelzebub. "And our new crew member can't exactly do anything. That steel he's been bound with was created by the gods, and unless we have the key to release him, which we do not, he's staying shackled until we get him back to Hell."

Lothar's brows lowered, his eyes flashing from gold to red as he stared down at the traitorous lord who not only tried to overthrow Lucifer but had captured two of his brothers, locking them in their hound forms, and had plans to use and possibly hurt the only female hound in existence. "You think Drake did this?"

Going by the way Beelzebub exploded, fighting against his restraints and letting out another muffled roar, he'd just given us the answer. "He literally had a monster chase us away, getting us as far from him as he could, then gave us what we wanted. Trying to protect himself and, I assume, hoping for leniency from Luci."

Lothar bared his fangs. "What do you want to do with him?"

"Nothing." I slammed the door, shutting Beelzebub back in the closet. "He can stay there until we reach land." Grabbing some clothes, I quickly dressed and strode out of the cabin, suddenly needing space. I had to get away from that bed and Lothar before I did something stupid. I needed to breathe in some sea air, clear my head, especially after he'd tended the scar on my side. It had brought back painful memories, more than I could take. Especially since this thing between us, that should have been erased, at least on his side, seemed to be growing in intensity every day.

Lothar dressed in record time, because his boots were thudding on the wooden floorboards after me, before I even reached the deck.

There was no getting away from him, though. We were on a gods-damn ship in the middle of the Night Sea. Quickly climbing the stairs, I rushed through the small cabin and out onto the deck, where I dragged in a breath, desperately trying to clear my head.

"You okay?" Lothar asked as he closed the space between us.

I gripped the railing and looked out at the ocean. The sun was going down fast, and we were headed for choppy seas. "Never better," I lied. He moved up behind me, his hands gripping the railing on either side of mine, trapping me against his huge frame.

He pressed his face against the crook of my neck and breathed in deeply. My eyes slid closed, my heart pounding furiously in my chest. He wanted me, I could feel how much. Not just in the obvious way but in the way he gripped the railing so tightly it was as if he were fighting for control, in the slight tremor moving through his muscled body, and by the way his heart pounded wildly against my back.

"I really don't smell bad to you anymore?" I asked, which could steer us into dangerous territory, but I wanted to know.

"You smell the same, but how it affects me is different, like something was distorting it or masking you, and I'm finally getting your true scent. I'm not filled with the urge to remove myself from your presence anymore."

Me stinking sure would help about now. I didn't know what this change meant, but it couldn't be good. I forced a careless laugh. "I'm glad I don't stink, but—"

"Let me have you," he said in a deep, rough voice, all beast. "Give yourself to me."

I shivered. Something had most definitely changed. Lothar was different, and it wasn't just the scent thing. "That's not a good idea." He was asking for more, for all of me, at least physically, but giving him that could be the catalyst to revealing the secrets I'd sacrificed everything to lock away forever.

"Have you ever been with a hound, Roxy?" His voice was all growl.

Oh gods. I squeezed my eyes closed tighter. "No." And that was the truth, not in the way he meant. Lucifer had forbidden me and Lothar to take it there. He'd ordered us to wait, adamant that the time wasn't right for our mating. We'd obeyed our maker, our king, and it was the second biggest regret of my life.

"I'll make you feel so good, kitten," he said against the side of my throat, his voice guttural.

He was using that name more and more, as if it came naturally to him, and every time he uttered it, it tore me apart. "Step back, Lothar. I need some space." This was getting out of hand. I'd already done things with him that I never should have. It was inevitable that he'd want more from me. I should have known. But, somehow, I had to douse the embers igniting between us.

"I'll fill you up, Roxy. So good, all you'll be able to do is scream my name and beg me for more." He nipped my jaw and nuzzled my cheek. "And I'll give it to you, baby, exactly how you need it, and when you're trembling and sweaty and your pussy's soaked from how hard I fucked you, from how hard you came for me, I'll slide back inside, and fuck you again, but this time, I'll take it slow, I'll make you feel every inch—"

"Stop," I gasped and spun, shoving against his chest. "You need to stop." Because I was seconds away from giving in, from dropping to my hands and knees and offering myself up to him, from begging him to do whatever he wanted to me.

"You want me, Roxy, just as badly as I want you." He took my chin in his roughened fingers. "I can smell it, smell just how badly you want everything I just described."

"Lothar—"

"I don't know why you're fighting it. It's just sex, right?" His gaze slid down to my mouth and back up. "Why can't we just enjoy each other?"

No, of course he didn't understand, and I didn't know how to make him. But we couldn't be together, despite my slipups, no matter how much I wanted it. The truth was, Lothar wasn't mine. The feelings he had for me were buried and never resurfacing. Desire was all he felt when he looked at me, and it was a spear to my chest. It didn't matter that I already knew this, or that this was how it had to be. Knowing that I was just someone to feel good with for a little while hurt like hell.

I'd given in to him on this trip already because I wanted to pretend that our past hadn't happened, because I'd fooled myself that I could handle it and not break my own heart, but I knew better now.

Taking this further would be a huge mistake. There was no going back to the way it was. It was impossible for several reasons.

I forced myself to hold his gaze and tried to make him hear me, to make him stop this. "Yes, we had some fun, but that's as far as I'm willing to take it. You need to respect that, and you need to back off. Now."

His eyes switched between gold and red, repeatedly, before finally settling back to normal. He flashed his teeth, or maybe he was gritting them, then he released the railing and stepped back. "If that's what you really want," he said, his voice pure grit.

"It is." Hounds were protective of females, to the extreme, and not only the females they knew. I'd just used that to my advantage. It was the only arsenal I had at my disposal when it came to him. The wind whipped through me, and forked lightning streaked through the sky above us. I hugged myself. "We're getting closer to land. We need to prepare for our arrival. The Outer Realm's still going through changes after Nox and Death's fight. Anything could be waiting for us there."

Lothar dipped his chin, and the muscle at the side of his jaw pulsed. "I'll go check on Beelzebub."

He turned and strode away, heading below deck, and I gripped the railing again as I finally caught a glimpse of land. I would get through this. It was almost over. I just had to hold on a little longer.

It had almost killed me, but I'd survived losing him once. Closing my eyes now, I prayed to the gods with everything I had that I could do it again.

The wind tore through us, and I hung on to the mast as rain pelted down. "We're headed straight for the rocks."

"We're gonna have to jump," Lothar roared over the storm.

"What about Beelzebub?"

Lothar's eyes lit with fury. "The fucker can drown."

That was a pointless thing to say since B was immortal. Sinking to the bottom of the ocean wouldn't kill him, and Lothar knew it. He'd been in a foul mood since our earlier conversation.

The roar of the storm suddenly silenced, and the ship seemed to come to a complete stop. The sound of the huge anchor chain rattling came a moment before the heavy iron plunged into the sea.

I spun around. "Are you seeing this?" The storm still

raged, I could see it, but it was outside of a four-yard radius around the entire vessel.

Something thudded against the side of the ship, and I peered over the side. A dinghy bobbed in the water, waiting. "Looks like Drake thought of everything."

Lothar grunted. "I'll get Beelzebub," he muttered, then strode off.

There was a rope ladder attached to the railing, conveniently positioned right where we needed it, and I shoved it over the side. It unraveled, stopping just above the dinghy.

Lothar appeared a moment later, muscles bulging, as he dragged the huge lord of Hell across the deck with one hand and carried our bags in the other.

"Guess we better go see what waits for us on land," I said when he reached me.

Lothar grunted, dropped the bags at my feet, hefted Beelzebub off the ground and, without hesitation, tossed him over the side of the ship. The sound of his large body landing in the much smaller boat bobbing below in the water made me wince. I quickly looked over the edge, expecting to see both the dinghy and B being swallowed by the sea. Instead Beelzebub stared up at Lothar with hatred, the little boat miraculously still in one piece.

Lothar was still pissed off. Hopefully he got over it quickly, though it definitely made it easier to resist him. If he was angry with me, he wouldn't be trying to get me to change my mind.

Sliding on my bag, I descended the rope ladder and jumped down into the boat. Lothar made his way down next, grabbed the oars, and we headed toward the shore. We were no longer protected from the storm now, though, and it raged around us, drenching us with the driving rain. The small boat bobbed around, threatening to capsize, but

Lothar sliced the oars through the thrashing sea, powering through, muscles bulging from the strain.

It didn't take long before we reached the shore. The sandy ocean floor scraped the bottom of the boat, and Loth jumped out into the frigid water and dragged the dinghy in the rest of the way.

I quickly got out and scanned our surroundings. The sky was dark with gunmetal clouds, and the thunder and lightning was a constant now, but at least the rain had stopped. The next flash of lightning lit up the sky—and the huge, glossy black tower we needed to head toward.

"This way," I called over the wind, pointing to it.

"What is it?"

"Accommodation for travelers."

The tower jutted up, imposing and incredibly tall. The top was obscured by low clouds, but light burned at the top, glowing behind them, making it serve a dual purpose of lighthouse as well.

"We're close to Limbo. We should keep moving," Lothar said.

"It's dark here all the time, but worse at night, and if any of Nox's creatures are still out here, this is when they'll be more active. Better to wait until morning before we travel."

Lothar nodded, then reached into the boat, grabbed the shackles between Beelzebub's ankles, yanked him from the dinghy and started dragging him across the rocky ground. Beelzebub roared behind his gag, flailing and fighting, eyes blazing. Lothar ignored him and kept walking.

Scanning the area around us, I kept pace beside him. "You gonna keep up this tantrum the rest of the journey?" I said, because I couldn't stand his silence and resentment much longer.

His gaze sliced to me. "Not a fucking pup, Roxy."

"I know that, but you're sure as hell acting like one right now."

He stopped abruptly, dropping Beelzebub's feet, and turned to me. "What is there to say? Apparently what I want is irrelevant, and I'm not even worthy of an explanation about why you've suddenly gone cold on me."

Hounds didn't get hurt, not emotionally, not before they found their mates. Was this reaction from residual emotion he'd developed back when we were together? Lucifer had fixed it when he took his memories of us. But it happened again when Lothar and Jagger sired pups, during Lucifer's experiment. Lucifer had cured them of the affliction then as well. This shouldn't be possible, yet the emotion I felt flowing from him was palpable.

Had Lothar somehow tapped back into it? Or was something else causing him to suddenly start feeling more than the limited emotions a hound should have. "I didn't think I was required to give one," I said, because I didn't know what else to say or do. He'd thrown me completely.

He crossed his muscled arms. "Yeah? Well, I want one anyway."

"We need to keep moving."

He grabbed my arm, stopping me. "Tell me."

"I just don't want to take this any further, okay?" I lied, panic rising inside me.

His grip tightened. "You really think you can hide what you truly want from me, Roxy? I can fucking smell it on you. Why are you refusing me? Why are you pretending you don't want me?"

Thunder boomed above us so loud, the ground shook, then the sky opened and rain poured down, instantly drenching us again. I pulled my arm from Lothar's hold and started up the rocky path. He growled but followed, dragging a furious Beelzebub with him.

We thankfully made it to the tower without being ambushed, and I jogged up the stairs and pounded on the wooden door. The imposing structure was supposed to be a safe place for travelers, a place to rest before sailing the Night Sea. Safe was definitely not the vibe this place gave off.

Beelzebub's head bounced up the steps as Lothar took them two at a time and joined me. The sound of someone coming, echoed from inside, followed by the door being unlocked.

Finally, it creaked open, and Horace, the demon in charge of the tower, blinked his red eyes up at me before they slid over to Lothar. Horace had somewhat humanoid features, but they were bulbous and exaggerated. That, and other things about his appearance, meant he'd been confined to Hell for his entire life. When a position had come up to oversee the running of the tower, he'd volunteered and Lucifer had granted his wish. I hadn't seen him in a very long time.

"My lady," he said, his voice almost breathless. "I am so delighted to see you."

I smiled. "It's been a long time, Horace."

"Indeed, my lady."

I took his cold hand in mine. "You look well, my old friend. I'll be pleased to report this news to Lucifer." His breed of demon was short in stature. He was even shorter than me. He had wispy gray hair that was so long it reached his waist and was just a shade darker than his gray skin.

The gruff male actually smiled at me. His expression was stiff as he flashed his black teeth, but it was definitely a smile. "I would be most thankful."

I kept hold of his hand. "I know I can trust you, my friend, but due to proximity, I also know you've developed a loyalty to Nox. I hope that won't be an issue for us? I'd be most grateful if she didn't know we were here, Horace." Nox was evil and vengeful. She'd smell Limbo on us as soon as she saw us and any "friend" of Death's was her enemy.

He looked scandalized. "I assure you, my lady, my loyalty is to Lucifer, to Hell, above all others."

I gave his hand a squeeze and let it go. "Be at ease, Horace. I know you'd never do anything to hurt your family."

"Never," he said.

"We were hoping you had a couple of rooms available for the night?"

"But of course." He shifted nervously on feet that were inordinately too large for his wiry and misshapen body. "There will always be a room here for you, my lady." His gaze slid back to Lothar, and like all demons, being around a hound obviously made him nervous.

"Lothar can be trusted," I said.

He nodded, then his eyes widened when they finally found Beelzebub.

He took a startled step back. "You have a lord, bound and gagged."

"He betrayed Lucifer," I reassured him. "We are returning him to Hell for punishment."

Horace nodded but couldn't seem to look away from B trussed up on his front steps.

"It's raining pretty hard out here, Horace."

He jumped. "My apologies." And he quickly stepped back, holding the door wide for us.

I strode in out of the rain and Lothar dragged Beelzebub unceremoniously through the door and into the foyer.

Horace quickly rounded his desk and unhooked two keys from the wall behind it.

"Your rooms are on the seventh floor. Sorry about the climb, but there is an added cell in room 102 that I thought would be useful for your prisoner."

"Fantastic, thanks so much." I took the keys.

"Would you like me to bring up a repast for you both?" the demon asked.

"That would be great. Just something simple, if it's not too much trouble. Bread, meat, some fruit and cheese, oh... and something to drink. Don't rush, though, I want to take a shower before dinner."

Horace inclined his head, and we headed up all seven flights of seriously steep stairs. Beelzebub hissed and roared behind his gag the entire way. When we reached the top, I held up the keys. "Do you want to watch over the traitor, or shall I?"

Lothar took the key for 102. "I will."

He wasn't going to get any complaints from me. I needed a long shower and a decent night's sleep. Lothar unlocked and opened his door, then dragged Beelzebub in behind him.

"I'll let you know when the food's here," I called after him. He kicked the door shut behind him without a word. "I'll take that as a yes," I called and shook my head as I opened my own door and shut myself in.

The decor was as memorable as I remembered. Apart from the beds, all the rooms were a little different. In this one, the walls were bloodred with a gold filigree design, the carpet a deep burgundy. There was a lot of dark wood and brass around the room, and several candelabras were already lit, as if the tower had a mind of its own and knew I was coming. I took in the large bed and screwed up my nose. The bed frame was a chaotic jumble of charred bones, with a skull in the center of the headboard, all collected from creatures from the many different realms, and most definitely not to my taste.

A fire blazed in the hearth, and somehow gave the macabre decor a warmth that wasn't easily found in this place. I stood in front of it and sighed, shaking out my tight muscles. If we left early and traveled nonstop, we could be back in Hell by tomorrow night.

Taking out my phone, I sent off a quick text to Luci, telling him where we were and that we had Beelzebub, though knowing Lucifer, he probably already knew.

I rubbed my hands over my face. When we got back and Lucifer tortured B until he told us who was behind all this, when it was all over, I'd request he send me somewhere else for a while. Just to get my head clear again and numb my heart to what I was feeling. It would take time, I knew that, but I could do it again. I had to.

CHAPTER
TWENTY

Roxy

I WAS RUBBING a towel over my hair when the knock at the door came. I rushed over to open it, and Horace gave me his crooked smile. It was kind of unhinged, but I appreciated the effort.

It was then he noticed I was only wearing an oversized T-shirt. "Apologies," he said, looking scandalized. "I can leave and return with your repast later, my lady."

"It's fine. Bring it on in."

"As you wish. Would you like me to alert your companion?"

The sound of a door closing came from across the hall. "No need," Lothar said and walked in.

Was he still angry with me? I wasn't sure I could handle moody Lothar right then, not when my heart already felt as if it'd been pulverized.

Horace unloaded the food from the tray onto the table at the window. "I'll return to collect the dishes."

"Thanks, Horace," I said and shut the door behind him. "Hungry?" I asked Lothar when I felt his gaze burning into me.

"Very."

I fought back a shiver at the rough edge to his voice, and what he was obviously implying, and took a seat at the table. I popped a piece of cheese in my mouth. "How's B liking his new accommodations?"

Lothar took his seat opposite me. "Seems like he has a lot to say. Thankfully, I can't understand any of it."

I chuckled. "The male always was a blowhard. He once told me that he wrestled and killed a pair of vysan single-handedly. Oh, and he likes to tell everyone that he was the one who got Lucifer's throne back when Diemos went rogue, and we all know it was the knights. The lords sat on their hands while we were locked out and did sweet fuck all to help us." I shook my head. "The male is delulu, seriously. I don't know what Lucifer has planned for him, but whatever it is, it's past due." I selected a grape and took a sip of my wine, then glanced across the table when Lothar hadn't said anything.

He sat back and crossed his arms, and his eyes went from red to gold and back again, doing that weird rapid switch they'd done earlier. It was as if his beast was fighting for freedom, which didn't make any sense at all. "Are you okay?"

When he said nothing, but also didn't look away, I rolled my eyes and made a show of selecting a slice of meat that had the perfect meat-to-fat ratio, when inside I was barely holding it together.

The silence dragged on, and I refused to be the one to fill it. I carried on eating, and he eventually did the same, but still he studied me the whole time. He wasn't doing it to intimidate me, that wasn't what hounds did, especially to females. It was as if he was searching for something, trying to figure something out, and that terrified the hell out of me. I tore off a piece of bread, put it in my mouth and forced myself to chew even though it suddenly tasted like sawdust. He wasn't himself, and he was changing more with every day we'd been on this hunt. If I didn't get away from him, and soon, I was afraid it was only a matter of time before Lothar remembered everything.

"You rolled your eyes at me before, why?" he said suddenly, breaking the silence.

I actually jumped, so deep in my own worries. "I know you have limited emotions, Lothar, but even you can't be that dense." The feeling of being backed into a corner, of what might happen if I didn't do something to stop this now, had my reply coming out a lot snappier than I'd intended.

He sat forward, resting his elbows on the table. "I get it, you want me to pretend I'm perfectly fine with you giving me the brush-off, but just so you know, I absolutely am not fine."

Heat rolled through me in a wave of anger and fear. I needed him to let this go. "This whole scorned-lover bullshit is getting old, Lothar. We fooled around a couple times, nothing more. You've said, more than once, it was only about getting each other off. Are you saying you want me to ignore my own feelings because of what *you* want? Are you saying you want me to force myself to be with you, and if I don't, you'll throw a tantrum and give me the silent treatment until I relent?"

His brows shot up. "That's not what I said. And do not

use the word *force* when it comes to you and me. I would never fucking do tha—"

"Well, that's the way you're acting. I thought, if nothing else, we were friends. Obviously that only applies when you get things your way."

He growled and reached for my hand resting on the edge of the table. I pulled it back right as someone knocked on the door. I shot to my feet, because, honestly, I didn't trust myself alone with this male, let alone him touching me. He was my Achilles' heel, the chink in my armor, my kryptonite, and I was afraid, even with everything I knew, that if he touched me again, if he kissed me, I wouldn't be able to resist him.

I rushed across the room and yanked the door open. Horace blinked up at me, an odd look on his face.

I scanned him from head to oversized feet. "Is everything okay?"

He jolted a little, then nodded. "I've come to clear away your dishes if you're finished?"

"We're done, thanks."

He hustled across the room, loaded up the tray, and headed back across the room, but before he walked out, he turned back, and it looked as though he wanted to say something.

"Horace? Are you sure you're okay?" I asked him again.

"I want you to know, my lady, that my loyalty to Lucifer has never and will never waver."

I smiled. "He knows that. That's why he granted your request to come here. He rewards loyalty."

The demon bowed his head and backed out, taking the tray with him. I didn't shut the door after him. Instead, I held it open and turned back to Lothar. "I'd like to get some sleep now."

"I'd like to continue our conversation," he said, his jaw stubborn.

"Well, I wouldn't. Please leave."

His eyes narrowed as he stared at me from across the room. I stayed where I was, continuing to hold the door wide.

"Roxy—"

"I need you to leave," I said again, more forcefully.

His nostrils flared, but he stood. He strode toward the door, then stopped in front of me, and I braced when he dipped his head and breathed me deep into his lungs. He growled low. No disgust on his face now, just hunger.

He made another sound, one that was utterly sexual. "We will finish this conversation later, kitten," he said, then he swaggered out of my room and disappeared into his own.

I woke with a jolt, a rolling boom fading into the distance. Lightning flashed through my room like a strobe light, and I shoved back the covers and rushed to the window. The thunder hit again a moment later, so violent I was positive the tower rocked from the force.

The weather here was always wild and stormy, but something seemed strange, off. Rushing back across the room, I slid my feet into my boots, opened my door and walked out into the hall. A loud crash came from somewhere downstairs at the same time another round of lightning lit up the darkness in a riotous show of eerie, glowing blue light flickering against the dark glossy walls.

Lothar's door opened, and he strode out, feet bare, and hastily pulled on jeans.

"You hear the crash downstairs?" he asked.

"I was just heading down to check it out."

He nodded and followed me down all seven floors to the foyer. A demon was at the desk and greeted us, and I strode over while Lothar scanned the area and scented the air. "I heard a loud noise down here, what's going on?"

The demon grinned, flashing his pointed teeth. "Apologies for waking you. The storms here are intense at times, one of our cleaning staff got a fright and dropped something—"

"Something really fucking big," Lothar said behind me.

The demon nodded. "Well, yes it was, you are correct, but I assure you, all is well."

"Where's Horace?" I asked.

"He's asleep. I'm working the night shift."

That made sense of course, but then again, Horace was devoted to Lucifer, and I couldn't imagine him resting, or taking time off with one of Luci's handmaids here. "I'm just surprised he'd leave his post tonight."

"I have been training under Horace for many years," the demon said and bristled. "I assure you I have everything well in hand."

"Of course, I meant no offense. We'll head back up now." I hadn't been here for a seriously long time. Things changed, but still an unease slid through me.

"Sleep well," the demon said, his lips curving.

We started back up. "I hate this place," Lothar said beside me.

"It's definitely not my favorite. Did anything seem off to you?" I said and tried not to look at his bare chest, or the trail of dark hair below his belly button that thickened, then disappeared behind his barely hanging-on zipper. The thing was straining, forced to do all the work without the help of a button, since he'd not bothered to do it up, and it was losing the battle.

"No more than when we got here. This whole fucking place seems off to me. If you're asking if I sensed anything new while we were down there? No. Nothing."

I relaxed a little...then his hand brushed mine, and I jumped, my gaze slicing up to his face. He was looking straight ahead, though. I bit my lip and looked down at my feet. *Don't look at him.* His hand brushed mine again, and my breath literally caught. I couldn't even handle the back of his hand touching mine, for fuck's sake, how could I possibly resist him if he did more than that?

"You smell really good," he said low.

My throat went dry. "Still no stink, huh?" I forced out.

He shook his head. "That's gone now. I think for good. This must be how you smell to everyone else."

We rounded the landing and headed up another flight of stairs, and his hand brushed mine again. I sucked in a breath. He had to be doing it on purpose. I tried to put more distance between us, but the staircase was narrow. "I guess I'll take that as a win. I'd rather not stink up the place."

As soon as the last word left my mouth, Lothar spun on me and advanced.

"What are you..." My back hit the wall.

His huge body pressed into mine, his chest pumping hard as he curled his arm around my waist. The other thrust into my hair, and he hauled me off the ground. "Kitten, you smell like clean cotton and soap, and something else, something I'd never been able to scent on you before, but it's exactly what I imagined you should smell like." He dragged his nose up my throat, breathing deep. "And blended with all of that, all that is you, is warm, welcoming female, and it is fucking intoxicating."

I shivered and desperately tried to catch my breath. *Welcoming female.* In other words, he could smell how much I wanted him, just from the sight of him walking out of his room a short time ago. "Lothar—"

He slammed his mouth down on mine, his knees bending as he curled his big body around me, his arms tightening like he thought I'd try to escape and was attempting to get me closer as he kissed me like a triumphant warrior home from battle.

I should stop him, but I couldn't do it, despite every reason that I should end this right the hell now. No, I threw my arms around his neck and pulled him closer.

Matching his hunger was impossible, though, I could only surrender. His fingers cradled the back of my head as his mouth devoured mine, his lips giving fierce, claiming kisses that made my head spin. In that moment, I lost my way to the power of his need for me, and I ceded to his will. There was no fighting this—not when his resolve to have me was far stronger than mine was to resist him.

Maybe I could have this? Just one more night.

We'd be going home tomorrow, and once we reached Hell, our time together would be over. I squeezed my eyes closed, praying for mercy, begging the gods to give us this one night without repercussions.

Just give me this one night, then I promise I'll give him up. I'll walk way and never come back. I'll give him up forever.

It was what I had to do. There was nothing else that would guarantee Lothar wouldn't get hurt. Lucifer said there would be dire consequences if he learned the truth. I had to protect him. That was more important than my feelings.

All I asked for, was tonight.

TWENTY-ONE

Roxy

LOTHAR'S KISSES were wild as he carried me up the last two flights of stairs and into my room. He kicked the door shut behind us, his beast vibrating in his chest as he strode across the room. He lowered me to the bed, coming down and covering me with his huge frame, so I was pinned to the mattress.

"Tell me you want me?" he growled against my skin.

As out of control as I was, I still had enough presence of mind to be careful. "I want you, I do, Lothar," I said, nipping at his jaw and lifting my hips, desperate for more friction. "We'll make each other feel good, but no...no sex."

He snarled a little. "Whatever you want, Rox." But when he spoke, there was no anger or disappointment in his voice. He cupped my jaw, sliding his thumb below my lower lip, then kissed me gently and lifted his head. "I just

218

need to make you come, baby. That's all I need. Promise I'll make you feel so good."

I was addicted to his mouth, to the way he kissed me. The long and slow, the wild and out of control, and the quick pressing of lips like the one he'd just given me. I curled my arms around his neck and pulled him back down for another, moaning against his mouth from how good it felt to be close to him, to taste his lips and feel his warmth pressed against me. I savored every moment, memorizing every touch, every sound to remember later.

His hand slid down my side, and he squeezed my waist, then gripped a handful of my oversized shirt and tugged it higher. His hand trailed up my thigh before hooking his fingers in the waistband of my underwear. My breath shook in anticipation. He didn't make me wait, he slid his hand down the front and I cried out against his mouth when he touched my needy flesh, gliding one of his thick fingers across my slickness.

I spread my legs for him, asking for more, and he growled against my throat.

"Love how fucking wet you get, Rox." He nipped my jaw as he slid one finger inside me.

I arched against the mattress and gasped. Gods, it felt too good. "Please..."

"Another finger, kitten?"

I whimpered and nodded. "More."

He pushed two thick fingers inside me, and I lifted my hips when he thrust deep, desperate for more. "Faster. Oh gods, more."

His thumb swiped over my clit, again, and again, leaving me gasping. "More?"

I couldn't get enough, nothing was enough. I whimpered. "Yes."

He withdrew his fingers, and when he slid back in, he'd added a third, and I cried out, my thighs shaking as he fucked me with them, fast and deep.

"You love that, don't you, kitten? You love feeling so fucking full you can barely catch your breath. That's how my cock would feel inside you. I'd stretch this pussy to its limits. I'd hit you so deep, you'd see fucking stars."

He shoved my shirt up the rest of the way and sucked one of my nipples into his mouth, then grazed the sensitive nub with his fangs. I broke then, my pussy clamping down hard around his fingers, and I cried out, coming hard for him.

"Tell me you want me to fuck you," he growled out. "Tell me."

I gasped, shaking my head, still recovering, still riding the waves of pleasure.

"You're telling me one thing, but this curvy, tight little body is telling me something else," he growled. "Let go, baby."

"I c-can't," I rasped, pleading with him to stop this before it was too late.

"Give in to me, kitten," he demanded.

"Please, Lothar, we can't."

He growled, then I was airborne, lifted onto his lap. He'd undone his jeans, and had shoved them down so there was barely anything between us, then both of his hands gripped my hips and he held me steady, thrusting his hard cock against my clit through his boxer briefs and my underwear. I wrapped my arms around his neck, my head spinning, wanting him still, needing more, and I rocked against him, meeting his out-of-control thrusts.

His fingers slid into my hair, and he took my mouth in a deep kiss that sent sparks igniting all over my body. Oh gods, I was so sensitive that it only took minutes before I tipped over the edge again. I tore my mouth from his and came, crying out his name, my heart shattering all over again at the thought of letting him go.

His fingers dug hard into my ass, and he rocked up against me, then held me there, thrusting almost brutally.

Oh fuck. Oh no.

I could feel it, through his underwear and mine.

What was happening to him only happened to a hound when he found his mate. Lothar had grown bigger, thicker, his beast trying to knot with his mate, a mate he'd never once gotten the chance to claim fully—a mate he had no idea existed. This shouldn't be happening, it shouldn't be possible, but it was. *Oh fuck, it was.*

"Roxy...fuck. Fucking hell," he rasped. His eyes widened. Something like shock, like understanding, or recognition flashed through his eyes, and then he buried his face against my throat and came with a low, agonized groan. His big body, wrapped around mine, shuddered, his muscles jumped, twitching all over his body, while his cock pulsed and throbbed against me.

Everything went silent, except for our panted breaths.

I squeezed my eyes closed.

What the hell had I done?

His hand slid up my back, into my hair, and he fisted, jerking my head back, forcing a gasp from me. His eyes were glowing red, burning into me. "My knot... I just..." He swallowed thickly. "You felt it..." He shook his head wildly, trying to clear his head. "That's never happened before. You felt me...you fucking felt it, didn't you, Roxy?"

I bit my lips. I didn't know what to say, what to do.

"You felt it, didn't you?" he said again, more forcefully.

I blinked rapidly, fighting back my tears. Don't cry. Do not cry.

He studied me. "But that's impossible, right? Tell me that what just happened is impossible, and there's an explanation for it, tell me," he said low, deadly.

His grip on me tightened as I shook my head. "I don't know—"

"No more fucking lies," he said and shook me. "Something is going on between us, something I can't explain. Shit has been fucked between us for months. But you know what it is, don't you? You fucking know."

Tears stung my eyes. "I...I don't. You're imagin—"

"You can't be my mate. Right, Rox? Because I'd know if you were. I'd fucking know, wouldn't I, Roxy?" He was all but roaring now.

A tear streaked down my cheek. "You'd know," I said, still trying to lie, even as more tears streamed down my face. "Y-you're confused. It's just this realm. We're not... we're not—"

He snarled. "Tell me the fucking truth," he bellowed.

The window shattered, darkness pouring in, bringing with it a freezing wind that blasted through the room. My hair whipped around my face as the darkness, the shadows, stopped moving, coalescing into tall imposing forms.

Wraiths.

Oh fuck. I pulled away from Lothar and dived for my blades.

An awful voice filled with agony and rage reverberated through the room. One so dreadful, it hurt to listen to. "You will come with us, or he will die." Something warm trickled down my face and I swiped it away. Blood, it was dripping from my nose, my eyes.

"Roxy!" Lothar roared from across the room.

I spun to him, shoving back my hair being blown every-where. Wraiths surrounded him, a blade of the gods pressed to his throat.

"Don't do it," he snarled at me. "Don't you dare fucking do it. Do not go with them."

"If you don't comply, the hound will die," the voice screeched.

I tried to shrink away from the voice, covering my ears. I had no choice but to do what they demanded. I wouldn't let them hurt Lothar. I wouldn't let anyone hurt him, not ever again.

As much as I wanted to fight, there was no beating this many wraiths, not without losing Lothar, and I couldn't let that happen. As long as he was okay, I'd be okay, no matter what happened next—even if that meant never seeing him again.

The wraiths whipped around me, tearing at my hair, my clothes, scraping over my skin. They lifted me, all tugging and pulling me in different directions as they dragged me toward the window.

Lothar's roar followed as they ripped me through it and into the cold night.

CHAPTER
TWENTY-TWO

Lothar

I ʀᴀɴ to the window and watched as seven stories below a swirling mass of darkness flew across the rock plains and toward the forest, carrying Roxy with them. Sprinting to the door, I shoved it open. Horace stood on the other side, eyes wide, his hands up. I didn't stop—and plowed into an invisible force that knocked me back so hard I flew across the room and landed on my ass.

Bounding back to my feet, I ran at it again, and it threw me back harder, my body smashing into the stone wall opposite.

"Master Lothar," Horace said. "Please, be calm."

I ran back and gripped the doorframe. "Where is she? Who took her? What the fuck is going on?" That's when I finally noticed the demon was bruised and bloody, with lacerations on his arms and legs.

He darted glances down the hallway and back at me

and leaned in. "I don't know how to free you," he rushed out. "She won't let me."

"Who?" I roared. "Who has Roxy."

"S-sss..." He grabbed at his throat, his mouth moving but nothing coming out. Blood bubbled through his gasping lips. He leaned over, and it poured from him. He looked up at me, his hand outstretched, choking, then he hit the ground.

A moment later, Horace turned to ash, silenced by whoever took Roxy from me. I slammed my shoulder into the invisible barrier between us, but there was no getting through. The door slammed in my face, and when I tried to open it again, I couldn't. I was trapped in this room, seven floors up, with no escape, and no way to get to Roxy.

Roxy

Beelzebub grabbed my jaw roughly. "Come on now, Rox, time to spill." His gaze drifted down my beaten and bloody body as he shook his head. "You look like shit." He lifted my hand, and I refused to wince as he prodded the fleshy ends where the nails had been torn off. "You have to be in a lot of pain?"

Whoever sent the wraiths for me had freed Beelzebub as well. They'd also taken Lothar's and my phones. They were shoved in Beelzebub's back pocket. Which meant Lothar couldn't get word to Lucifer.

I didn't know how Lucifer's powers worked, even after

knowing him as long as I had—why sometimes he knew things and sometimes he didn't. I could only hope he sensed something was wrong now, but even then, he might not help me, not because he didn't want to but because sometimes things needed to be left to play out, no matter how horrific.

Lucifer saw the big picture, and occasionally that meant making sacrifices—even if that sacrifice was me. So as awful as this was, and as hard as it was to accept and not feel abandoned by him, I had to trust that whatever happened next was how it was meant to be.

I hadn't said one word to Beelzebub since I was brought to this place, this hideous onyx fortress. The energy it was giving off told me it was new, created by someone immensely powerful and with seriously shitty taste. Whoever this place belonged to had claimed the Outer Realm as their own. Which meant it had to be someone at least as strong as Nox or someone with something she wanted. Yes, Nox had retreated from this realm when she and Death had their showdown, but she wouldn't want anyone else this close to the Night Realm, not without reassurances of their allegiance to her.

Beelzebub planted his hand on my head and jerked it from side to side. "Are you listening to me?"

I glared straight ahead. Without the wraiths to help him, I would have made the motherfucker beg for his life. They were the only reason he'd managed to capture me and chain me up. Many had tried over the years, because of my closeness to Lucifer, but none had succeeded until now.

"Looks like I'm gonna have to make you scream, Roxana."

Never.

No matter what he did to me, I would never scream. I would never give the enemy that satisfaction.

Beelzebub clicked his fingers at the demon guarding the door. It was the same demon who'd attacked me in Skull Forest. "My friend here has nice sharp teeth," he said. "I think it's time he used them."

"Long time no see, hog face," I rasped and grinned, but with how swollen my face was, I wasn't sure he could tell.

The demon rushed over, his furious gaze burning into me before it sliced to Beelzebub. B nodded, giving the demon the go-ahead.

Hog face grabbed my left hand and slid my pinky into his mouth and sucked, making an *mmm* sound.

"Do it," Beelzebub said.

I braced, right as he bit down at the knuckle, his sharp teeth lacerating skin and flesh. I ground my teeth as sharp agony sliced across my palm and shot up my arm. The sound of bone crunching was nauseating as he bit through, then wrenched his head to the side, tearing it off. Blood poured from my hand all over the floor.

"Eat it," Beelzebub said.

The demon chewed, loudly.

"Pigs will eat a-anything," I choked out. "By all means, if you're hungry, bon appetit."

He offered me a bloody-toothed sneer.

I grinned, giving him the same in return. "Joke's on you. I p-pick my nose with that one."

Beelzebub grabbed my jaw again. "You think you're funny? How many fingers are you willing to lose?"

All of them, motherfucker.

Lucifer was my creator, my friend, my family. He was everything. My love for him was indescribable, unbreakable. I would sooner die than betray my king, before I gave them the means to hurt him.

I kept my mouth clamped shut and the hatred burning bright inside me. I would never give them the ammunition they needed to take Luci's throne. Never.

Beelzebub chuckled. "You'd die for Lucifer, wouldn't you?" he said as if he'd read my mind. "Such loyalty to someone who would never give you the same. If only you knew the truth." He dragged his claws lightly over my swollen face. "If only you knew what he did—"

"Beelzebub," a female voice snapped.

My entire body stiffened. Seraphina. Of course it was her. I'd known, hadn't I? Even before the wraiths made an appearance in Oldwood Forest. There was the verahn attack in Hell, that should have been a warning. The way hog face had vanished after he and his friends had attacked me, only someone seriously powerful could have done that. But the biggest flashing red light should have been when Lothar started acting strangely. She'd been purposely trying to break us both down, by slowly exposing the emotions Lucifer had locked away in Lothar. Trying to make him remember. Yes. I'd suspected it was her, but I'd tried to convince myself it couldn't be true, and when Lucifer hadn't been able to get the information from the angels we needed, I told myself she still had to be locked away, that there was no way she'd be able to escape her prison in Heaven—yet here she was.

I'd never encountered a colder and more heartless being in my long life. I would die today, but not before she'd made me endure torture so horrific, I would almost definitely lose my mind first.

"The wraiths?" B asked her.

"They fulfilled their end of the bargain. I set them free," she said.

Beelzebub looked relieved. Having been brought here by them, touched by them, I understood why. But if they were free and now available to the highest bidder, we were in serious trouble.

"It's been a long time, Roxana." Her frigid stare chilled me to the bone. "Too long, yes? I had hoped to do all of this without getting my hands dirty, but, sadly, Poe and Tarrant weren't quite as clever as they thought they were, and with Beelzebub forced to flee Hell, it seems I have to do everything myself."

I kept my chin up, refusing to be weak in front of her, despite the condition I was in after Beelzebub's beatings.

She lifted a hand, palm up. "We have a fun day planned for you, Roxy. I'm excited to get started." An orb appeared, hovering above her open hand. It grew in size steadily until it was at least a yard in diameter. Black smoke swirled behind some kind of invisible barrier. "Keep watching," Sera said as the smoke began to thin, then dissipated completely.

My room at the tower came into view. I jerked against my restraints when I saw Lothar. His hands were a mess, cut and bloody, his hair wild, his chest heaving. He looked up then, blinking, eyes glowing red, aimed right at me.

"Oh look, he's spotted you," Seraphina said.

Lothar's mouth opened on a soundless roar. He ran at the orb, slamming into it, then hammering his fists against it over and over again.

"Stop," I cried when his knuckles split open. "Lothar, please. You need to stop."

Sera chuckled. "You can see each other, but he can't hear you." Her head tipped to the side. "How far can we

229

push him, do you think? How long before he fractures completely and the truth of what you and Lucifer did to him comes rushing back like a nightmare?"

"Don't," I choked out. "Please."

"She speaks," she said. "But not soon enough, sadly." She shook her head. "Remember when you betrayed me? Remember when you had me imprisoned? Left to rot alone for centuries. That can't go unpunished, Roxana, you have to know that."

She'd lost her damned mind. I had nothing to do with her imprisonment, and neither had Lucifer. It was her own fault she was caught.

"What's it going to be? Are you going to help me over-throw Lucifer, like I should have done a very long time ago, or are you going to rend your mate's psyche in two?"

They were going to hurt me and make Lothar watch. They were going to force him to break since I wouldn't. I jerked against my restraints.

Either option was unthinkable. If Lucifer lost his throne, ripples would be felt through every realm, the balance between Heaven and Hell would be lost, and every-thing would descend into chaos.

I met Lothar's wild, panicked stare through the orb and tried to communicate how sorry I was. He opened his mouth on another silent roar. A hot tear streaked down my cheek. I wouldn't survive this, but Lothar would. Lucifer would put him back together, I had to believe that. However broken he was after this, I knew Lucifer loved me and he loved Lothar, we were both his creations, and he wouldn't let Lothar suffer.

Seraphina nodded to hog face when I kept my mouth clamped shut, still refusing to give her what she wanted, and the demon came forward, lifted my hand, slid my ring finger into his mouth and crunched down, tearing the next finger off as well. Lothar exploded with rage on the other side of the orb. Veins bulging, fangs extended, silently roaring as he slammed into the orb's surface repeatedly, trying again and again to get to me.

"Time to get a little more creative," Seraphina said, a chilling smile curving her perfect lips. "But first." She handed Beelzebub a knife, one made by the gods—the same blade she'd used to slice open my side all those years ago, causing a wound that had almost killed me. I was in no doubt that her escape was the reason the wound had grown painful and raw again. "Let's make sure those fingers don't grow back."

Beelzebub took the knife and pressed the flat side of the blade to the bloody stumps. I clenched my teeth, jerking as the Heaven-made weapon sent toxic power surging through my Hell-born body. The pain only made my hatred for them burn hotter. I smiled, still refusing to scream.

Sera's fury rose. Good, maybe she'd be so furious, she'd burn herself out quicker.

When the torture began, I closed my eyes, so I couldn't see Lothar and what this was doing to him.

If I saw how this hurt him, it would weaken me, and I needed to hold on, because despite the odds—I would not just give up and die.

›)›·●·(((

Lothar

231

My knees hit the floor, blood dripping onto the tiles from my torn-up hands. Panting, I blinked back the red rage and took in the destroyed room. Smoke drifted around me. The walls were charred, the furniture nothing but ash. In this, the beast and I were in perfect harmony. We'd fought to escape this room, going as far as using my hellfire to try to burn this fucking room to the ground, anything to get to Roxy while they fucking tortured her relentlessly. Even after the orb vanished, I hadn't stopped.

I had no idea how long ago that was. The rage and fear had been so overwhelming, I wasn't sure when I last had a lucid thought or how I was managing it now, honestly. I had to think. It was the only way to help Roxy. The beast snarled and fought inside me now, and I wasn't sure how much longer I could hold it back.

Being forced to watch as Beelzebub beat and cut, and had that fucking demon from the swimming hole bite Roxy —and not be able to do anything to stop it, to help her— was more than my sanity could endure.

Yes, she was sweet and small and looked easy to break, but despite her size, Roxy was a fierce and brutal warrior. She was powerful, immensely strong, and loyal to a fault, which meant she could sustain immeasurable pain and torture and not give an inch. Nothing Beelzebub and the bitch with him did would make her crack. Nothing would get her to help them overthrow Lucifer. It would never happen. Roxy would die before she did that.

Which was why I was so fucking terrified.

What were they doing to her now? How much suffering would they make her endure?

With a roar, I ran at the door again, claws extended, and hacked at it, battered it with the full force of my body, but nothing I did would open it and nothing would smash the glass in the window.

I'd tried repeatedly to call for Lucifer, but he hadn't come.

I picked up a chair and hurled it at the window, then charged it and was thrown back, tossed across the room again as soon as I reached it.

Roaring, I gripped the sides of my head.

How much longer could she survive?

CHAPTER
TWENTY-THREE

Roxy

SEVERAL DAYS HAD PASSED since Sera took over my torture. She'd had B use my phone, pretending to be me, and text Lucifer to say there's been a holdup, that I'd be hard to reach for a while, and that I'd be in contact soon.

Lucifer had to know something was wrong, though, and if he wanted to find me, or any of his handmaids, he could. He knew when we were in real trouble. Which meant there was a reason he wasn't here now, a reason only he knew and one I had to trust in.

My muscles twitched and cramped from being in the same upright position, chained to this wooden rack for so long. And the wounds Sera had sliced into my flesh with some rusty old blade weren't healing because she'd smeared some noxious slime into them, and they were beginning to fester, throbbing incessantly.

My thighs trembled, my body weakened to a point it

never had been in my life, but at least I could feel my internal injuries starting to heal.

I held my chin up as Seraphina closed the space between us and stared deep into my eyes. There was a tug at my subconscious as she tried to probe deeper, to find the information I refused to give her. She never would. I'd had centuries to prepare for a moment like this, to strengthen my mind. Everything she wanted from me, all the information on Lucifer she craved, was locked away in a vault of my own making, unreachable to anyone but me.

"I'd hoped we'd be friends once upon a time. I don't trust easily, but I trusted you and Lucifer, and you both betrayed me."

Bullshit. While she'd been locked up, her warped mind had rewritten history.

"Because of you I fell, because of you I lost my place in Heaven. You must pay for your crimes, Roxy, if you want my forgiveness."

She could stick her forgiveness where the sun didn't shine. She fell because she was a treasonous, honorless bitch. It had nothing to do with me or Lucifer.

"Time for the next phase," she said and tilted her head to the side, studying my face. "You really are a pretty thing... well, you were." She smiled. "I never could figure out what Lucifer saw in you, Roxana, why he thought you were so special. Maybe if you survive what comes next, I'll have the opportunity to find out?"

I didn't hate easily, and the number of beings who had managed to incite that emotion in me were few, but I hated this bitch in a way that defied comprehension. Cruelty for the sake of it wasn't my thing, and Seraphina was among the cruelest beings I had ever encountered.

"Why does Lucifer love you so much?" she continued.

"Why did the fates choose such a handsome and strong male as your mate?" She laughed huskily. "Oh...that's right, you never did mate in truth, did you? You don't even know what it's like to fuck him." She leaned in, her mouth half an inch from my ear. "I do." She bit my ear, hard, then licked it. "But you saw that for yourself, didn't you? You saw what you were missing out on when you walked in on us." She lifted her head, her eyes flashing with evil delight when she saw the pain her words caused.

I tried to hide it, but I couldn't, and that split-second show of weakness was all she needed.

She sneered. "You never got over his faithlessness, did you? You've enjoyed watching him suffer. You've relished watching him slowly unravel before your eyes while you were on your little hunt together," she said, her cool breath brushing my cheek.

What the hell was she talking about?

Her eyes widened dramatically. "Oh dear, you don't know?"

"Know what?" I bit out, unable to stop myself.

Sera smiled triumphantly. "I can't believe you haven't noticed." She circled me slowly. "The way his eyes keep flashing red, the way he growls constantly, the way his beast rolls beneath his skin, wanting to get free."

She was right, that's exactly how Lothar had been behaving. I'd seen how tenuous the grip was he had on his control, but I had no idea what it meant, not really. I thought that maybe the truth of our past was in danger of resurfacing if I didn't put some space between us, and that maybe that was messing with him, but Sera meant something else, didn't she?

"His beast knows who you truly are, even if Lothar doesn't," Sera said finally, answering my unspoken question. "Lucifer may have suppressed Lothar's memories, but he can't stop fate. He can't suppress the instincts of a beast who has been separated from his mate for centuries, or the kind of damage a torment like that can do to the animal side of a hellhound, what it has been doing to *your* hellhound."

Nausea cramped my belly at what she said, at what Lothar must be going through. Oh gods. He must be so confused right now. Lothar's behavior, the strange way he'd been acting, it was impossible not to believe what Sera said. He'd been unraveling, and I hadn't seen the fracture between him and his beast.

Sera was the catalyst. She was the one who started him down the road to self-destruction when she escaped her prison, and she was the reason I'd started to struggle when I was around him again, why I was feeling so much anger again. "You did this to us," I said.

"It's nothing you don't deserve. You only have yourself to blame." Her gaze sharpened. "Because of you, he's splitting in two, Roxy. Two separate psyches. The beast is fighting to get to his female, even if that means tearing free. What do you think will happen when he finally succeeds? What do you think the beast will do when he's in charge of them and I release Lothar from that tower?" She leaned in, tucking some of my blood-soaked and matted hair behind my ear. "What do you think he'll do when he finally gets his hands on you?"

Oh gods. My heart slammed into my ribs. "Please, don't," I rasped past my dry throat. "Please, Sera, don't do this to him." I didn't beg, ever, but I would if I had to, to stop her from doing this to him.

"Are you going to give me what I want?"

I wanted to fucking scream in rage. I'd never felt so

helpless. But I couldn't give her the means to take down Lucifer. Doing so would affect so much more than just him and I.

"No? Then it's time to set the beast free and offer him his prize, right here for the taking." She lifted her hand and the orb appeared again, showing me Lothar in the tower.

He was naked and looked utterly feral. He'd watched Beelzebub and Sera torture me. He'd seen every slice and bite, every break, every twisted evil thing they'd done to me. He'd shifted from hound and back to his human form repeatedly while it happened, shredding his clothes and his control. And as soon as he saw me now, his eyes began flashing between gold and red, and his body jerked and contorted. Fur sprouted across his forearms and thighs, his feet elongating, and his fangs punched down, looking longer and more vicious than I'd ever seen them. He wasn't all Lothar, not anymore, and not all hound either—he was something else.

I could see Lothar was fighting it, but he was so close to breaking, it wouldn't take much to tip him over the edge completely.

Sera crooked her finger at Beelzebub, who'd been watching and listening to us silently across the room. The huge demon strode over, anticipation lighting up his harsh features. She held out her hand, and he placed his knife in it. Sera circled me, stopping at my back, then wrapped her arm around my neck, took my chin, and jerked my head to the side. "Look, he's watching us," she said against my ear.

I looked up and his eyes locked on mine, full of fury and fear and pain. I gritted my teeth and fought to hold on, to believe that Lothar would be okay, that whatever happened, he would get through this.

"Once he breaks, I'm not sure he can be put back

together," she said as if she were reading my thoughts. "Last chance to talk, and save both of you unending pain."

Lothar was the strongest male I knew. If he broke, he would find his way back. He would. I had to believe that now more than ever, because I was a second away from betraying Lucifer, from giving Sera everything she wanted and letting Hell fall, allowing all the realms to descend into chaos and destruction.

"Still no?" she said.

I clamped my mouth closed.

"Very well." She pressed the knife to my skin.

As soon as she did, Lothar lost his mind. I couldn't hear his roars through the orb, but his chest kept expanding and his mouth was wide open, the veins and tendons in his throat bulging from the force of it.

Sera sliced then, and I gritted my teeth as she dragged the blade across my skin just below my collarbone. Blood immediately bubbled to the surface and slid down my chest.

"Lick it up," she said to Beelzebub.

He chuckled and leaned in, swiping his tongue over my bare flesh, licking up my blood. I thought Lothar had lost control before. Not even close. More fur burst across his shoulders, and vicious claws punched through, replacing his fingernails.

He gripped his head as his eyes flashed between gold and red repeatedly, then finally—stopped.

The gold was gone. Bloodred irises remained, staring back at me.

The beast was in control.

"Come now, beast," Sera said and flicked her hand carelessly.

As soon as she did, Lothar's head spun to the door. He

tilted his head back, and I didn't need to hear him to see he was howling, then he was gone.

Oh fuck. Sera had freed him.

He was coming for me.

I was naked and filthy, and instead of the rack, I had been shoved into a cell below her fortress, iron bars holding me helpless.

Sera wanted to destroy Lothar and me both, for what she saw as a betrayal. She wanted Lothar to tear me to shreds, and if he managed to regain control, she wanted him to live with the knowledge of what he'd done. She wanted us to suffer, but mostly, the person she wanted to punish was Lucifer.

I wouldn't let that happen. I wouldn't let her hurt Lothar or Lucifer—whatever it took.

A howl echoed in the distance.

Lothar was close, and quickly closing in. My scent was all he'd need to find me, and he'd been locked in my room for days, with nothing but my scent surrounding him. He would've known exactly where I was before Sera even released him from the tower.

I pulled myself to my feet, ignoring the aches and pains throbbing through me as Sera walked into the room and strode up to the bars separating us.

"Are you excited? You and Lothar are about to be reunited." Her eyes sparkled with twisted pleasure. "He's got those big claws, and those really long fangs, what do you think he'll use on you first? I can't wait to see."

Another howl came. Closer.

The sound of splintering wood echoed from upstairs.

"He's here." Excitement burned in Sera's eyes. "Have fun, won't you," she said, then she strode across the room and through a door. As soon as she shut it, it vanished, blending seamlessly with the walls.

Nerves throbbed through me. I was injured, but I was still strong. I could take it, whatever happened next. I could withstand it.

A loud, hollow boom had me gripping the bars, bracing, a moment before the steel door across the room buckled. There was another boom, the steel giving some more—then it exploded open.

I sucked in a ragged breath, goose bumps lifting all over me when I finally saw him in the flesh. He was huge. His body looked a lot like it usually did, strong, heavily muscled, but now there was fur on his shoulders, thighs, and forearms. His face was the one I loved, but his brow was heavier, and his fangs were longer.

His gaze locked on me, then he leaped across the room and thrust a hand thought the bars, trying to grab me.

I stumbled back. "Lothar?"

He snarled and swiped at me wildly.

"I know you're in there," I said. "I know you don't want to hurt me. I need you to fight. I need you to fight for me. Come back to me."

He arched his head back and howled, not hearing me, not understanding. I walked closer but still out of reach, so I could try and make him listen.

"Lothar," I snapped, louder. "Listen to me." He stopped swiping his clawed hands at me and stilled. His red eyes burned, predatory and utterly intent. "That's it. Listen to my voice. Lothar needs to come back, you need to let him come back."

241

His eyes flickered to gold, just for a split second, before it was gone again.

"I know you're fighting, Loth, don't stop, okay? I need you here. I need you to come bac—"

The metallic slide of a lock being opened, froze me in place. My gaze sliced to the door just as it swung open.

Oh fuck.

The beast didn't hesitate, he burst through, and came straight for me, eating up the space between us, and slammed me against the wall with so much force, I was surprised he didn't crack my ribs. I gasped for breath and reached up, grabbing his face, holding his wild, red stare. "Lothar," I yelled. "Come back, right the fuck now!"

There was another flash of gold, but again, only for a split second.

He dragged his nose along my naked shoulder, and a deep rumbling sound vibrated from him. "My female. *Mine,*" he said in a distorted and garbled voice, then he roared in my face.

Fucking hell.

My heart was pounding a furious beat as he scented me again, then nipped at my shoulder and licked my skin. His head jerked back, his gaze locked on one of the deep cuts Sera had made in my upper arm, and he snarled at it, as if he could intimidate it into vanishing. He licked the wound. "Heal you," he said roughly and licked me again, his instincts to take care of me distracting him.

Okay, maybe things would be okay? If I could keep him focused on my wounds while I worked out what to do next — His hard cock prodded at my tightly clenched thighs.

Fuck.

"Lothar?"

He lifted his head with a snarl, and his eyes flashed

gold. "Roxy," he snarled, confusion slipping through, fear as well, then the gold was gone again. "Mate," he said next, his voice back to the beast. "Claim," he said and ground his hard cock against my stomach.

His head jerked back suddenly, his mouth opening as his jaw extended into its hound's snout, then retracted and went back to normal. His fangs slid back in, then thrust back out. Lothar was right there, right below the surface, and he was fighting with everything he had, but the beast was strong—and right now, that part of him, the part that knew who I was and had been cruelly suppressed for so very long, was winning.

I was sure Lothar could hear me though.

"Whatever happens," I said, gripping the sides of his face and making him look me in the eyes, "it's okay. I'll be okay. This is not your fault, none of this is your fault."

Even as I tried to reassure him, I called for Lucifer in my mind, begging him to come, to stop this.

Lothar's eyes flashed gold again, and he pulled away with an agonized cry and dropped to his knees. He tilted his head back and looked up at me. "Roxy?" He shook his head, confusion, realization, betrayal, heartbreak, it all flashed across his face, and gods, I felt it, it was like everything he was experiencing in that moment had been shot directly through my chest.

"Lothar, I'm here. Stay with me."

He gripped his head with a roar, but when he looked back up, he was gone. The beast shot back to his feet and hauled me up against him, dragging my legs around his waist. I didn't fight him, I would never let him think he forced this on me. His beast was driven by the instinct to claim his mate. I was his mate, his female, kept from him for far too long.

243

A tear slid down my cheek as I wrapped my arms around his neck. "It's okay," I said again. "You can do it. You can claim me." The alternative was fighting him, and with him in this state, there was a good chance I'd lose. The result of that would be devastating. I would not do that to Lothar.

He shoved his face against my neck with a growl. "Kitten," he rasped, Lothar breaking through again. "I'm...I'm sorry." Then he snarled again.

When he lifted his head, his eyes were flashing red, then gold, not holding one color while the beast and hound inwardly battled it out. Lothar was terrified, he had to be so scared of what was happening, at what he couldn't stop from happening.

Pain washed through me when I realized Lucifer wasn't going to stop this. Gods, that hurt, so fucking badly. Maybe there was a reason, some greater good right then. But I didn't care about the greater good. I only cared about Lothar and what this would do to him.

"It's okay. I'm yours," I choked out again, giving him the permission he needed. "I'm yours to take. Claim me, claim your mate."

His chest vibrated against mine as the thick head of his cock prodded between my thighs. I held on tighter, bracing as he pressed me against the wall with force—then slammed inside me.

I cried out at the intrusion. Lothar was huge everywhere, and if I were anyone else, I would have been torn in two. But I was Hell-born, and most importantly, I was made for him. I clung on tight as he thrust wildly into me, as if he had no control at all, had no choice but to claim me like the animal he was right then. He snarled while he licked and nipped at my throat, my shoulder, and I did the only thing I could, I yielded in every way possible, and held on to him, choking down my gasps and cries of pain, and doing my best to reassure him the only way I knew how.

Lothar would never hurt me. He'd never force himself on me, and I refused to let Seraphina win, for her to hurt us both this way. This wasn't his fault, it was Sera's, and that bitch was going to pay.

"I-I can't stop," he said harshly against my cheek. "Oh fuck, kitten, I c-can't stop."

Lothar was talking to me while the beast claimed me for the both of them. I wrapped my arms tighter around his neck and pressed my mouth to his ear. "You don't have to stop. I don't want you to stop, my love," I rasped as more tears slid down my face. "Everything will be okay," I said, desperately trying to reassure him, to get him through this, to get us both through this, but not knowing if what I said was true.

He lifted his head, and his red eyes hit mine. "Mate," the beast said, but it was softer. "My mate."

"Yes," I said and took hold of his face again. "I'm yours."

He rubbed his face against the side of mine, marking me with his scent, and eased up the intensity of his thrusts. "We don't want to hurt our mate," he said and slid his thumb over my cheek.

Lothar was getting through to the beast, somehow, they were communicating.

"Your mate appreciates that," I said. "This feels much better." And as fucked up as this whole thing was, it did feel better. The pain of his initial intrusion was gone, and in its place a warmth slowly unfurled, spreading through my belly and between my thighs. It was pleasure, steadily building inside me. I gasped, but this time, I didn't choke it down, because it was the good kind.

The beast groaned. "Mate feels good. Smells good." He slid deep and ground his hips, his panted breaths quickening. "We want mate to come," he said and ground his hips against me again. "We want mate to come with us."

We. That had to mean they were both here now, even if the beast was still dominant.

Heat washed through me—despite my wounds and barely healed body, despite this being the very last way I would have wanted to mate with Lothar in truth—and pleasure built, swirling low in my belly. My thighs trembled as Lothar began to thicken inside me, stretching me to my limits. I clung to his shoulders as he thrust deep over and over again.

When he tried to slide out next, my hips were tugged forward with him. He instantly stopped trying and instead pushed back in, rolling his hips against mine while he panted.

"Feel us," he said roughly. "Feel our knot."

"I f-feel it." I groaned. Oh gods, we were locked together.

He ground against me more forcefully, and hot seed jetted into me, filling me up. I cried out, hooking my arms and legs more fiercely around him, giving both the beast and Lothar what they wanted, what they needed, and came hard with him. I gasped, and he groaned as we ground against each other, locked in place, our orgasms seemingly never-ending. He dragged his mouth over my shoulder, sucking, kissing, licking my skin. I knew what was coming, and there was no stopping it.

He sank his fangs into me and exploded into a wild frenzy. His jaws sunk deeper into my flesh, and he tore into my shoulder in his excitement. I bit back my cry of pain, not wanting to make this worse for Lothar. When he finally released me, he licked his bite, stopping the bleeding, but this wound was different, this was the only wound his saliva couldn't heal. I'd wear it for an eternity, so everyone knew I was his.

He stayed where he was, holding me tight, a low rumbling sound rolling from him while we were still interlocked.

Several minutes passed before his knot finally released me, before he could slide his cock free.

He didn't move, though, even as seconds ticked by. He didn't speak, either, he just stood there panting, large body trembling, every muscle hard as granite.

"Lothar?" I whispered.

He jumped, like I'd yelled his name, then finally, he lifted his head. I could feel his struggle He was barely holding on, he was still fighting back the beast, but his eyes were burning bright gold now, and they bored into mine.

"Lothar?" I said again.

His chest heaved, that golden gaze searching mine. "What did you do, Roxy? What the fuck did you do to me?"

Then the gold was flooded with red, and he was gone.

CHAPTER
TWENTY-FOUR

Roxy

ONE OF THE wheels on the cage dropped into a pothole, jerking it to a stop. I tumbled to the side, my shoulder glancing the silver bars, burning my skin. Pain rolled through my body instantly, and I jerked away, wrapping my arms around my knees. The silver was angel blessed, and given that I was spawned in the depths of Hell, prolonged contact would turn me to ash. The demons pulling the cart heaved, and the cage finally bounced free with such force, I left the floor, then crashed back down, narrowly missing the bars a second time.

The silver not only kept us caged, it smothered our powers, making us almost as helpless as humans, and slowed my healing even more. My hand and scar on my side were the worst. My shoulder throbbed from Lothar's bite, but I tried not to touch it. If Lothar was in there, watching, I didn't want him to know it was bothering me.

He sat a couple feet away, his gaze trained on me. He seemed to have moments of lucidity, moments when the wild obsession left his red gaze and instead shone gold—and were full of anger, but worst of all horror.

I turned away from him, again, watching Seraphina and Beelzebub being carried ahead of us like ancient gods in their palanquin. The wooden box had velvet curtains, and it rested on the shoulders of four muscle-bound demons forced to bear their weight as they traipsed over uneven terrain. Several more heavily armed demons walked alongside our little party, including my old friend hog face, supposedly protecting us from the creatures with fangs who lived here in the Outer Realm. Though, by my count we'd already lost at least two along the way.

"Lucifer, he suppressed my instincts, my knowledge that you were my mate?" Lothar asked, and I jumped. He'd been quiet now for over an hour. "And you both kept it from me for centuries?"

His beast-roughened voice grated across my skin. It had always been deep and rough, but not like this. In these short cogent times, his voice didn't seem to have time to go back to normal.

"Yes," I said without looking back at him. He'd already asked the same question several times. I didn't know if he forgot that he'd asked between those lucid moments or if he was just so fucking stunned that we'd done it to him, that he was hoping for a different answer.

He snarled. "Why?"

"It was for the best," I answered, giving him the same answer I had several times now. The truth wouldn't help him. Knowing what he had done could only hurt him, and I'd hurt him enough already.

"It was for the best?" he bit out. "Did you think it was

for the best when I was driven to...to..." He swallowed audibly and hissed.

"Stop." I turned to him. "You didn't do anything wro—"

"The beast took hold of me, forced me to shove you against that cell wall and...and force you..." He groaned in agony, then panted as if he were trying to stop himself from throwing up.

"You didn't force me, Lothar, and you didn't hurt me. Please, I'm okay. I let you—"

"You let me?" His gaze dropped to where his bite was, to the mark a male gave his mate, and he bared his teeth. "I gave you no fucking choice."

My shirt covered how big and jagged it was. Something else that would cause him distress when he finally got a good look at it.

But that would not be now, because like the last time his emotions got the better of him, his eyes flashed red and the beast returned, taking over and pushing Lothar back. His hand shot out, and he grabbed my arm and pulled me over to him. I didn't resist, I let him plaster me to his side, if that helped him somehow. The beast sniffed my hair and pressed his lips to the bite he'd given me. His tongue swiped over the part that was exposed before he wrapped a huge arm around me and held me there, his chest vibrating with a low growl of warning as he stared at the demons around us.

Over the next hour, he snarled a lot, sometimes punching the side of his own head before his hold on me would tighten. No doubt Lothar was in there telling him to let me go. I took his hand and tried to soothe them both, not sure what else to do.

Lothar knew that Lucifer had hidden what we were to each other, yes, but that's all he seemed to know, and that's the way it needed to stay. If he hadn't remembered everything else yet, I could only pray to the gods that meant those memories were gone for good. The truth would serve no purpose now but to hurt him. Too much time had passed, and he'd paid more than enough of a price without knowing all the awful details.

Sera shoved back the curtain on her palanquin and called down to one of the demons carrying her and Beelzebub. They stopped instantly and lowered the box to the ground. The demons carrying our cage stopped as well. Another demon rolled out a carpet so Sera didn't dirty her precious little feet, and she disembarked and strode toward us.

Lothar snarled at her and tightened his hold on me.

"Now, now," she said. "We used to be such good friends, Lothar, and despite all your growling, I have a feeling we will be again, but until then." She held up a collar. "This will have to do."

No fucking way.

"Take it," she snapped at me.

"Fuck off," I said. "And shove that bullshit up the wind tunnel between your legs."

Her hand shot up, her fingers curling into a fist. I grabbed at my throat, instantly choking. It was as if she had an invisible grip around my neck and was squeezing tight. Lothar's beast roared, confused. He grabbed at me and shook me, so hard he almost broke my spine in his attempt to save me.

Sera eased off, and I gasped for air. The blessed silver had weakened me so much more than the torture had. Anything Heaven touched did that, and I had no way of protecting myself or Lothar from this evil fucking bitch.

"Put it on him now or he spends the night with this lodged between his ribs." She held up several short spikes.

They were made from the same silver, a couple inches long and pointed at both ends. They'd burn into his flesh, eventually making their way through muscle, then bone. They wouldn't kill him, but they'd do a lot of damage and cause horrific pain, but that would be nothing compared to the agony of extracting them.

"Okay," I said, because she would do it, and she'd love every moment of my distress. I slid my hand through the bars and took it from her, then turned to Lothar. "I need to put this on you, okay?"

I lifted it to his neck, but he snatched it away and tossed it through the bars and onto the ground.

"I thought we might have an issue," Sera said and waved her hand.

Demons swarmed forward and grabbed Lothar's arms through the bars and held him there. He fought and roared as his skin sizzled, burning against the silver. Sera handed me another collar.

"Put yours on first, so he understands." I had no choice but to do as she said, the silver could kill him.

It was a struggle without two of my fingers or any nails, but I managed to secure it around my throat, and as soon as I had, the demons released Lothar. He snatched me up again, ignoring his burns, and instead attacked my collar, yanking at it, snarling, and choking me in the process.

"Lothar," Sera snapped.

He ignored her, still grappling with my collar, getting more and more worked up. My oxygen was restricted enough that I was starting to see black spots. I was going to pass out.

Lothar roared suddenly, jolted, and dropped me. I

gasped and choked, desperately sucking in much needed oxygen.

One of the demons held a rod, like a fucking cattle prod.

"Lothar," Sera snapped again and held up his collar. "If you are in there somewhere, best you persuade the beast to put this on. If you don't, your mate will lose her head." She waved her hand and long, thin silver spikes, blessed like the bars, burst from the inside of the collar she was holding.

If she did that to the one I was wearing, the spikes were long enough that they'd burn right through, until I eventually lost my head completely, and that wasn't something I could survive.

"Put this on, beast, or your mate pays the price." She tossed it into the cage, and Lothar's beast picked it up. Then snarling at it, he tried to do as she said, fumbling and struggling with his claws and thick fingers, then finally held it out to me.

I took it and put it on him.

"How sweet," Sera said, then gave me a cold smile. "Try to get some sleep, won't you, we have a big day tomorrow." Then she clicked her fingers at Beelzebub.

The demon's gaze slid to me, and his lips curled up. He was going for bravado, but I saw the truth he was trying to hide. If Seraphina failed, he was toast. "Lucifer's going to make you scream, you know that, right, B?" I said to him and smiled.

There was a flicker of fear in his eyes, but it lasted for just a split second.

"You should be more worried about yourself, Roxy. Shit isn't looking too good for you right now." Then he scooped Sera up and strode to the huge tent her demons had hastily pitched for them and disappeared inside.

· · ·

It didn't take long for oppressive darkness to descend on the Outer Realm. I was hungry and cold and exhausted. I tried to fight the tiredness, but in the end, I lay down in the center of the cage, so I wouldn't accidentally touch the bars and curled into a ball.

Lothar's beast had been preoccupied with snarling at the demons and into the shadows for the last couple of hours, but now that the demons were gathered around a fire several yards away, he'd calmed down some.

Shivering, I looked at the fire and wished I could feel its warmth.

"Mate cold," the beast said, then lay down beside me and pulled me into his arms.

I didn't resist. He was so warm and, thankfully, wasn't squeezing too tight since the demons weren't as close. "Thank you."

He nuzzled my neck. "Smell good," he said, and I felt his hard length now pressed against me.

I quickly turned in his arms, and he let me. I looked up at him, into those red eyes. "You don't want to hurt your mate, do you?"

He shook his head, bared his teeth and growled, as if he wanted to attack himself at the very idea. Then he nuzzled my neck and ground his erection against me again. "Mate, open legs for me."

The pills Ursula had given me, concealed in that cheap ring I'd given Drake, would have come in handy right about now, but they were long gone. My clothes had been wet, covered in blood, stripped off, tossed aside. I had no idea where they'd ended up. Since sedation was off the cards, I had to somehow convince Lothar's beast that sex wasn't a good idea. "I'm still in some pain from being tortured, I need to rest. Being with you that way could hurt me right now." I wrapped my arms around him. "Will you just hold me? Like this?"

The beast flared his nostrils, but then slid his arms around me. "Like this?"

He sounded more like Lothar than the beast that time, even though his eyes were still red. "Yes, just like that. Thank you." I pressed against him tight and squeezed my eyes closed. "I'm so sorry," I whispered, and hoped that Lothar heard me.

Yes, he'd broken my heart all those years ago, but I'd broken him, too, in so many ways. The punishment he had suffered didn't fit the crime. Taking his memories, forcing him to live in ignorance, driving his beast to madness, was too much for anyone to suffer, and now he thought he'd forced himself on me as well.

My guilt was unbearable. Somehow, I would find a way to release him from the mating bond. He deserved a good female, someone like Asher, someone worthy of him, someone who would fight for him and cherish him. What he'd done had seemed unforgivable at the time, and even now it hurt to think about it, but he didn't deserve this. No. Better he thinks I am an evil, selfish bitch than blame himself for one more thing.

I felt the bond between us now, so strong, but it was as fractured as Lothar was. It wasn't flowing easily between us because Lothar was resisting it with everything he had.

He hadn't chosen this. First the option was taken from him, now it had been forced on him.

I didn't deserve him, didn't deserve his love, and even if there was no way to release him, he'd never truly be mine, not now. Not with how fucking messed up this was.

The beauty of what we could have shared was long

gone. It was a path not taken, a chance missed and lost forever. We'd both destroyed it, disrespected it, long ago.

Squeezing my eyes closed, I dropped my arms from around him and, breathing deep and slow, I started the slow, painful process of rebuilding the walls around my heart.

Lothar had been through enough, and I'd do whatever it took to save him from more pain.

To save him from me.

CHAPTER
TWENTY-FIVE

Lothar

DAWN TURNED the black night of the Outer Realm into a deep gray. Roxy was pressed against me, she had been all night. I needed to let her go and move away, but she felt too good.

Thank fuck the beast had started to listen to me now, when it came to being gentler with her, but more importantly, when he wanted to mate with her last night. I wasn't sure I'd be able to stop him, but somehow Roxy had gotten through, and he'd ignored his driving need to rut and held her instead.

This morning the beast seemed farther away and content to let me take the lead. He was still there, and pushed forward every now and then, but since yesterday I'd been able to take the lead more easily. I had to assume it was because Roxy was now my mate in truth. The beast had been calmer since, except of course, when he thought she was in danger and wanted to protect her. While I'd been in fucking turmoil, the beast had stepped up to do what I couldn't.

It was slow progress, but I could feel him coming back to me, as if bit by bit, that part of me was latching back on, wanting to make us whole again, like I did.

I shuddered. I thought for a while there, that I'd lost myself forever.

My gaze dipped to Roxy's hand, to where they'd taken two of her fucking fingers. She'd used a strip from the bottom of her shirt to wrap it. The rest of her fingers were missing nails, looking raw and bloody. My lips peeled back, my fangs sliding down. The pain she must have suffered, the fear—I looked at her shoulder and shuddered deeply. I could only see the edge of my mark, and the urge to slide her shirt to the side to get a better look at it, to check on it, had my fingers twitching.

I lifted my hand, unable to stop myself—Roxy groaned, her ass wriggling back and pressing firmly against my cock. I jerked my hips back, and Roxy jolted awake.

"What's going on?" she asked groggily.

She'd been so cold last night, her hands had been like ice, and it'd taken an hour of me holding her before she stopped shivering. The blessed silver cage plus her injuries were steadily weakening her.

"I can hear Sera and Beelzebub stirring in the tent," I said low.

She spun to face me. "Lothar?"

Having her this close was torture. I wanted to beg her for forgiveness. What I'd done in that cell was utterly unforgivable. I had also never *wanted*...or fucking *despised* someone more in my life. She and Lucifer had messed with my mind, lied to me, manipulated me, and what they'd turned me into as a result, would fucking haunt me for eternity.

I shuddered again, and my stomach rebelled at the thought of Roxy's much smaller body pressed against that cell wall while the beast snarled in her face, while he spread her thighs and shoved them around his hips...

No. I couldn't allow myself to think about that, not now. I shoved it down deep. We had to get through this first. We had to take down Sera and Beelzebub, then I could deal with the horror on repeat in my head. "I'm finding it easier to take control and hold it," I said low, swallowing thickly. "You should be safe now. I won't..."

"Lothar, what happened between us—"

"Is your hand okay? Are you in pain?" I said quickly, cutting her off, sure as fuck not wanting to go there.

"Nothing I can't handle."

"Good." I glanced back at the tent. "When they come out, don't let on that I'm back in control, yeah?"

She bit her lip and nodded. "Understood."

The fallen angel thought she could control me, but she was fucking wrong. "Before she put me in here, she called me her dog of war." I touched the collar around my throat. "She means to control me. She knows the...the mated bond will drive me to protect you, and plans to use these to bend me to her will."

Roxy's throat worked. "I thought as much."

Her hand pressed against my chest, and I sucked a rough breath in through my nose. "Don't touch me," I choked out. I was in control, but it was still tenuous.

She quickly pulled her hand away. "I'm so sorry, Lothar."

"You're sorry?" There was a snarl in my voice that I couldn't swallow.

"Yes, I'm sorry, you have no idea how much."

The sooner I could put distance between us, the better. "You think an apology could ever make this right?"

Her eyes were wide. "No, of course not, but I need you to hear me, really hear what I'm saying."

"I don't want to talk about it," I said.

"Well, we need to talk about it. I need you to understand that you didn't force yourself on me, you didn't—"

"I did, and we both know it. I don't need more of your lies to appease me. I was reduced to a rutting beast, Roxy. I shoved you against a wall, and I forced you to mate—"

"Stop it," she snapped. "Do I look traumatized to you? Do I look hurt or afraid?"

I ground my teeth. "We don't have time to talk about this."

"Yes, we do." She shook her head. "Lothar—"

"Maybe you're just used to fucking monsters against your will?" I fired at her. "Lucifer made you his whore, anyone he chose for you, right? So maybe you're not the best judge in this case."

She flinched.

I was so fucking angry with her that I'd been intentionally cruel. Every word had been said to cause harm. I was as much a monster as the ones I'd thrown in her face. I'd already physically hurt her multiple times, but obviously that wasn't enough for me. "I didn't mean that," I rushed out.

"You hate me, and I get it. Believe me, I hate myself more, but if you hear nothing else that I say to you, if you never speak to me again, please hear this—you did *not* force yourself on me. For better or worse, you are my mate, Lothar, and in that cell, in that moment, I submitted to you in every way. I submitted willingly. I wanted you too."

I was desperate for that to be true, to believe that she'd wanted me, too, that I wasn't the worst kind of monster a male can be. "I want to believe that."

"Believe it."

That was why she'd avoided fucking me, wasn't it? The times we were together on this trip. She was afraid that I'd work it out, that my body would give away the truth, which is exactly what had happened. "Then why?" I snarled. "Why did you and Lucifer fuck with my head? Why did you hide the truth of what we were for so long?"

Her slender throat worked. "You still can't remember anything of that time?"

"Obviously not."

She chewed her lip, and I hated that even now, even after the betrayal and the lies, I still wanted to kiss her so badly it fucking hurt.

"I...I thought it was the right thing to do at the time," she said.

In other words, she chose Lucifer over me. Like she would always choose Lucifer over everyone and everything. She'd tossed me aside, as if the sacred bond between us was nothing, to serve her king, to put his needs and wants first, and she didn't even have the courage to admit it.

"No, you and Lucifer decided to take that choice from me. Everything you do is for him, right? He comes first, always." I released her and sat up, fucking desperate to put some distance between us. The beast was still volatile, and with all the new emotions that had been awoken inside me when we mated, I was struggling on a whole new level.

"Lothar, please." She touched my arm.

I jerked it back, hissing with rage, with confusion. My mind spun and my body ached for a mate who had never truly wanted me. I fucking despised myself, despised her, for how much I wanted to pull her close again.

"We're mated, but that's where it ends," I growled out, unable to even look at her anymore. "You and Lucifer can have your happily ever after together. I'd rather be alone for eternity than be with someone who was so disgusted by the idea of being mated to me that she'd rather wipe my fucking memories, suppress my fucking instincts, and lie to me for centuries." I lifted my head and met her wide-eyed stare. "I may still be trying to figure out all these new emotions hammering me, but I'm pretty sure I've worked out the one I'm feeling the strongest right now. Hate. I fucking hate you, Roxy, for what you did to me. When we get out of this, I want you to stay the fuck away from me."

CHAPTER

TWENTY-SIX

Lothar

ROXY SLICED HER HAND, then curling her fingers into a fist, she closed her eyes and let her blood drip on the stones by her feet. They immediately rumbled to life, rolling and reforming, until they created our gateway from the Outer Realm back into Limbo.

I watched from the cage as Rox trembled, her powers still so weak after being surrounded by blessed silver for so long that she was struggling to maintain her hold on it. Seeing her like that lit fire in my gut and sent my fury higher.

Sera grabbed her arm before she could step through and shoved Roxy's confiscated phone into her hand. "Contact Death's mate, tell her you and Lothar are passing through, that you have Beelzebub and can't stop for pleasantries."

Roxy took the phone. "If I use the word pleasantries, she'll think I've been body-snatched by someone with a stick shoved up their ass, so how about you leave the script to me."

Outrage transformed Sera's face. "Watch how you speak to me, handmaid."

"What are you gonna do, torture me?" Roxy said, not looking up from her phone as she typed out her message. When she was done, she handed the phone back to Sera. "Does that meet your approval?"

Sera read over it. "Send it."

Roxy took the phone back and hit send. "I forget sometimes how behind you are with technology. I guess when you were last walking the earth, they were still using parchment and ink?"

"Are you trying to anger me, Roxana? Because I assure you, you won't like—"

Roxy's hand shot up when her phone beeped, cutting her off. "We got a reply." She clicked open the message. "She gave us the go-ahead." She looked up at Seraphina. "So what's your plan? We just waltz on through and cross our fingers that Death won't notice there's a fallen angel in his realm?"

Seraphina looked as if she were ready to tear Roxy apart. I'd guess it'd been a long time since someone had disrespected her like that. I didn't know what was going on, but it seemed like Roxy was pushing her, testing her. Either that or she'd developed a death wish.

The beast snarled, unhappy, wanting to get closer, to protect her, but I was able to subdue him without too much effort. Something had definitely changed. He wasn't as loud, like his thoughts and feelings were muted by my own, especially when we weren't in full accord. I was sure, no, positive, that we were almost completely one again. It couldn't happen fast enough for me.

"You'd love that, wouldn't you?" Sera said, a triumphant look on her face. "But my powers have only strengthened, even during my confinement. Death will only know I'm in Limbo if I choose it." She turned to Beelzebub then. "Get in the cage," she snapped, before her gaze slid to me. "You'll be pulling the cart, and if you or Roxana attempt to escape, I will activate your collars and you will both lose your heads."

Beelzebub opened the cage and I got out. The buzz in my head and the drain on my powers eased instantly. I stretched and cracked my neck, then kicked the cage shut behind Beelzebub, locking him inside, where that fucker belonged.

Sera let her robe fall then, underneath she wore leather pants and jacket.

"Who are you supposed to be?" Roxy asked, taking in the outfit that was almost exactly the same as hers.

"If we're stopped for any reason, you will tell Death that I'm one of your sisters," Sera said.

Roxy huffed out a laugh. "No one would ever believe that."

"I'm dressed exactly like you," Sera snapped.

"Yeah, but we're warriors, and you're just a cunt playing dress-up."

Sera's arm shot out in front of her, and Roxy dropped to the ground. Sera advanced, lifting her hand, and Roxy grabbed at her throat as blood slid down from beneath her collar.

"Stop," I roared and charged forward.

Sera's other hand shot up, aimed at me. "Stop where you are, beast, or I decapitate your mate."

I stopped in my tracks and snarled, watching as Roxy gasped for breath. Then, still holding her throat, Roxy grinned wide, blood coating her teeth. Then she lifted her other hand and flipped Sera off.

"Stop," I roared again, and not just at Seraphina.

All I wanted to do was tear the angel to bloody shreds, but Sera needed us both, and I had to believe that she wouldn't be stupid enough to kill Roxy, not yet anyway. I curled my fingers into tight fists as the evil bitch leaned in and said something for Roxy's ears only.

Rox bared her teeth but nodded.

Finally, Sera released her hold, and going by the way Roxy's body slumped in relief, Sera had retracted the silver spikes she'd at least partially shoved into Roxy's throat.

Seraphina straightened, her face a mask of twisted serenity. "This is where we part with our demon companions. Get ready to tow that cage," she said to me.

Roxy pushed herself to her feet, and Sera grabbed her arm and shoved her through the gateway.

"Hike, dog, hike!" Beelzebub said when I towed the cage after them.

I didn't react, though it fucking cost me. Sera thought I was still controlled by the beast, that I was nothing but an animal, and that's exactly what I wanted her to think. I kept the beast's red irises front and center, which wasn't hard to do when I was so full of rage. But more importantly, I needed her to trust me, to think she had all the control.

I stepped through the gate, and it closed behind us. Ignoring Beelzebub's complaints about the bumpy ride, I followed Roxy and Sera.

Roxy walked with all the arrogance of the fierce warrior she was, letting Sera know that although she was being compliant, she needed to stay on guard. And as furious... bitter, hurt... Fuck, I couldn't name all the emotions swirling inside me yet, but despite what I was feeling, I had to fight not to smile when I thought about the shit she'd said to Seraphina. At least her confidence managed to put me at ease. I had a tentative plan, one that might fail miserably, but it was all I could come up with, and Roxy would need to play along when the time came.

I refused to let Sera and Beelzebub take Hell, and I'd do whatever necessary to stop them, not for Lucifer but for my brothers and my pack, because losing Hell to Sera would fuck us all, not just the selfish fuck currently sitting on the throne.

There was no doubt in my mind that Roxy felt the same way, just for very different reasons. She'd protected her home in the past, many times, and she'd put herself last over and over again to serve and protect her king—even going as far as wiping our bond from my memory. So yeah, she'd be down to do whatever necessary to protect her beloved Lucifer.

I dragged the cage over a fallen log with a snarl, the wheels bouncing off the ground. Beelzebub cursed me out, and I ignored him and carried on. Once this was over, I'd put as much distance between me and Roxy as I could. I'd give her all the fucking freedom she wanted so badly.

How long had she known I was her mate before she had Lucifer wipe all knowledge of our bond? Had I known before they fucked with my head? My memories of that time were hazy, he'd obviously fucked with them as well. What did she think I'd do to her? Lock her in my den and keep her barefoot and in pup? I never would have asked her to leave Hell, or her sisters. Did she truly think so little of me? I had no idea, since she wouldn't tell me any-fucking-thing.

Roxy shoved her hand under her jacket and rubbed at her shoulder, right over my bite—and I finally got a good look at it. It was big, ragged, raw. The beast had been careless, he'd torn at her flesh in his excitement, and shame washed over me stronger than before.

My gut tightened painfully. The scar would be setting in, there was no fixing the mess I'd made of her shoulder. Usually a male would tend it regularly, lick it to keep it clean and stop our mates from feeling any irritation. She'd taken so much from me, so many things that I'd only allowed myself to hope for in quiet moments on my own. I'd imagined what it might be like to find my female, to win her trust, to finally make her my mate, to feel my knot for the first time, and give her my mark, a mark she'd wear with pride, like my brothers' mates did. I'd imagined a female carrying my pups, of climbing into bed with her at night and pulling her into my arms, of how the scent of her skin would call to me, no matter where we were.

Instead, I'd gotten lies and shame and pain.

My gaze slid down Roxy's strong body, and my heart slammed hard in my chest when I realized that's what I'd been feeling, the connection to my mate, and why the more time I spent with her, the more I'd been drawn to her.

The way she tasted was addicting, the way she fit against me as if she was made to be there, and yeah, her scent after it changed, had all been flashing red lights, but I'd been incapable of sensing the bond.

The scent thing, that'd been Lucifer as well, hadn't it? He'd made her smell in a way that repelled me, so I'd stay the fuck away from her. I growled again, and I realized the sound was all me. The beast and I were again one, and thank fuck for that.

If Roxy and I were going to get through this, if we were going to defeat Seraphina, I needed to be in total control over my actions. My gaze slid to Roxy again, and my stomach tightened. *Easier said than done.* She hadn't looked or spoken to me once since I spewed all my fucked-up, twisted-and-tangled emotions at her earlier. I shouldn't regret what I'd said, she'd more than deserved my anger, but I did. I told her I hated her, but what I felt wasn't that, I didn't know what it was. Despite everything, she was my mate, and hurting her in any way felt utterly wrong.

Nothing made sense. I was confused and angry. She was giving me the distance I'd demanded. Still, I didn't fucking like it. I wanted her to look at me. I thought I might actually needed it, as if her eyes on me had become some vital part of my survival.

Look at me. Turn around and look at me.

She didn't, of course, she couldn't read my mind. Thank fuck.

I forced myself to look away from her. Being mated meant nothing, not for us. She wasn't truly mine.

And she never would be.

))) · ● · (((

Roxy

We made it through Limbo without issue. Shame. I'd been hoping Death would appear, grab Seraphina by the throat and squeeze until her head popped clean off. Sadly, she was just as powerful as she boasted, and yes, far more powerful than she had been before her incarceration, which honestly didn't make sense to me. If anything, she should be weaker.

We reached the end of Limbo's skull path, and I cut my

hand and opened the gateway that would take us to Roxburgh. I glanced back, my hopeful little heart still wanting Death to come barreling around the bend—Sera shoved me—but he obviously wasn't coming.

"Let me out of this fucking cage," Beelzebub barked as soon as we walked through to Oldwood Forrest and the gate shut behind us.

Sera nodded at Lothar, and he immediately did as she bid.

His eyes were glowing red, but it wasn't the beast looking out of them, no, it was all Lothar, something Sera was too blind to see, and thank fuck for that.

"What now?" I asked, then motioned to Beelzebub, the giant, red asshole beside her. "We can't very well walk into the city with him looking like that, and the moment he sets foot in Hell, Lucifer will be all over him."

Sera kind of froze.

She hadn't thought that far ahead.

The panic in her eyes made me happy, even if it was only short-lived.

Lothar turned to us, baring his fangs and rolling his shoulders. To anyone looking, it seemed like he was struggling with his control. He was faking it. I'd been up close and personal with the beast, and that wasn't him.

"I know someone who'll help us," he said.

"Who? How?" Sera snapped out.

"Lucifer's grandson."

Holy shit. He had a plan.

Beelzebub growled. "His much beloved grandson? You're fucking full of it, hound. Don't fall for his tricks," he said to Sera.

"How much time have you spent with Zenon?" Lothar growled at Beelzebub.

The big demon scowled. "I may not have spent time with him, but I know—"

"You don't know shit. Zenon hates Lucifer. He blames him for his father's downfall. He plays nice, but if he had a chance to make him pay for what he did to Diemos, he'd take it."

Every word Lothar had just said was a complete lie. Zenon had nothing but contempt for his father, a male who had descended so far into darkness, he was now locked up in Hell with no chance of ever getting out after the horrific shit he'd done. Zenon and Lucifer were tight, it had taken time, yes, but they were family.

"Bullshit," Beelzebub said.

Lothar's red gaze sliced to me. "Tell them."

"What the hell are you doing?" I fired at him, playing my part. Whatever Lothar had planned, I trusted him, but they'd never believe I'd betray Luci willingly.

"I don't owe Lucifer shit after what he did to me," Lothar snarled. "Sera can fucking have that asshole's throne. I'm done with him."

"Tell me what you know," Sera fired at me.

Lothar's red eyes bored into me. He knew as well as I did, I'd have to get them to force me to speak. Torture hadn't worked, but a threat to Lothar, my mate, could. My stomach churned. I had to get them to hurt him to make this believable. "Fuck off," I bit out. "I'm not telling you anything."

Right on cue, Sera gave Lothar what he wanted. Fisting her hand, she aimed it at him. He gasped, dropping to his knees, clawing at his throat, and blood instantly slid down his chest.

"Stop!" I yelled, and I didn't have to pretend to be

distressed. Seeing him like that was killing me. "Leave him alone."

"Talk or he loses his head."

I dropped to the ground beside him. I also knew first-hand how much pain he was in. "Fine!" I yelled at her.

"And, Roxy, you will tell me how to take Lucifer's throne," she said, now that she knew my weakness. "Or he's dead."

"Whatever you want. Just stop hurting him."

Sera released Lothar and he fell to the ground, gasping for air. I pulled this head into my lap, holding his red gaze, and instantly got pulled deeper. I brushed his hair back, my hand shaking uncontrollably. "Are you okay?"

He swallowed thickly, then hardened his eyes and nodded.

"Talk!" Sera yelled.

"It's the truth, okay," I fired at her. "Zenon hates Luci... he was a knight of Hell before he knew of their connection."

Seraphina stilled. "I'm listening."

The knights were half demon, half angel, created long ago to control the first demons who escaped Hell and invaded Earth. "My granddaughters, they're both mated to knights, they live in the same compound as Zenon, and they...they told me the truth. Zenon has never stopped hating Lucifer. I just never had the heart to tell Luci." I let tears slide down my face, piling it on thick, though the tears came easily, like they'd been waiting for me to give in and let them fall for days. "The knights despise demons, obviously, add in Lucifer's, at times, careless attitude and self-serving decisions, well, it only managed to push them farther away. Zenon formed a close relationship with the angel Silas and his brothers eventually did the same. They chose where their allegiance lies. Lucifer just doesn't want to see it."

"Silas lost his wings," Sera said. "That angel certainly doesn't align them with Heaven."

"Exactly, it doesn't, because they want no part of Heaven or Hell. They came together due to their mutual distain of Lucifer, and to add insult, Silas lost his wings because of him," I said, piling on the lies. "Silas was in love with Ursula, one of my sisters, but she was only using him for information. Heaven found out he was consorting with the enemy, and he paid the price." Half-truths worked best. Silas had most definitely been in love with Urs, but Lucifer had no part in their short-lived relationship.

And with Sera being on the outs with Heaven, there should be no way for her to confirm my story.

"Roxy's going to tell me how to overthrow Lucifer, what do I need with his grandson?"

"I can tell you Lucifer's weakness, but you'll need more than that, you'll need an army. He's strongest in Hell. If you truly want to take his throne, you'll need to get him above-ground, and this is the only way to do it."

"What do you think?" she asked Beelzebub.

His cold gaze slid over me, then Lothar. "I don't know." He shook his head. "If they're telling the truth, we could have some powerful allies. The knights have always wanted Hell and its demons under tighter control. If you can reassure them that's what you want, too, as well as taking down Lucifer, it could work. But if Roxy's lying? If Zenon is Lucifer's devoted grandson"—his nostrils flared—"we're dead."

"Roxana's right, we'll need an army," Sera said. "We have demons willing to fight with us, but if we had the knights and the hounds as well? We'd have an excellent chance. Will your brothers join you, Lothar?"

His nostrils flared. "When I tell them what Lucifer did to me, yes. I know they will. We're pack. If you fuck with one of us, you fuck with all of us," he growled out. "And just so you know, Sera, that includes you as well. Best you think about that the next time you threaten to take my fucking head."

My stomach knotted. The hounds were all going to hate me as much as Lothar did once this was over. Relic would despise me for what I'd done to his sire. My heart broke a little more, and I quickly shoved down the pain. I couldn't think about that now.

Sera's gaze sharpened. "You suddenly seem a lot more in control, Lothar."

He bared his fangs, his eyes still glowing red. "I can control myself just fine...now." He thumped his chest.

"And who am I talking to? Lothar or his beast?" Sera asked, eyeing him shrewdly.

"Both," he said. "We are in full accord when it comes to Lucifer."

I grabbed his arm, doing what I had to, playing the part of wounded mate and loyal warrior to Lucifer. "Please, don't do this."

He jerked his away. "You don't touch me unless I tell you to. The mating bond is what's keeping you alive, and that's the only thing, understand?" he snarled.

He was walking a fine line. He had to convince Sera that his drive for revenge outweighed his connection to me, despite his instinct to protect me, and in that moment, I didn't know if he was acting anymore.

Sera's gaze slid between us, her eyes sparkling with

sadistic pleasure. She liked what she saw. "Why doesn't Zenon take Hell for himself? Make it all he wants, control the demons from the inside?" Sera asked.

"Because the last time Zenon tried to enter Hell, it almost killed him. I saw it myself." That was the truth. He had been as close to death as an immortal could get without decapitation.

She advanced on me. "Show me," she demanded, then placed her hand on my head, her nails scraping my scalp. I'd been locking her out all this time, and the idea of letting her into my head in any way made my skin crawl, but showing her this memory could be the only way to get her to go along with this.

I called the memory forward, showing her Zenon entering Hell, the panic from his brothers, the horror, then finally, him being tossed back out a while later, lifeless and on the verge of death. Sera tried to prod for more, but I slammed the doors on her, shutting her out.

She studied me for several moments. "I think it's worth meeting with this Zenon and testing the waters," Sera said to Beelzebub, then tossed me my phone. "Set up the meeting, but do not tell him what it's about. And he must come alone. I want to see with my own eyes how he reacts to what I have to say."

"Where?" I said.

"I'll sort it," Beelzebub said. "Tell him you'll get back to him with a location."

I nodded and opened my family text chain with Eve and Kyler and quickly typed out a message.

Then handed it back. Sera looked down at it. "A surprise party for Lucifer?"

"Zenon hates him, but he plays the devoted grandson

well. This way no one will be suspicious of me asking him to contact me directly."

When my girls read that, they'd be instantly suspicious, which was what I was banking on.

Now all we had to do was wait.

CHAPTER
TWENTY-SEVEN

Lothar

Zenon called Roxy back within the hour. Their conversation had been brief, but he'd agreed to meet with her. If Zenon thought this whole thing was fucking strange, which he absolutely would, he didn't let on. We'd seen him not that long ago at the bar. He knew we were on a mission for Lucifer and I was banking on him playing along when the time came.

I hadn't had much time alone with Roxy, but she assured me the message she sent her granddaughters would've made them suspicious. The male wasn't stupid, he had to know something fucked up was going on and would come prepared.

"How much longer must I wait?" Sera said, pacing back and forth in the ramshackle cottage we were now holed up in. Since Beelzebub couldn't leave the forest and risk being seen, he'd called on the demons who lived out here and ordered them to provide us with shelter.

"He should be here any moment," Roxy said.

The cottage was surrounded by demons. Beelzebub sat outside while they all buzzed with excitement, like he was a fucking celebrity.

I glanced at Roxy again. On the outside she appeared calm, almost serene. I knew better. It was almost as if I could feel what she was feeling. Somehow, I knew her belly was in knots and her heart was racing. I also knew she was afraid—for me.

Sera paced across the room again. If she was worried that Zenon would be suspicious by the location Roxy had asked him to meet, she hadn't said. Maybe she was just that naive after being locked up for so long. I got the feeling she was confused by a lot of things when it came to relationships between people, but then most angels had pretty shitty people skills. She was extremely powerful, yes, but she'd been locked up a long fucking time, she said and did things that came across as gullible. Or maybe she was just blinded by her thirst for power?

A commotion came from outside.

I strode to the window as Zenon landed right in the middle of Beelzebub's superfan gathering. His leathery batlike wings folded in, and he reached a tattooed hand back to the handle of one of his battle-axes, his yellow eyes sliding over Beelzebub. His long black hair fell forward as he tilted his head to the side and curled his lip. "You lost, Lord Beelzebub?"

Roxy rushed over and shoved the door open. "Zenon! I'm so glad you came."

He stared at Beelzebub for several more seconds, while B sat frozen under his cold-as-fuck stare.

"Please, come in," Roxy said.

Zenon turned to her, finally releasing the lord from that frigid gaze, and strode into the cottage. He spotted me and his head jerked up before those yellow eyes, so like Lucifer's, landed on Seraphina.

"Zen, brother," I said.

"Loth." He curled his fingers tighter around the handle of his axe.

"Appreciate you coming," I said.

"Yeah?" He looked between me and Roxy. "Someone want to tell me what the fuck's going on?"

Sera stepped forward. "I am Seraphina."

"I don't give a fuck," he said. "Start talking."

She bristled. "I understand you are Lucifer's grandson?"

He said nothing, just stared her down. Not that many years ago, the male avoided making eye contact. A lot had changed since he'd found his mate, Mia.

"I also understand that you don't think very highly of him?" she said.

Zenon didn't flinch. His gaze sliced to Roxy, then me, then back to Sera. He knew that was a lie. He also knew how much Rox loved Lucifer, how loyal she was. It would have only taken him a split second to work out where this was going. "You're accusing me of something pretty fucked up there, Seraphina," he said. "How about you get to the point."

Seraphina straightened her shoulders. "I have a proposition for you."

"No shit."

"Roxy tells me you are resentful of Lucifer after his actions toward your father, and that you wouldn't be unhappy if someone were to remove him from his throne... that you despise him, in fact."

He tilted his head to the side. "Roxy's had a lot to say, apparently." Not denying it, playing along like I hoped he would.

"I didn't give up that information voluntarily," Roxy rushed out.

Sera threw out a hand, and Roxy flew back against the wall, hitting it hard before she was pinned there.

Every muscle in my body went rock solid, and Zenon's nostrils flared, but thankfully he saw Roxy's subtle head-shake, telling him to let it go.

"You will be silent," Seraphina snapped at her.

"I know you hate him, Zen," Roxy rushed out. "But think what unseating Lucifer would mean. Please, don't listen to her." She was playing her part perfectly.

Sera hissed and swiped her hand through the air, and Roxy's belt was torn from around her waist, flew up across her mouth, and wrapped around her head. Sera turned back to Zenon, waiting to see what he'd do, if he'd rush to Roxy's aid or leave her to suffer.

Zenon didn't move a muscle. Didn't try to help Roxy, and I knew it had to be killing him, but nowhere near as much as it was killing me.

"You have my attention," Zenon said, turning back to Sera. "But if you want to do this, you better have a solid plan. Taking that fucker from his throne won't be easy."

Sera smiled.

›››·◉·‹‹‹

"How am I supposed to sleep with that still going on?" Roxy muttered on the other side of the cottage.

Several hours had passed since Zenon's visit, and we'd

spent that time chained on opposite sides of the room while Beelzebub and Sera *celebrated* their win.

Unfortunately for us, the walls were paper thin. I screwed up my face when Sera barked another order at Beelzebub, then moaned wildly.

I lifted my head so I could see Roxy, something I'd purposely avoided doing, and as soon as I laid eyes on her, all I could manage was a grunt. I'd filled her in on our plan, then I'd avoided talking to her. I was afraid if I spoke to her again, I might say something I shouldn't—like, maybe we should talk? Or please just tell me why you chose Lucifer over me?

What a fucking fool. How could I ever trust anything she said?

Laughter came from outside. There were demons out there drinking around a fire pit. Beelzebub had ordered them to guard the cottage. If anyone came for us, they'd be utterly useless, and the blessed-silver manacles and chains we were wearing had drained us of power, leaving us weak and without the ability to protect ourselves. The mating bond humming in the back of my skull wasn't helping the feeling of helplessness, and making the small distance between me and Roxy more than I could take.

The circumstances of our mating didn't matter to the beast. A newly mated hound was ruled by his protective instincts, and seeing Sera hurt Roxy today had shredded me. If I hadn't already regained control over the beast, I wouldn't have been able to stop myself from attacking the bitch, and more than likely would have gotten myself killed.

A hound forced to be parted from his mate physically fucking hurt, and having her so close but not being able to touch her made the beast very fucking unhappy.

I rubbed my hands over my face, dropped back down to my pallet and shut my eyes. If I didn't look at her, then maybe I could ignore this knot in my gut? I drew in a breath to calm my racing heart and got a lungful of her perfect, drugging scent.

"You're going with the silent treatment, now?" Roxy said. "Really?"

Fucking hell. "Not in the mood to talk, Roxy."

She blew out a long breath. "I get that, I do, but how the fuck can you say nothing when Beelzebub and Sera are getting freaky in the next room and are spouting some of the most bizarre dirty talk known to man?"

I smiled before I could stop myself. She wasn't wrong.

"He called his own dick a flaming hot Cheeto, Lothar. I mean, dude, say you have a little red, weirdly shaped, finger dick without saying you have a little red, weirdly shaped, finger dick."

A laugh rolled from me, taking me by surprise.

"The shudder I shuddered when she told him to 'eat mommy's ambrosia,'" she added.

I barked out another laugh. "I'm still trying to work out what was happening when he was making that fucked-up noise—"

"Like a happy seal," she finished and giggled.

"That's the one." Another laugh rumbled from me. I didn't laugh, not like this. It was a good feeling, though. Really good. Roxy's giggles were like music and made my chest feel warm, my belly tight—and made my dick hard as fucking iron. All humor vanished, and I listened as her giggles died down.

"That's a good boy," Sera cooed from the other room. "That's my very good boy." Then all noise in the other room finally stopped as well.

A shudder slid through me, something about her tone lifted the hair on the back of my neck, and my skin felt as if a million ants were crawling all over me. A feeling, a moment, that I couldn't see or reach flashed in my mind for a split second, then it was gone, out of reach, and no matter how hard I tried, I couldn't call it back. What the fuck was that?

"Lothar?" Roxy called, breaking the silence.

"Yeah?"

"I'm sorry everything's so messed up."

"Me too," I said, my voice rough as hell.

Several more minutes of silence filled the space. "If I could go back and change what happened..."

"But you can't."

And I could never forgive her or Lucifer for it.

TWENTY-EIGHT

Lothar

SERA CROWDED ROXY, and I could tell Rox was struggling not to punch the bitch in the throat. Instead she calmly handed Sera back the phone.

"What did Zenon say?" Sera snapped.

"His brothers want to meet with you before they commit to this. He said you can bring your demons if it makes you feel safer, but nothing moves forward until this meeting."

Sera's eyes were filled with excitement. "We've got them, haven't we?" she said to Beelzebub. "The knights will join us. With them and the hounds, we can't lose this."

"I'll need to talk to my brothers as well," I said. "I'll have to explain the situation. They won't just follow me blindly." I rattled my chains. "But I won't do it, if this"—I held up my bound wrists—"is what's in store for us. If you treat us with respect, we will be loyal to you, but if I show up to speak with them chained and guarded, there's no way they'll agree."

Her cool gaze slid over me. "You'll need to prove yourself to me, Lothar, if you want those chains removed." She walked closer, not stopping until the points of her nipples brushed my chest. I had to force myself not to shudder in revulsion. She grabbed my jaw. Roxy's chains rattled on the other side of the room, her growl of outrage making my stomach clench. Was her reaction real or for Sera's benefit? "Will you kiss me, Lothar, to seal our deal? Will you prove to me that I'm more important to you than your pathetic little mate?"

I curled my lip, giving her a cocky smile, when all I wanted to do was shove her away. If I didn't do this, she would send me with a guard, or she'd keep me here chained up when I needed to warn my brothers, so I did the only thing I could, I slid my hand up her spine and gripped the back of her neck, and instead of snapping it, like I wanted to —because the bitch wouldn't die that easily—I leaned in and kissed her, hard.

Everything in me violently recoiled, utterly repulsed, but when I released her, looking down at her flushed face and her now red, puffy lips, I smirked at her heavy, lust-filled eyes. "That proof enough for you?"

"For now." She licked her lips. "You always did know how to kiss a girl," she said huskily.

The way she said that made it sound like I'd kissed her before, and I'd sure as fuck remember that horror if it'd happened. Had she seen me with Roxy? That didn't seem right either. The way she said it implied the past, a past that she was part of. "You think so?" I said, not sure what to say, and not wanting to question her directly and risk pissing her off when I thought I might finally be winning her over.

"Oh, I never forgot. Memories of you kept me going long into my imprisonment."

Memories of me? What the fuck was she talking about? Roxy made a pained sound, and I turned to her. All color had drained from her face. She was gripping a chair beside her, as if she was struggling to keep her feet under her. I searched her face, the wild look in her eyes. Was the mating bond affecting her the same as it was me? She had to know that kiss was bullshit. That I'd fucking hated every second of it.

"Feels like history repeating itself, huh, Rox?" Sera said and laughed, a cold grating sound that made my skin crawl, like it had last night, that same feeling coiling in my gut, the sense of wrongness.

No, Roxy's reaction wasn't just about the kiss, it was something else. That same flash of memory that I couldn't hold on to burst through my mind, and the hair on the back of my neck lifted.

Sera grabbed my jaw and forced me to look at her again. "If you disappoint me, if you betray me, I will slaughter your entire pack, but I'll make them watch as I disembowel their mates and their children, and anyone else they love first," Sera said. "I have shown you but a fraction of the power I possess, and I will unleash it upon you and yours without question, if you fail me." She slid her hand down my chest. "You have one hour. If you're not back by then, or if I get even a whiff of deceit, Roxy will be the first to go, and mark my words, she will die screaming. Understand?"

Somehow I contained the fury burning inside me. "I understand."

She waved a hand, and the silver manacles around my

wrists, and the collar buckled around my throat, fell away, freeing me. "If you succeed, Lothar, there will be a prominent place for you in my court. You will sit at my side and know riches and glory like you've never imagined. I will reward you beyond your wildest dreams." She lifted to her toes and pressed her lips to mine, then dug her nails into my shoulders. "You have my sacred word." She smiled. "Now go."

I nodded and strode for the door.

"And, Lothar?" she called before I could walk out.

"Bring the alpha back with you. I'll need to hear it from his own lips."

I jerked up my chin and strode out.

Growls echoed loudly around the room. I'd quickly shared everything that'd gone down since Roxy and I left in search of Beelzebub, and my brothers were as furious as I knew they would be.

War crossed his arms. "We'll fight, we'll do whatever it takes to stop her, but you know this fallen better than us, what's the play here, brother?"

"Should we send someone for Lucifer?" Relic asked.

I shook my head. "We can't risk it. I have no idea how powerful she is. I've felt it, though, it flows from her like a constant current, ever growing. If she's stronger than Lucifer, if she's capable of taking him out, the chaos that would flow across the realms would be unimaginable. I think our best option is to get word to the angels, telling them what's going down tonight and they need to come pick up their trash. They have to be searching for her."

War nodded. "Agreed. Silas?"

"That's what I'm thinking. He's fallen, but he'll have a way to make contact."

"What can we do?" Willow said, striding into the room. The alpha's mate was not one to sit idle when shit was about to hit the fan, and neither were Jagger's and Relic's mates. Fern and Sutton were standing with Wills, looking just as determined.

War shook his head, and both Jag and Relic looked far from happy.

"You need an army, and we have two powerful covens at our disposal," Willow said.

"There are females and pups here that will need protecting if shit goes south. If this doesn't go the way we want, you're gonna have to ward the fuck out of this place and keep everyone safe."

I nodded. "The fight alone, with someone as strong as Seraphina, will cause unrest. There's no telling how a loss of balance, or even just a ripple, will affect the humans and demons in this city when she lets loose. This compound will need to be defended."

Willow's eyes were locked on her mate, as if they were silently communicating. She nodded. "I'll call the family here, so we're all in one place."

"Can you have someone get Lenny and bring her here?" Jag said.

Kurgan's female lived alone, and Jagger kept an eye on her.

"Of course." Wills turned to me. "Where's Rox?"

"Sera's holding her."

Willow frowned at my brothers when several of them growled at the mention of her name. "What's the problem? Why does Rome look like he's sucking a rotten egg?" She turned back to me. "Loth? What the hell's going on?"

"Roxy's my mate," I said, because there would be no hiding it. "We mated a few days ago."

Her eyes widened. "What? How is that possible?"

"She and Lucifer concealed the connection between us from me, a really long time ago. They wiped my memories."

"They did what?" she snapped, fury burning in her eyes.

"If you can find a way to break the bond, I'd really fucking appreciate it."

The fury in her eyes turned to pain. "Loth, no, there has to be a way for you both to—"

"She lied to me, Wills. She and Lucifer for *centuries*. There is no coming back from that."

She studied my face, then nodded. "I'll see what I can find out."

War strode over to her after that, for a private word, no doubt to tell her he was leaving with me. He pulled her into his arms and kissed her, and I turned away and caught sight of Relic doing the same with Fern, and Jag with Sutton. Seeing them like that, Roxy's face immediately filled my head, and fuck, yeah, that was a knife to the chest.

I couldn't think about that now. I couldn't imagine myself with her that way, that was not our future.

"Relic, you go share our plan with the knights. Tell them everything, tell them to lock down their compound, and have Zenon call Silas," I said.

He nodded, and after giving Fern one final kiss, he came to me. He gripped my shoulder, and for the first time, I recognized what was in his eyes, what was flowing from him. Relic loved me. My son loved me like a pup loved their sire. There was fear there as well, for me.

"Be fucking careful," he said gruffly. "You fucking hear me, Loth?"

I swallowed thickly, my new emotions taking hold of

my throat and gripping my chest, and I nodded. "You, too, son."

His nostrils flared, his gaze sharpening, and I knew he could see the same thing in my eyes. He squeezed my shoulder, then he walked out.

As War and I left the clubhouse a short time later, Willow was already on the phone with her family, calling them in.

CHAPTER
TWENTY-NINE

Roxy

WAR WALKED IN, Lothar right behind him. The hellhound alpha's gaze instantly sliced to me chained to the wall, and his lips peeled back. His unhappiness could be one of two things. Being a hound, he hated seeing females being mistreated, so it was either that or Lothar had told him what I'd done to him, and the sight of me induced rage.

My guess, a little of both. Seeing me chained would set off his protective instincts, whether he liked it or not.

I fought down the shame and guilt that had been steadily digging its thick roots inside me and watched as Sera preened and War shook hands with Beelzebub, like he wasn't the biggest and most traitorous piece of shit on the planet, and pretend he was on board with betraying Lucifer.

Lothar's plan was a good one—if it worked. If it didn't? I couldn't bear to think about it. The hounds and knights didn't have enough firepower to take out Seraphina on their own, and I hated relying on fucking angels. We all knew Lucifer getting anywhere near Sera was a bad idea, but he was the only one with enough power to take her on if everything went to shit.

"You will come to our meeting with the knights. Seeing that the alpha hound is joining this fight will help our cause," Sera said.

War jerked up his chin. "We'll be there."

Lothar kept sliding glances my way, then back to Sera, a strange look on his face. What that twisted bitch had said to him before he left earlier, after she'd forced him to kiss her, had him searching his mind for answers. I could literally see it in his eyes.

"It's time to leave," Sera said. "Roxy will remain here with our new friends to keep her company," she said and smiled like the evil cunt she was.

Lothar growled at me, then strode over. He looked down at me, baring his fangs. "Nothing you don't deserve, isn't that right, Rox?" he said to me, then crouched, crowding me. His hand shot out, grabbing me by the throat, just above the collar.

My hand flew up, gripping his wrist. "I'm sorry," I choked out, tears filling my eyes, because this hurt so fucking much. He wasn't on Sera's side, but he wasn't on mine either.

"Keep your worthless apologies," he snarled.

That's when I realized his hold on my throat wasn't tight, and that there wasn't rage in his eyes but determination. His gaze dipped, and I followed it. His knife stuck out from the top of his boot. He gave me a subtle nod. As soon as he released my throat, I fell forward, dramatically, clutching my throat, and grabbed his legs.

"Please, please forgive me," I said as I slid the knife free and tucked it under my thigh.

He shook me off, gave me a hateful look, then strode back to Warrick. They'd planned for this, guessing that Sera might decide to leave me here. I was chained, my powers drained, but I was Roxana the Blade, and the fuckers she was leaving here with me didn't stand a chance.

Still, as Lothar headed toward the door, he glanced my way again, and I could see the fear in his eyes, for me. "Maybe we should bring her with us," he said. "For collateral."

Sera grabbed his jaw, forcing him to look at her. "We don't need her and neither do you. She is nothing. You are mine now, Lothar."

Warrick's gaze hardened, but he managed not to screw his face up in disgust and, somehow, I managed to stay completely still and not explode to my feet and tear my own hands off in my desperation to get free of my manacles and take a bite out of the carotid artery pulsing delicately at the side of her neck.

Lothar nodded, but his hands were curled in tight fists.

"Come now, lover," Sera said to him, then strode ahead.

Lothar froze as soon as she said it, his head jerking up, his eyes clashing with mine.

Horror filled me.

He was remembering.

Oh gods, he knew.

Lothar took a step toward me again, and I shook my head.

Warrick planted a hand on his chest. "You need to keep walking," he growled low.

Every vein and tendon visible strained as Lothar fought with himself.

"Go," I mouthed.

"Fucking move, before Sera sees you," War snarled.

Lothar let War shove him out the door, but the look on his face broke me in two. Our love story was a tragedy, not some beautiful romance where we'd walk into the sunset hand in hand, and it was as impossible now as it was then. We'd hurt each other too deeply, there had been too many lies, too much pain. We'd incinerated any chance of a happy ending.

There was no time to think after that, because the demons outside the cottage had moved to the windows, realizing I was here alone. I stood, gripping the knife that had once been mine, that had been covered in Lothar's blood the last time I held it. At least the chains were long enough for a little movement, not much, but enough.

The door burst open and the biggest demon walked in. "Daddy's home," he boomed and bared his pointed teeth.

Lothar

I had to fight not to throw up as memories flooded back.

They were still hazy, but I knew we'd been in love. Roxy and me. We'd loved each other. Nights with her in my arms spilled into my mind, kissing, touching, whispered words in the darkness. Planning a future together, being forced to resist the urge to mate in truth, because Lucifer insisted that we wait.

We'd obeyed, like the loyal soldiers we were.

Handmaids weren't meant to have mates, but fate had overridden Lucifer and he'd been furious.

The memories around what happened right before it all went wrong were still jumbled, pieces missing. Lucifer had asked me to "charm" Sera, that if I got her to tell me what she had on him, he'd finally let us mate in truth. He'd convinced me that I wasn't being unfaithful because we weren't mated yet. He'd said that Roxy would understand, that she had seduced many people for him over the years, that it was for the good of Hell and would ensure his throne, that it was for the good of my brothers, but more importantly, it would ensure that Roxy would remain safe.

I didn't remember the details, but I did know that I did it. I did what Lucifer wanted.

I rubbed at my chest, phantom pain slicing through me as if it were happening now, not centuries ago.

Roxy hadn't done anything to me.

I was the one.

I'd done this to us.

I'd been too weak to tell Lucifer to shove his assignment up his ass, to ignore his orders and make Roxy my mate. I was the one who'd ruined everything.

"Loth?" War said quietly. "What's going on?"

The sun had gone down, and we were in a van. Relic was driving. Sera was beside him up front. Beelzebub took up the seat behind them, while War and I sat in the far back. I shoved my fingers through my hair. "Do you remember me and Rox together?"

War frowned. "No." Then his brows shot up like a fucking light went on.

"You remember something?"

His gaze sliced to Sera and his brows shot up. "What the fuck?" He shook his head, confusion all over his face. "I do."

Hatred filled his eyes. "How? What the fuck is going on? How did I not remember until now?"

"I'm assuming whatever block Lucifer had in place has broken. He took my memories of me and Rox, but not just from me, from everyone who knew what we'd been to each other." I swallowed, my throat dry as hell. "The specifics are blurry still, but I remember enough."

He cursed. "Why did he do it? What happened?"

"I betrayed her, War, in the worst way."

"Fuck," War muttered.

"How am I ever gonna make this right?"

He curled his fingers into a tight fist and tapped my leg. "We need to get through tonight, brother, then you have an eternity to win her back. For now, you need to focus. You need to win this for her."

I tried to take a steadying breath and failed. "She's back there, all alone."

"She's a warrior. Even chained, those demons don't stand a chance," War said, then he opened his phone and turned the screen to me. "And she has backup coming."

He'd texted Asher.

Thank fuck.

The van pulled into a large empty lot on the outskirts of the city. Seven huge males stood waiting. The knights had arrived. Zen and Chaos stood a couple feet in front, their brothers right behind them.

Sera almost vibrated with excitement. As soon as the van stopped, she shoved the door open. We quickly followed. There weren't many streetlights out here and the edges of the lot were drenched in heavy shadow.

Seraphina strode up as if she already owned them. "Zenon, introduce me."

Hatred burned in Zen's yellow eyes, but I watched as he

physically controlled himself. "Chaos," he said, motioning to the big male with a shaved and tattooed head beside him. "He leads us. Lazarus, Gunner, Tobias, Rocco, and Kryos stand behind us," he said, not looking back.

A huge smile curled her lips. "I am pleased to meet you all," she said. "I know of your origins, that your mothers were all fallen angels like me. Except, of course, for you, Zenon." She held out her arms. "I want...hope that eventually you will think of me as a mother figure to you all. I promise your fealty, your devotion to me will be rewarded in ways you could only dream of," she said, giving them the same kind of bullshit speech she'd given me.

Chaos's gaze slid to Beelzebub, then back to Sera. "We can't enter Hell. I'm not sure how much help we can be."

Her shrewd gaze slid around the knights. "Two of your brothers can, I can feel it. They've been there already. I can see it on them like a stain."

"That was a long time ago," Chaos said. "We stick together."

"I'm sure that's what you'd prefer, but I will need them to follow me into Hell, Chaos." Her eyes narrowed. "I need to draw Lucifer out, and I'll need protection. The more of you that can follow me the better. There is no other way."

Chaos was stalling, while my pack closed in, surrounding us.

We just had to hold her until the angels came, then this would be over.

As soon as they took Sera back to her prison in Heaven where she belonged, I could go to Roxy—and I would fucking beg her to forgive me.

)))●(((

Roxy

I slashed my knife and demon blood sprayed my face.

His hand flew to his throat and he snarled. "Bitch!" Then he charged at me again.

I ducked, hooked my chain around his neck, wrenched his head back and plunged my knife into his heart, his stomach, his genitals repeatedly, then spun back and let him drop to the floor with the three others I'd already taken care of. It wouldn't kill him, but it would incapacitate him for some time. The knife wasn't big enough to hack off his head, not easily, and I had three more demons surrounding me, hissing with fury.

"You come any closer, you'll end up with punctured balls like your buddy down there." I needed to get out of here. I needed to get to Hell, to Lucifer, and tell him what was happening. Something was wrong with this whole thing. I had a niggling feeling that wouldn't leave me alone. We were missing something, I was sure of it.

A howl echoed in the distance. Not hound, wolf.

The three demons in front of me froze, and the one closest to me tilted his head, listening.

"Sounds like backup just arrived," I said. "Now would be a good time to run."

"Fuck," the demon growled, then spun, and they ran for the door, bursting out and heading for the cover of the forest.

Four wolves exploded into the clearing before they could make it, and the sounds of their snarls and demon screams came next as the pack members tore them to shreds. I recognized one of the wolves instantly.

Asher.

She shifted, and naked and covered in blood, strode into the cottage. Her gaze landed on me. "You okay?"

"I'm good," I said and forced the growl from my voice. Asher was a good female, and Lothar's friend. Jealousy was not the emotion I should be feeling now, so I squashed it ruthlessly.

"War told us you might need help." She eyed the demons flailing on the floor. "Sorry we didn't get here faster." She held out a hand, and a hunting knife was tossed to her from another wolf just outside the door. She went for the closest demon, fisting his hair. "We were on the other side of the forest when I got the text," she said as she hacked off his head.

The demon turned to ash.

"Looks like you had it handled though," she said as the next demon's head hit the floor, then turned to ash.

"I appreciate the help. I have somewhere I really need to be."

Ash nodded, then dealt with demon number three. "Lothar okay? We heard from Willow, she told us to lock down the keep."

I wanted to tell her not to say his damned name, but again that was born from jealousy, from finally being mated in truth. "He's okay, but yeah, there's some serious shit about to go down, Ash." An angel fighting, using powers like Seraphina's in this realm, could cause some major problems. "The sooner you can get back to your pack and protect them, the better. The demons here might start acting weird, they might feel emboldened. Honestly, I don't know what will happen, but you need to be prepared."

She nodded. "Gotcha. Let's get you out of those chains, then we can do what we need to do to get through this."

I yanked at my chains. "Our best bet is to pull them from the wall. These aren't coming off, not without some serious magic. The collar, though. I think we can get it off. It's buckled on."

Ash closed in, her hand going to the fastening.

"You're going to have to do it fast. There are needles imbedded in it, made from blessed silver that will shoot out as soon as you undo it. I need you to tear them from my flesh as fast as you can or they could decapitate me."

Asher froze. "The fuck?"

"I can't enter Hell with this on, either, or same thing will happen, and Hell's where I'm headed."

"So no pressure, then?"

I laughed. "Nope. Just the fate of existence as we know it."

"You're being serious, aren't you?" Ash said.

"If I die before I can get to Lucifer, and things don't go the way we need them to, our world, the realms, will never be the same again."

Asher took a deep breath and shook out her hands. "Okay, then, Rox, let's get you to Hell in one piece, yeah?"

"I'd really fucking appreciate it, Ash."

"You got it. My count?"

I nodded.

"On three." She cracked her knuckles. "Three...two... one."

Fuck.

CHAPTER
THIRTY

Lothar

MY BROTHERS WERE HERE in the shadows and closing in. The plan was a simple one, hit her with every bit of firepower we had, distract her long enough for the angels to come and take her back. Between us and the knights, we had this.

"When do you want to draw Lucifer out?" Chaos asked Sera.

She opened her mouth to answer, then spotted Relic walking out of the shadows. Her gaze flew around the parking lot as my brothers walked forward and circled around us. She smiled, still convinced she was in control. "Excellent, the pack's all here. My pack."

Warrick crossed his arms and shook his head. "My pack."

"Now, now, Warrick. When I take the throne, you will all belong to me."

He bared his fangs. "You'll have to do it without us. Turns out, we've had a change of heart."

Her eyes grew wild as they took in the big males surrounding her, power snapping from each one. "What do you mean, a change of heart?"

"I mean, we would never betray Lucifer for you, Seraphina. To even think it shows just how fucking stupid you are."

"Did you really think we'd want anything to do with you?" I snarled. "You fucking disgust me. Kissing you was almost as repulsive as fucking you." The way I loathed her made me shake, and saying this shit felt good, but it wasn't the reason I was trying to piss her off. Most beings with powers had limits. If we could get her angry enough to let loose the majority of it in one big initial blast, then we might have a chance against her.

Wind whipped around her as the fury of her power snapped through the air. The knights spaced themselves out, stepping back and blocking her way. "You have made a monumental mistake," she shrieked.

Beelzebub roared, and Relic and Dirk shifted and pounced, tackling him to the ground, while Jagger bound him with iron forged in Hell, strong enough to hold him while we ended this.

Dirk stood over him, while Relic and Jagger took their places again.

"Looks like you're on your own, Sera," Chaos said.

"You think you are strong enough to defeat me?" she said and laughed maniacally. But the humor dropped as fast as it came, and she lifted her arms and screamed in rage, releasing a blast that knocked every male there on his ass.

I bounded back to my feet, and we all ran back to our

places, forming a circle around her again. Chaos and Zenon started first, blasting her with power from either side of the circle. Jagger and Rome next, then Kryos and Gunner. Over and over we took turns bombarding her. Keeping her off-balance, knocking her back.

She shrieked and blasted us with another wave of her power. We managed to keep our feet this time, pushing back with everything we had. Gritting her teeth, she squeezed her hands into fists. Jagger grabbed his throat and so did Rocco. I called my hellfire forth and blasted her with it. She screamed, but didn't let up.

"Where the fuck are the angels?" Chaos roared.

There was no sign of them, and Seraphina seemed to have a fucking endless supply of power. My brothers called their hellfire forth as well, and as one, we sent it at her, not stopping until she was engulfed in flames, fucking near burning ourselves out.

As soon as we lowered our hands, the flames died, and the knights hit her all at once, sending her wave after wave of crushing pressure, enough to bring down a fucking skyscraper, but still she remained standing.

Our power was dwindling, we couldn't hold her for much longer.

Sera spun to me and her arm shot out. Her power wrapped around my throat, and I was dragged toward her with invisible hands.

"You're all going to die," she screamed, then bared her teeth. "But you, lover, will be first."

Relic leaped forward, wrapping his jaws around Sera's side and shaking her. She sent him flying, slamming into a brick wall hard enough to shatter every bone in his body. I roared.

"The angels should be here," Jagger snarled.

303

"They're not coming. They're not coming for her," War roared to Chaos as I was shoved to my knees in front of Seraphina.

He was right. They weren't coming.

And now I was about to die without telling Roxy I was sorry, without telling her how much I loved her.

Roxy

I burst through the door to Lucifer's quarters. He was sitting on his chair, Mini resting along the back.

As soon as he saw me, he shot to his feet and strode over. The chains attached to my wrists fell away as he gripped my chin and lifted my head up and to the side, checking out the damage to my throat, then snatched up my hand. "Your fingers."

I pulled away. "Blessed silver." I wriggled the remaining fingers on my left hand. "And demon teeth," I said. "We need to go, you need to come with me."

"Why is Beelzebub not secured?" he said, because he knew we'd found him and he knew the lord of Hell was aboveground. Lucifer always fucking knew. He frowned. "You've been through a lot, my precious one, I felt your pain, but he needs to be locked down…" He stilled suddenly, before I could answer, and closed his eyes, breathing in deeply. When his eyes snapped open, they were glowing. "A loss of balance. I can feel it."

"It's Seraphina, you didn't know?"

His gaze burned with fury. "The angels wouldn't tell me anything. No matter what I tried. No matter what I offered. I've had blind spots this entire time, to what was happening, there was so much I couldn't see."

"She escaped Heaven. She's making another play for your throne. She's the one who's pulling Beelzebub's strings. Right now, the knights and the hounds are fighting her to protect it, to protect you. You need to help them before she brings down the entire city."

Lucifer's eyes flashed. "I can't believe those mother-fucking angels are behind all of this. They set her free."

Lucifer tried to touch me, and I jerked back before I realized I was going to do it.

His yellow eyes bored into me, probing inside my head, and when he flinched, I knew what he'd seen.

"Lothar knows what we did," I choked out. "That we took his memories from him, that we hid who I am to him. You said you've had blind spots, was I one of them? While I was gone, did you know what was happening to me? To Lothar?"

"Yes," Lucifer said. "You and Lothar are mated."

"Do you know how it happened?"

"Yes."

The betrayal almost fucking choked me. I hugged myself. "Even though it's the last thing you wanted, you let it happen anyway? And worse, the choice was taken from Lothar again, because of what we did to him."

His expression didn't change. "What will this mean going forward?"

For him. What did it mean for him, he meant. I still loved him, but Lucifer was a selfish being. He always had been. "It means, I'm leaving. You, Hell, this city, to free Lothar from me."

"The fuck you are. I won't allow it," Lucifer growled.

Again, all he cared about was himself. "You said you sent me to that room to catch Lothar and Seraphina so I'd know the truth," I fired at him. "But you sent me there so you could keep me all to yourself."

He said nothing.

Pain sliced through me, the rest of it unraveling. I'd never wanted to believe it, but I knew it was the truth. "But that's not all, is it? You put Lothar up to sleeping with Seraphina, didn't you?"

"Roxana—"

"Answer me."

"I gave him a choice. I didn't force him to do anything. You can blame me all you like, but Lothar could have refused me."

"Really? And what were his options? Fuck Seraphina or what?"

His features were calm. "I needed information. Sera always had a soft spot for him, you know that. I gave him the choice to charm her, to get the information I wanted, and as payment, he would be free to mate with you."

Rage rolled through me so strongly, I shook. "And if he didn't?"

"He could never have you," he said without a shred of emotion.

I grabbed for the wall, my heart breaking all over again. "That's not a choice," I cried. "Especially since you never planned to honor it. You made him think we'd finally be together, in truth, then you sent me to find them so you'd get what you wanted, anyway. So you'd keep me here, tied to your side." Then the rest of it finally hit me. "Oh gods," I choked out.

"Let me explain," he said. "You're misreading—"

"I'm not fucking misreading anything! For the first time, I'm finally seeing the truth." I held his stare. "The deal you made with Sera that day, the one where she gave you the gem that you'd convinced me could harm you, the deal where I agreed to give up Lothar to protect you..." I gripped my stomach, feeling fucking sick. "You didn't need to make a deal, did you?"

"The gem can, and still could harm me."

"That's not what I'm talking about."

"Roxana," he said, shaking his head. "Stop this."

"You didn't need to make a deal, because the angels were already there, waiting to take her. You'd already made a deal with them. You took Lothar's memories of me, his knowledge of our bond, *because you could*, because you didn't want to share me, because I was too valuable an asset for you to lose. You used the situation with Sera to manipulate me."

"My precious one, you need to listen to me." He cupped the side of my face, and I jerked back again.

"You told me if Lothar ever learned who I was, if he one day got his memory back and knew I was his mate, there'd be dire consequences...but for who, Lucifer?" I demanded, my voice shaking as hard as I was.

He said nothing.

"For you, right? The dire consequences were you losing me, *right*?" I demanded louder.

"Losing you would destroy me," he said roughly.

I shook my head. "You made me think it was my idea. You played me. You used Sera's attempt on your throne back then to kill two birds with one stone. I have been devoted to you, protected and worshiped you, Lucifer, my entire life. You are my family, my king, my maker, the first being I ever loved." I looked up at him, holding his beautiful yellow eyes, and my heart cracked in two. "I would have done anything for you, and I have, over and over again. I've given my body, my blood, devoted every moment of my life to you and what you wanted, yet you couldn't let me have one thing for myself? You couldn't let me have Lothar."

He flinched, the first and only sign of real emotion. "Roxy, please—"

"You have destroyed any chance Lothar and I had to be together. We have hurt each other beyond measure. He hates me now, because of you. He despises me. There is no future for us. You've ruined the rest of eternity for me, and you don't even care. I would have laid down my life for you, Luci. Don't you see, I would have remained your most devoted servant until the end of time. Loving Lothar doesn't take away the love I have for you. They are not the same. You are my king and my family. Lothar is the love of my life."

"Why do you think I sent you with Lothar on this mission? It is because I knew you could reawaken the bond between you both. Yes, I could have stepped in at any time while you and Lothar were away, but I let it play out, I stayed away because I knew the outcome. I wanted you to find your way back to each other. I regretted what I did to you both back then, and this was my chance to make things right."

"I don't believe you."

He sucked in a breath.

I'd hurt him, but I wasn't going to take it back.

"It's the truth," he said roughly.

"Even if I did believe you, it's too little, too late," I rasped.

"No, it's not."

"Yes, it is. Because now I've lost both of you."

"You will never lose me," he said, his gaze wildly searching mine. "I'll always be right here."

"But that's the thing, Luci, I won't be." I shook my head. "I'm already gone."

"No." His yellow eyes flared. "I won't let you to leave."

"The only way you'll stop me, is killing me."

He cupped my face, and this time I didn't shove him away. "I was trying to make things right and I hurt you again. That is the last thing I wanted. I'll do anything you want, Roxy, to fix this."

Nothing could make this right. Nothing. Still, I gave him an answer, because time was running out. "Kill Seraphina."

By the time we exited Hell, the city was in chaos. The power was down. Humans ran around looting and fighting. Fire alarms were going off, cars were left in the streets haphazardly, while demons prowled, taking advantage of the mayhem.

We ran toward the source of the surging power, until we were finally close.

Lucifer snarled when he saw Seraphina, glowing, her intense strength rolling off her.

"She isn't this strong," he bit out. "The angels did this. They increased her powers. Then those fuckers set her free."

"The forgotten prophecy," I yelled over the storm whipping around me.

His jaw hardened. "Yes. They want to change the course of fate."

A roar reached me through the storm. Lothar. I searched for him, and my heart almost burst from my chest when I saw him. He was on his knees in front of Sera, his body at an odd angle, while his brothers and the knights blasted her with their power over and over again, trying to get Seraphina to release him.

Fury burned through me as I drew knives from the sheaths at my hips. I needed to move now, while she was distracted. "I'm going in. Be ready," I said to Lucifer.

He nodded. "We always have been a good team, Rox."

"Just be ready," I said, and in the cover of shadow, I sprinted around the perimeter of the lot until I was behind her. Lothar roared, blood sliding down his face from his eyes, nose, and mouth. Her powers were depleting, but she was still incredibly strong, and she was killing him.

I gave Lucifer the nod, then gritting my teeth, sprinted at her and leaped in the air.

She dropped Lothar, sensing me, and spun before I could reach her. She slashed her hand through the air. It had the same effect as a blade, and I felt the scar at my side tear. The pain was nothing compared to my rage, though, not even close. I slammed into her, wrapped myself around her, and thrust my blade into her temple, jerking it around and scrambling the bitch's brains.

It wouldn't last long, not with her healing abilities, but long enough for Lucifer to do what he needed to.

He strode forward, his immense power flowing from him. He was incredibly strong, but with the angels' interference, he wasn't strong enough to destroy Sera on his own, not like she was. Now he had a fighting chance.

His eyes glowed brightly, and beams of light burst from him, from all around him. He was incandescent as he lifted his hands and, baring his teeth, sent all that power straight at Sera. It slammed into her chest, and she screamed, struggling as he lifted her off the ground. I didn't let go of her, twisting my blade, not letting her rapid healing abilities unfuck her mutilated gray matter.

I felt her body heat, so hot it burned my skin, but I refused to let go. No, I clung tighter and pressed my mouth to her ear. "Bitch, just so we're clear. Lothar is *mine*," I snarled.

Seraphina shrieked in outrage—and exploded. Her body literally blowing apart.

I dropped, landing in a crouch, and spun, searching the lot, making sure she was truly gone. When I turned back, the hounds and the knights were staring at me.

"Holy fuck, Rox," I heard Roman say.

I ran to Lothar, dropping to my knees beside him. "You alive?" I choked out. He had multiple broken bones and was bleeding badly.

"Take more than that to kill me," he choked out.

I let out a sigh of relief. Sera's powers would make his recovery slow, but it wouldn't be fatal.

Bright light flooded the lot, and I looked up as three angels landed several yards away.

"You're a little late," Lucifer said and strode toward them. He took them in from head to toe. "We don't even warrant an archangel or two? They sent you three chuckle-heads instead?"

The one in the middle bristled. "We are more than powerful enough, I assure you."

"Well, it doesn't really matter now, does it? You missed all the fun."

"We came as soon as we could," another one said.

"Sure you did," Lucifer said. "You also let her think she'd escaped prison all on her own and boosted her powers to levels Seraphina should never have possessed."

They didn't bother to plead their case and were gone a moment later.

"They were watching the whole fucking time, weren't they?" Zenon growled. "They had no intention of taking her back."

"What does this mean?" War added.

"It means that we need to be on guard. The angels want change, and they are willing to do anything to get it," Lucifer said.

I tried to stand, and Lothar grabbed my arm. "Where are you going?"

"I'll be right back," I said and smiled down at him as I gently pulled from his hold. Rome said something to him, and I quickly backed up and walked into the shadows, my heart shredding even more.

My phone beeped, and I pulled it out of my pocket.

Luci: *Don't leave. Come home.*

I looked up. Lucifer stood across the lot from me, Sera's scattered remains between us. I quickly typed my reply.

Roxy: *I will always love you, Lucifer, but I'm not sure I can forgive you. If you love me, too, you'll let me go.*

He looked down at his phone, and I turned mine off and shoved it in my pocket before he could reply. Lothar was still on the ground and I heard Relic ask where I was, which was my cue to leave.

I spun around and sprinted away. I didn't look back.

Lothar told me he wanted freedom, and I loved him too much to force him into something he didn't truly want. I'd taken so many choices from him, but not this one.

To make him happy, I would give him his freedom—I would set him free.

CHAPTER
THIRTY-ONE

Lothar

"HOW MUCH LONGER WILL I be confined to this fucking bed?"
I growled.

Willow poured out a measure of some foul-smelling
shit. "Another day, two at most." She poured it into a mug
with water to dilute the putrid taste and handed it to me. "I
know this sucks, but these aren't normal injuries, so normal
rules don't apply. You need to be patient."

I chugged back the potion. No, they weren't normal. I
hadn't healed like I normally did. The lacerations had taken
a week, the broken bones, so far, almost two. Due to the
prolonged exposure to blessed silver and my injuries
caused by a fallen at her most powerful, my body had taken
a serious hit.

Being a fucking invalid wasn't something I'd ever experienced before, and I felt more insane now than I did when

my beast had taken over and used me like a motherfucking puppet.

"I put a sleep draft in there as well," Wills said.

Fuck. "I don't want to sleep. I want to get out of this bed and find Roxy."

She sighed and stood. "Well, you can't, and you haven't slept for days. That won't help your healing, and when you are ready to get up in a day or so, you'll fall over from exhaustion. So stop complaining and go to sleep."

I'd fallen over several times while trying to leave, reopening my wounds and refracturing my femur. I rubbed my hands over my face. "Has anyone heard from her?"

Willow shook her head.

"Any word from Zenon? Lucifer still hasn't talked to her?"

"No."

"What about her granddaughters? Urs? Have they heard from her?"

"No, Loth, no one has." She gave my shoulder a squeeze. "I promise if we hear anything, you'll be the first to know." Her eyes softened. "You'll find her."

The door opened and Relic walked in.

"Excellent," Wills said to him. "You can stop him from trying to get out of bed. And don't even think about helping him leave, his bones aren't finished healing. This is where I remind you of what happened last time. His bones need another twenty-four hours. He'll manage a few steps, then be flat on his back again, and we'll be back to square one." Relic had had a lot more broken bones than me, but his healing hadn't been hindered, and he'd been back to full strength in a matter of days.

Relic smiled. "His ass will be staying where it is."

I growled.

They both ignored me.

"I've given him a sleep draft, so with any luck, he'll sleep and we'll all get a nice break."

Relic chuckled as she walked out, then sat in the chair they'd put beside my bed. I had a constant stream of visitors, or more around-the-clock guards making sure I didn't try to go anywhere.

"Anything?" I asked him as soon as she shut the door.

He shook his head. "None of us have been able to pick up her trail. She has to be in another realm or there's something or someone concealing her."

"Fuck." I snarled. "I can't take much more of this. I need to find Roxy. I need to find my mate. There's still so much from that fucking day missing from my memory. I know there's more. I can fucking feel it...here." I thumped my fist against the center of my chest.

Relic sat back. "I get it. I know what it's like firsthand, and yeah, I'd lose my fucking shit if I wasn't able to go after Fern immediately. At least you know Roxy can protect herself, yeah?" He leveled me with a stare identical to my own. "It might take you a while to find her, not trying to piss you off, but Wills is right. You need to let yourself heal or you won't get far. One more day's rest, you're almost there, and you'll be good to go."

My fucking eyes drooped. Willow's sleep drafts were strong as hell, or at least the ones she gave me. She'd knocked me out when they first brought me back here after the fight. I fought to leave then, even though I couldn't fucking stand. In the end, War and Relic had held me down while Willow poured that shit down my throat. I'd refused it since, which was why she'd taken it upon herself to slip it in my drink.

I rubbed at my eyes. "I can't sleep right now."

Relic chuckled. "You sound like one of the pups, you grumpy old fucker. Shut your damned eyes and get some rest."

My lids drooped again, and I snarled. "When I'm better, I'm gonna kick your ass."

"Impossible. I'm the newer, stronger, highly improved version of you. It'd be like you trying to win against a supercharged version of yourself."

Somehow, he always managed to make me smile—even as my head tipped to the side and my body had become a deadweight. I blinked heavily.

Relic stood, lugged my huge ass down the bed, tossed the extra pillow aside, and pulled the covers up. "When you wake up, you can go find Roxy."

I tried to answer, but only muttered incoherently.

Relic patted me on the fucking head and chuckled. "Sweet dreams."

The nightmare rushed forward instantly.

Sera shoved me on the bed, climbed up and started riding. My stomach rebelled. I wanted to throw the fuck up. Her scent was disgusting and made the churning in my stomach worse. If Lucifer hadn't given me a powerful tonic, I would be lying here flaccid and emptying my stomach all over her sheets. The concoction was the only reason I was able to get hard.

I gritted my teeth when she dug her nails into my chest and moaned.

I was doing this for Roxy. I was doing this for us, so we could be together like Lucifer promised.

I squeezed my eyes closed. I didn't want to think about Rox, not now, not while Sera touched me, not while she called me hers. I would never be hers.

"Good boy," she crooned. "You're mine now, aren't you, Lothar."

The door crashed open on the other side of the room.

Sera spun around with a hiss.

Oh fuck. No. I shoved Sera off as Roxy flew across the room with a bloodcurdling scream.

She slammed her fist into Sera's face with another cry, right as the angel snatched up a blade from the bedside table and thrust it into Roxy's side, then dragged it downward.

With a roar, I shoved Sera away, grabbing for Roxy, clutching her to me.

She swayed on her feet, then looked up at me, her big blue eyes wide and filled with agony.

She shook her head wildly. "Roxy, please, I can explain—"

"No." Her hand was a flash of movement, she drew it back, and that's when I saw the knife she held, a split second before she thrust it into my heart.

She dropped her hand, leaving it imbedded in my chest. I clutched at it, gasping for air. It wouldn't kill me, but the pain radiated through me so fiercely, I fell to my knees.

She held my gaze, and a tear streaked down her face. "Now your heart feels like mine," she choked out, then stumbled from the room, leaving a trail of blood in her wake.

My eyes snapped open with a gasp, my hand fisted against my chest.

The dream, the memory, those images flashed one by one through my head. I slid my hand away and looked down at the darker patch of skin there. I'd never known what it was. I assumed it had always been there. There had been nothing special about the blade, it shouldn't have been able to leave a scar, but it had. That knife, it was the same one I'd been carrying around with me since, that I hated being without, the same knife Roxy had now. I rubbed at my chest. I realized I'd been carrying Roxy's pain around, a physical manifestation of the agony I'd caused her all this time and I'd had no fucking clue.

Roxy had lived with this, these memories, this pain for so fucking long. She thought I'd betrayed her. And I had. I thought I'd felt broken and desperate, the last couple of weeks, but that had been nothing.

The full force of the loss we'd suffered crashed over me, a jagged ball of agony settling like stone in my chest. All this time, since my memories were taken, I'd been pushing her away. I always pulled away first when she'd hugged me. I'd avoided her, turned her down when she just wanted to hang out. Fuck, I couldn't believe she wanted to be anywhere near me, let alone hug me after what I'd done. I couldn't fucking bear to think about it. My female had been pining for me, for her male, a pathetic fucking male who had *betrayed* her, and I'd shoved her aside, over and over again.

I would not wait another moment to look for her. Not one more fucking second. I shoved back the covers and was relieved when there was no shooting pain through my legs and back. Finally. I snatched my phone off the bedside table and checked the time. *Motherfucker.* I'd slept twenty-four hours. I'd have been pissed, if it hadn't actually worked.

I felt rested and my body was finally and completely healed. Showering quickly, I dressed, shoved my phone in my pocket, and strode from my room.

"Whoa, where do you think you're going?" Willow said, walking toward me.

"To find my mate," I said, with a little more growl than I intended.

She stopped in front of me, her eyes narrowing. "You look a lot better this morning."

"I am."

She curled her fingers around my forearm. "Glad to hear it."

"Thank you for taking care of me. I know I didn't make it easy," I said, because I wasn't sure how long I'd be away, and Willow had put up with me, hadn't given up on me when I acted like a giant asshole.

"That's what family's for, right?" She pulled me in for a tight hug, and when she stepped back, she smiled up at me. "Now go find Roxy and bring her home."

I nodded and strode up the stairs, through the club-house, and headed for my bike.

"Loth!"

I turned to find Relic jogging toward me.

"Good to see you on your feet," he said when he reached me. "Don't think you're going to have to walk far on those newly healed legs, though. Pretty sure I know where Roxy is."

CHAPTER
THIRTY-TWO

Roxy

"How are you feeling today?" Eve said as she walked into my room. Lysander held her hand, jumping and skipping along beside her, and Revere clung to his hand, the pair of them giggling the whole way. They were cousins, less than a year apart, but behaved and looked more like twins.

Kyler followed, carrying a tray laden with food. "You need to eat."

I hadn't meant to stay here. After I ran from the battleground, I'd come here to say goodbye to my girls, but they'd seen how upset I was and convinced me to stay. They'd tended my wounds, fed me, loved me. Eve's mate, Lazarus, had even made me a leather guard for my hand, since the stumps where my fingers had once been were still sensitive. At least my fingernails had grown back and my scar had returned to how it was before Sera escaped. I was counting that as a win.

I crouched down. "Hello, my babies."

"Lovey!" Ly and Rev ran to me, giggling and squealing.

I scooped them up and smothered them in kisses. "You make your lovey so happy," I said, giving them more kisses.

"I'll never get used to that," Ky said. "You don't look old enough to be anyone's grandmother."

We looked the same age, and we all had the same black hair and blue eyes. We could be sisters, if it wasn't for the centuries that separated us. "Yes, my darlings, you are stunning, and you can thank me for that," I said and grinned.

Eve smiled, but her eyes were gentle, concerned. "Relic's been calling the compound. Zenon lied and said he hadn't seen you, but I think he suspects something."

I rested a large toddler on each hip and went to the window, looking out. "What about Lothar? Has he called?" If he'd called me, I wouldn't know. I'd blocked his number the night I ran, like a coward, afraid of what he'd have to say.

"Nothing yet," Ky said. "He's still healing, according to Relic, but I'm sure he will—"

"He won't." I needed to leave. I had to stop waiting, hoping that he'd change his mind. Of course he wouldn't. He'd never forgive me for letting Lucifer steal his memories, from stealing our connection the way I did, and I didn't blame him for that. I turned back. "I don't want to cause trouble for Zenon, or for your mates. I don't want anyone to have to lie for me. I'm behaving like a coward." I pressed a kiss to Ly's forehead, then to Rev's. "I love you both very much, my sweet babies, don't ever forget that," I said to them, then put them down.

"You don't need to leave," Eve said, reading me easily. "Please, stay a little longer."

My eyes stung, but I refused to let the tears fall. "I can't

be here in this city with him. I just can't, it hurts too much."
I grabbed my jacket from the chair beside me and slid it on.
It was Lothar's, the one I'd been carrying around for
centuries. I'd even risked going back to Hell to retrieve it
before I came here. I lifted the collar to my nose and
breathed deep, positive I could still smell him on it. "I need
some space, some time away to...to..." Get over it? That
would never happen, and I refused to allow Lucifer to take
the pain away. Taking it away would make it as if Lothar
was never mine, and I never wanted to not have that, no
matter how painful it was.

Eve and Kyler came to me and wrapped their arms
around me. I hugged them back, tight.

"Promise you won't do anything reckless, or put yourself in any danger," Kyler said.

"I promise."

"And make sure you call and text," Eve said.

"I will."

I stepped back as a howl echoed in the distance. I froze.

I had to be hearing things.

Lysander howled, imitating the sound, then Rev copied
him, and they both giggled uncontrollably.

"I didn't imagine it, then?" I rasped.

"Definitely not imagining it," Eve said and rushed to the
window as another howl rang out. "Rox, I think you need to
see this."

My heart was in my throat as I strode over to her and
peered out the window.

Oh gods.

Lothar had climbed up onto the tall fence that
surrounded the compound. He stood on it, shirtless, chest
heaving as he drew in a lungful of oxygen, tilted his head

back, and let out another mournful howl. I shivered, goose bumps prickling across my skin.

The knights had gathered below him, standing in the large lot just beyond the underground garage. They obviously hadn't opened the gate for him, but they weren't attempting to stop him, either, and nothing got over that fence.

"Why aren't they stopping him?" I choked out.

"I think...I think because they know what it's like to be mated, and they don't need to have been separated from us to know how much they'd hate it."

I scanned Lothar's body, tattooed and muscled, and now with several new scars. "But...why would he come here?"

"Why do you think?" Kyler said, squeezing my hand. "He's calling for you, Roxy. He's calling for his mate."

Eve wrapped her arm around my shoulders. "Go to him."

"What if—"

"No what-ifs. Talk to him," Ky said. "If you don't, if you leave without hearing what he has to say, you'll always regret it."

She was right, of course. There was no way I could leave, not without hearing what he had to say first, even if it was "Get the fuck out of this city and leave me the hell alone."

"Okay." I tried to calm my racing heart. "I'll talk to him." My legs shook as I walked from the room, down the hall and took the elevator to the underground parking lot. Shoving my hands in the pockets of my jacket, I walked up the ramp, through the opened garage doors and outside.

Zenon turned when I surfaced and elbowed Roc. I

nodded, and the knights walked away, heading back into the building and leaving me standing there in the quiet lot.

Lothar stared down at me, breathing hard, the veins and tendons bulging under his skin as he watched me. He jumped, dropping from the tall fence and landed with ease. He'd fully healed. At least he was okay. He straightened then and strode toward me, a determined look on his face. His eyes were locked on me, wild, and as he drew closer, I took a step back, then another. He was angry. I thought I could absorb his rage, but now confronted with it, I wasn't sure my heart could take it.

I spun, about to run, but he hooked me around the waist and hauled me up against him. His mouth pressed against my ear. "Oh no you fucking don't. You are going to stay right here and hear me out."

I gasped, pain washing through me, and then I was struggling, trying to get away because I couldn't bear to hear how much he despised me. With a growl, he prowled into the parking garage and spun me around, pressing me against the wall.

"I know you're angry, and you have every right to be." I struggled, the multitude of ways I knew how to escape a hold like this, every defensive move I knew, vanished from my mind. I was helpless in his arms, helpless against the warmth of his skin, even with his fury crashing into me. "I'm leaving. I'm going now. I promise—"

"Roxy—"

"You won't have to see me again."

"Roxy," he growled, so loud I startled.

I blinked up at him.

"You are not going any-fucking-where, you hear me?"

I shook my head and the tears fell, no matter how hard I

tried to fight them. "Why? Why would you want that? I can't...I can't be here, and not...while you..."

"While I what?"

"While you hate me."

He moaned, the sound distressed, broken. "Hate you?" He shook his head and dropped to his knees in front of me, his massive arms wrapping around my waist. "I'm not angry at you, I'm fucking furious with myself. I'm here, kitten," he choked out, "to beg your forgiveness. To fucking plead with you not to leave me. I remember, baby, I remember every moment with you, every fucking beautiful second we spent together." He made a rough, wrecked sound in the back of his throat. "And I remember what I did, I remember how I got this," he said and pressed his fist to the center of his chest, over the scar there. The scar I'd given him. "How I fucking blew us apart."

I stared down at him in shock. I shook my head, confused, scared, but gods, hopeful. "I wasn't thinking straight," I rasped. "Sera followed me, she offered Lucifer a deal... I should have said no, I should never have agreed to it, but I hurt so much and I...I couldn't breathe, I couldn't move, I just wanted the pain to go away, and Lucifer..."

"Lucifer used the situation to get what he wanted."

I nodded.

He rose and lifted me, pressing his forehead to mine and gripped the front of my jacket, his jacket. "I've hurt you, kitten, in the worst fucking ways imaginable. I don't deserve your forgiveness, but I'm begging you for it all the same." He swiped his thumbs over my cheeks, over my tearstained face. "Please, Roxy, please give me a chance to prove to you that I'm worthy of you, that I'm worthy of your love."

I stared into his glowing eyes. "The price you paid was

more than you ever deserved," I choked out. "You didn't want Sera, you never wanted her. I know that now. You did it for me. Lucifer gave you an impossible choice. I forgive you, my love. I forgave you a long time ago."

He shuddered against me, his huge body trembling. "You won't leave me?" he said with hope in his voice. "You'll stay?"

I wrapped my arms around his neck. "For centuries, I have loved you from afar, craved you, missed you. Being right here, by your side, is all I've ever wanted."

He closed his eyes, an agonized sound coming from him as he cupped my face and pressed his forehead to mine.

"I can't believe this is happening," I said.

He slid his thumbs over my cheeks. "Neither can I." Then he kissed me, slow and deep. His breath shook when he finally lifted his head. "Can I take you to my den, baby? Will you come home with me? If you wanna go to Hell, that's okay too. Whatever you want, I'll give it to you, Rox, yeah?"

I shook my head. "Take me to your den, Loth. I want you to take me home."

CHAPTER
THIRTY-THREE

Lothar

I GRIPPED Roxy's hand as we walked into the clubhouse. War's head shot up, and Relic, who stood beside him with his mate, took a step forward. Fern grabbed his hand and shook her head. Realization lit his eyes before a huge smile curled his lips.

My brothers hung back, not stopping us as we took the door down to the dens and rushed along the cavern. Good thing, too, because there was no stopping me. Our mating had been something I wouldn't wish on my worst enemy. I had assaulted my female. She submitted, but she'd done that for me, to protect me. I hadn't given her any other fucking choice. We could never go back and change that. We could never get that moment in time back.

So I would make this mating the one we remembered.

"Roxy?"

We spun around at the sound of Lucifer's voice. I snarled, fury lashing through me.

He lifted his hands, rings glinting off the wall sconces. "I know I hurt you both, beyond measure, and I will never forgive myself for my selfish act. Seeing you together..." His gaze slid to Roxy and he swallowed thickly. "I'm happy for you. I wanted this for you, both of you."

"I'm not going back to Hell with you," Roxy said, her voice instantly full of pain.

He shook his head. "I know that, and I know it may take you a lifetime to forgive me." He dipped his head, his yellow eyes shadowed but glossy. "You may never forgive me, and that, my precious one, will break my heart, but I understand it." He shook his head. "I know this is no excuse, but I was so fucking terrified of losing you, Rox. You and your sisters, you are everything to me. You were mine. My perfect creations. You were never meant to leave me. It should have been impossible, but I could feel you slipping away. Fate was taking you away from me, and I knew your sisters would follow, one by one. I felt it and I acted out of fear. I know I can't take back what I did, but if you will allow me, I'd like to do one small thing toward making this right."

"There's nothing you can do," I growled.

"Roxy's mark," Lucifer said. "I can take it away—"

"The fuck? Don't you fucking touch her?" I snarled. Roxy pressed her hand to my stomach when I took a step forward.

"You misunderstand me, brother," Lucifer said. "I want to give you a clean slate, as it were. You will still be very much mated, but when you both look at the mark she'll carry for eternity, it won't be one made in fear and horror."

Roxy looked up at me, her eyes wide. She wanted to do

it, I could see she did. Her mark, our first mating was my greatest shame. But it was a shame I'd carry for the rest of eternity. I'd always see it, no matter what we did now. The females with mated marks wore them with pride, showing them off proudly. When a female had a mark like Roxy's, one that showed how rough her male had been with her, others whispered under their breath, or outwardly showed their disgust. I deserved that, and I'd carry it, if she chose not to do this, but the decision had to be hers. "Whatever you want to do, kitten, it's up to you."

She chewed her lower lip. "I want to do it." She lifted her hand, resting it over the mark she carried now. "This isn't you, it isn't us."

My throat went dry, and somehow, when I thought it was impossible, Roxy made me fall even more in love with her than I already was. I turned to Lucifer. "If this is some kind of trick—"

"No trick. On the lives of all those I love most, I promise you this is done in good faith, and hopefully a step forward, toward healing for all of us."

Lucifer was sincere. He'd never make a promise like that otherwise. He'd also never usually allow me to disrespect him, question his motives and show full-on aggression. He loved Roxy, that was the truth, and I didn't think he'd risk doing anything that would push her farther away than she already was. "Do it."

He closed the space between us, and with a tender look in his eyes, he placed his hand over Roxy's mark. A wave of power flowed from him like a gentle wave, then he lifted his hand.

"It's done." He took a step back, watching her carefully. "When you're ready to see me again, I'll be waiting," he said, then he opened a gateway and was gone.

When Roxy turned back to me, there were tears in her eyes.

I swiped them away. "If it hurts too much to be parted from him..."

She shook her head. "I don't want to talk about him." She squeezed my hand and led me to the door of my den. "Make me yours again, Lothar, please."

I trembled as I led her into my den, but everything inside me eased as soon as I closed the door behind us. The beast rumbled with contentment in my chest as I backed her toward the bed. I slid my hand over the worn leather of the jacket she wore. It was far too big, but I'd recognized it as soon as I saw her in it. "You kept it," I said. "After all this time?"

She slid it off and placed it on the chair beside us. "It was all I had left of you."

I groaned, my heart unable to take it, what we'd missed out on. So much fucking lost time. I needed her right then in a way that was impossible to articulate. I knew what I needed, what she needed in that moment. "I want you on your hands and knees, Roxy. Will you do that for me?"

Her lips curled up and she nodded.

"That's how it should be done," I said roughly. "When I mark you this time, I want to do it covering your body with mine. I want to feel your back arch against my chest and stomach, and your ass cushioning my hips as your pussy clamps down on my knot."

A soft whimper fell from her lips, then she ran at me, leaping up and wrapping her strong, little body around me. Her soft, perfect mouth came down on mine. Groaning, I gripped her ass with one hand and the back of her head with the other, kissing her, tasting, licking, devouring her.

Striding to the bed, I lowered her to the mattress, coming down on top of her.

Utterly without finesse, I clutched her to me, unable to get her close enough. This mating was centuries in the making. Finally, I would claim my mate the way we were meant to so fucking long ago.

We tore at each other's clothes until we were both naked, our hot flesh pressed against each other. I couldn't get enough of her—the texture of her silky skin, of the satin of her thick, black hair. I kissed her jaw, her throat, sliding my hand over her smooth flesh, squeezing her waist and ass, her supple thigh.

I ached for her so fucking badly. "I need you, kitten," I groaned. "Please, tell me you want this, tell me how much you want me." I needed to hear it. I'd hurt her, more than once, in the worst ways, and I couldn't fucking bear it. It was selfish of me, asking her to put my heart and mind at ease when she was the one who had suffered, but I needed that from her so badly.

She held my face in her hands. "I have never wanted anything more in my life, Lothar," she rasped. "You're all I want, all I'll ever need." She swiped her thumb over my cheek, smoothing her hand over my beard. "We have to put the past behind us, okay? No more looking back. We hurt each other, Loth. It went both ways. We have to start here, now. Today. Promise me, you'll try to do that?"

I nodded, even though I wasn't sure how I would get past the shit I'd done, but I would try, for her. For her, I'd do anything.

She smiled up at me, and it was soft and sweet and sexy as fuck. "Now, make me yours. Mark me."

I lifted a little, giving her room, and she flipped to her stomach. My cock was hot iron, fucking throbbing as she lifted to her hands and knees. I slid my palm down her smooth back, over her perfect ass, and back up to grip her shoulder, where my beast's mark had once been. She arched, lifting her ass higher and giving me a prefect view of her pussy, pink and smooth, and wet as fuck.

"You look so fucking beautiful like this, Rox." She made a needy little sound, and I gripped myself and, shaking like hell, pressed the head of my cock to her pussy. I groaned just from the heat of her, then I tilted my hips and eased the head inside her. My fucking thighs trembled harder. Roxy undid me. She owned me, in every way, and finally making her mine like this was almost too much.

"More," she moaned.

Her plea eased my wild emotions, and the only thing that mattered was her, making this good for her. "I'm gonna take care of you, kitten," I rasped. "I'm gonna make you feel so good." Then I slid inside her, slow and steady, until I'd given her every inch.

She gasped and rolled her hips. "Please, don't stop."

As soon as the words fell from her lips, my hips jerked back and powered forward. I tried to ease up, to not fuck her like a beast, but Roxy shoved her ass back, setting the pace, hard, and deep.

My head spun as our bodies slammed together, over and over, her scent, her cries of pleasure for more calling to the beast in me. This time, though, I had control, because we were one, like we should be.

Tingles shot down my spine and along my shaft. My cock thickened, making me gasp and jerk my hips, and when I slid out, I tugged Roxy back with me. I quickly thrust forward again, staying deep, and swiveled my hips.

Roxy fisted the covers and cried out, about to come. I planted one hand on the bed beside hers and hooked the other across her chest, gripping the opposite shoulder. Then dragging my nose along her shoulder, I growled a warning and quickly sank my fangs into her flesh, this time with care.

Roxy screamed and came hard around my pulsing cock, wringing my orgasm from me, taking me with her. My seed shot deep inside her, filling her up while we rocked and slid against each other.

Finally spent, I held her to me and shifted her so we were lying on our sides, my arms wrapped around her while we were still locked together. I kissed her new mark, licked it gently, then pressed my mouth to her ear. "I love you, Rox, my precious mate, so fucking much."

She took my hand, threading our fingers together. "I love you too. Gods, my heart is full to bursting," she said, her voice shaky.

My warrior mate was still soft and sweet, and yeah, she could kill a hoard of rogue demons on her own, but she still needed to be treated with care. I pressed my hand to her chest. "You may not need me to protect you from the monsters of this world, Rox, but just know, I will always protect this beautiful heart of yours." I brushed her hair back and kissed my mark again, gently. "Just knowing it holds a place for me is an honor beyond measure, and one I promise I will never take for granted."

I finally slid from her body, and she turned in my arms. Her blue eyes glittered with emotion. "You hold more than a place in it, my love, you *are* my heart."

Then she wrapped herself around me, as though she couldn't get close enough, like she was trying to make up for centuries of us being apart, holding me with all her might.

I held her back just as tightly and reminded myself that we had an eternity ahead of us.

EPILOGUE

Roxy

Two years later
December 10th

HOLDING THE DOOR FRAME, I swung into the common room. "Anyone know where Lothar is?" Was I talking too loudly? I felt like I was talking way too loud. Gods, my heart was racing so fast.

"Check the pit," Rome called from the alcove where he had all his tattoo equipment set up.

"Thanks!" I rushed off, then broke into a run, because I couldn't hold this in another moment. The smile on my face probably made me look maniacal, but I didn't care.

The sounds of fists meeting flesh reached me before I rounded the corner and ran into the huge cavern.

War, Jag, and Relic stood to the side, watching on while Lothar worked with Brick in the fighting pit. Brick was still young, a pup as far as I was concerned, but he was a good fighter, quick, and like all young hounds, a complete hussy.

"Rox, hey," Relic called, a huge, affectionate smile on his face.

"Hey, Scrappy," I said, grinning, using the name I'd given him when he was a tiny pup.

He was chuckling as he strode over, then slung his arm around my shoulders. "You look happy with yourself."

"Oh, you have no idea," I said as I turned to face him and reached up so I could hold his precious face in my hands. "You know Mommy loves you, don't you, Scrappy?" I said. It was a running joke we all had, but for some reason, my eyes started stinging. I was pretty sure I was going to cry.

Relic laughed, then his smile slipped a little when he noticed. "Rox? Are you okay? What's going on?"

"And no one can ever replace you," I said, still trying to carry on the joke and failing miserably because another tear streaked down my face. "And that you'll always hold a special place in my heart."

"Why are you talking like that?" Relic said, alarm in his voice. "Are you hurt? Fuck, are you sick?"

"I'm okay, I promise." Though I'm not sure I was very convincing, since a sob broke free, taking me by surprise.

Relic's eyes widened in alarm, and his gaze sliced down to the pit at the same time as I heard boots thud behind me. A moment later, Lothar spun me to face him, his gaze was wild as he took me in.

They both crowded me, concern sharply etched on their faces.

"What the fuck is going on?" Lothar demanded.

"She just started crying," Relic said. "And she's saying a bunch of stuff that—"

"I'm o-okay," I stuttered, then hiccuped, and then I was crying and laughing, and I couldn't get the words out.

"Something's wrong with her," Lothar said, taking my face in his big hands. "Kitten, talk to me. Did Lucifer do something?"

I'd been hanging with my sisters, and it was the first time I'd spent any real time, quality time with Lucifer.

He'd been walking on eggshells, and I hated that I felt bad, that I wanted to make this better for him. It was ingrained in me to put him first, but as much as I still loved him, he didn't hold that position anymore. My mate did, and he currently looked as if he was on the verge of a nervous breakdown. I quickly shook my head, and another sob-laugh fell from me. "N-nothing's wrong," I managed.

Lucifer had shared some information with me, though, right before I left, and he was never wrong about these things. Still, I'd confirmed it myself, just to be sure.

His expression turned to one of disbelief. "Bullshit. You're fucking hysterical. Tell me what happened? Are you in pain?"

I shook my head.

"Are you hurt?"

I shook my head again.

"Are you sad after seeing Lucifer?"

I shook my head a third time.

His face fell. "Fuck, it's the 10th isn't it? Fuck, baby, I'm sorry I should have been with you—"

I pressed my fingers to his lips, stopping him. It wasn't that. I didn't need to mourn another year without Lothar, because he was mine.

His gaze went to Relic, and Relic shook his head, looking confounded.

"So it's not the date? You're not sad?" Loth said.

"I-I'm happy," I managed between sobs.

Lothar's head jerked back, his frown deepening. "Then, baby, why the fuck are you crying?"

I was too emotional to get the words out, and honestly, too afraid to say them out loud as if the universe or fate would snatch it away if I did. So I did the only thing I could —I took one of Lothar's big, rough, beautiful hands in mine and placed it on my belly then beamed up at him like the sun was shining through me. Gods, I felt as if it was.

Relic broke out into a huge grin, instantly working it out, then slugged Lothar in the shoulder.

Lothar looked at his firstborn, then back at me, still frowning. He blinked, then his brows shot up. I nodded, and another watery laugh burst from me when his head jerked back again, and his eyes widened.

His fingers spasmed against my belly, and the other shot up, locking around the side of my throat. "You're...are you saying... are you pregnant?"

"Yes!" I said and laugh-sobbed again.

Lothar hauled me off the ground, wrapping me in his huge arms, holding me to him. "You're truly having our pup?"

I pressed my mouth to his ear. "Yes, my love. Finally. Oh gods, Lothar. I'm so happy I can't stand it."

Lothar

My kitten was trembling against me as I strode from the cavern and along the cave towards our den. My sweet mate had wanted a pup so badly. We'd been trying for almost two years without success. She tried to stay upbeat about it. Roxy was always gifting everyone with her smiles, but I saw the longing, the pain in her eyes.

I'd wanted so badly to give her this. I'd wanted us both to have this, to experience this together, but I'd started to believe it wouldn't happen for us. It kept me awake at night, wondering how I could make this okay for her.

"Are you happy?" she said against my throat, because her arms were wrapped so tight around me.

"Happy doesn't cover it, kitten."

She trembled harder. "For me to find out this news today, of all days...I kind of feel like we're getting back some of what was taken from us." She lifted her head and planted a sweet kiss on me. "We can never get back the time we lost—"

"But no one will ever take away one fucking moment, not one, of the eternity we have laid out before us, never again."

She trembled harder against me, as I strode into our den and closed the door behind us. Laying her on the bed, I came down on top of her and wrapped her in my arms, tight, the way she loved it. "You're going to be the best mom." My throat went fucking tight. "Our pup is going to be so fucking lucky to have you to love and protect them. Talk about mama bear," I said and chuckled roughly.

Her smile was soft as she brushed fingers over my beard. "And you're going to be the best papa a pup could have."

I'd only known Roxy was pregnant for a matter of minutes, but I already knew that I'd protect the tiny pup she was carrying with my life. "I can't wait to meet them."

"Me either," she whispered.

Her black hair was fanned out around her gorgeous

face, her cheeks pink, her eyes puffy from crying. I'd never seen a more beautiful sight in my life. I held the side of her face and swiped away the tears dampening her cheek. "I fucking love you, Roxy, but you are stubborn as fuck, so warning, I'm going to be on the over-protective side, and I'm gonna need you to let me."

She laughed, sweet and musical. "You crack me up."

"I'm not joking, Rox."

"Right," she said, still laughing, then pounced, getting me in some insane hold, and flipped me to my back, reversing our positions, then grinned down at me. "Good luck with that, big guy. Now take off your pants."

I wrapped my arms around her and pulled her close, while we both laughed.

Also by Sherilee Gray

Fallen's Rebellion

Black Hills Pack:

Lone Wolf's Captive

A Wolf's Deception

Axle Alley Vipers:

Crashed

Revved

Wrecked

Rocktown Ink:

Beg For You

Sin For You

Meant For you

Bad For You

All For You

Just for You

The Smith Brothers:

Mountain Man

Wild Man

Solitary Man

Lonesome Man

Lawless Kings:

Shattered King

Broken Rebel

Beautiful Killer

Ruthless Protector

Glorious Sinner

Merciless King

Boosted Hearts:

Swerve

Spin

Slide

Spark

Stand Alone Novels:

Breaking Him

While You Sleep

About the Author

Sherilee Gray is a kiwi girl and lives in beautiful New Zealand with her husband and their two children. When she isn't writing sexy contemporary and paranormal romance, searching for her next alpha hero on Pinterest, or fueling her voracious book addiction, she can be found dreaming of far off places with a mug of tea in one hand and a bar of chocolate in the other.

To find out about new releases, sales, giveaways and other cool stuff, sign up for my newsletter!

www.sherileegray.com